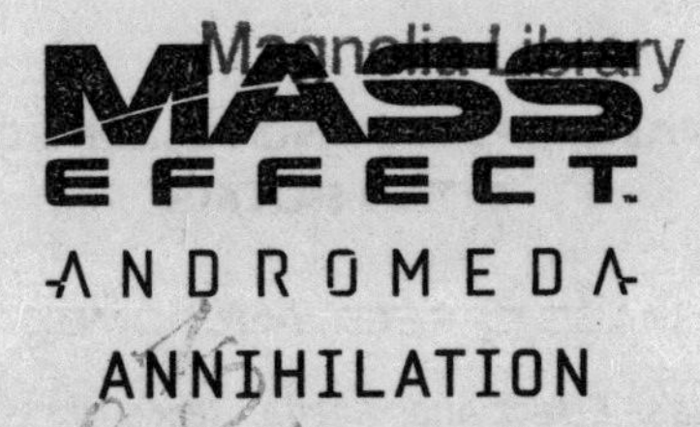

ANNIHILATION

MASS EFFECT NOVELS FROM TITAN BOOKS

MASS EFFECT ANDROMEDA

Mass Effect Andromeda: Nexus Uprising
by Jason M. Hough and K. C. Alexander

Mass Effect Andromeda: Initiation
by N. K. Jemisin and Mac Walters

Mass Effect Andromeda: Annihilation
by Catherynne M. Valente

MASS EFFECT™

ANDROMEDA

ANNIHILATION

CATHERYNNE M. VALENTE

TITAN BOOKS

MASS EFFECT ANDROMEDA: ANNIHILATION
Print edition ISBN: 9781785651588
E-book edition ISBN: 9781785651595

Published by Titan Books
A division of Titan Publishing Group Ltd
144 Southwark St, London SE1 0UP

First edition: November 2018
10 9 8 7 6 5 4 3 2 1

Editorial Consultants: Chris Bain, Joanna Berry, John Dombrow,
Cathleen Rootsaert, Mac Walters, Karin Weekes

A CIP catalogue record for this title is available from the British Library.

Printed and bound in the United States.

MASS EFFECT
ANDROMEDA
ANNIHILATION

PROLOGUE

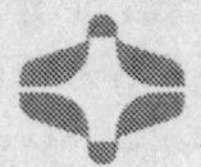

HEPHAESTUS STATION: CALESTON RIFT

Tech Specialist Second Class Oliver Barthes looked down at the hazy, glittering sweep of the galaxy far below him. Stars and red-orange astral dust clouds reflected in the flat, polished surface of his omni-tool. It was late: 0300. He hadn't finished his work and he would have murdered his best friend for a piece of real meat and a mug of real gin just then, if he had a best friend. Or a mug. One more round of calibrations and he could sleep. But Oliver just stood there on his tiny silver access platform, transfixed by the stars like a dumb kid breaking orbit for the first time. A chunk of the galactic arm glowed against his own very human, very un-celestial forearm like a ropy piece of muscle. Or a wound.

Of course, it was not his first time. Not even close. If he tried hard, Oliver Barthes could just barely remember a time when his life was not mainly a series of shuttles, cruisers, stations, forms, contracts, someone else's kludgecode, and tiny viewports in endless dull walls. A time when his life was green and warm and kind. When he could smell real dirt under his fingernails as he drifted to sleep in a real bed every night.

But that was then. That was Eden Prime. This was after. This was Hephaestus Station.

Even at 0300, Hephaestus's dry-dock facilities buzzed and hummed with people. This was the techies' witching hour. The machinists and engineers and cargo loaders and nosy passengers-to-be were all snug in their favorite bars or berths. Now the *real* work could get done. Not that anyone else saw it Oliver's way. They only saw the plasteel that separated them from the vacuum of space. They saw the power of biotic blasts that could rip that space apart with the twitch of an eyelash. But they couldn't see the code that made it all possible. Code was invisible, and therefore forgettable. And coders were more than forgettable. They were ignorable, expendable, and tragically low paid. Kids were practically born programming these days. Why pay someone a fortune for something as basic as eating and drinking?

Until something went wrong, of course.

The massive hull of the *Keelah Si'yah* crawled with codeslingers like barnacles on an old sailing ship. Each one clung to an open nodeport, accessing the ship's deep banks directly for maximum security. Oliver instructed his omni-tool to dose him with a last wave of stims. His veins flooded, opened, relaxed. He forgot about the stars' reflections in his omni-tool, about real meat and real gin and green fields ready for planting. Tech Specialist Second Class Oliver Barthes stretched up his arms toward the starboard hull of the quarian deep-space vessel as though he meant to give it a bear hug. His hands moved over the gleaming plasteel as he activated the gravity flexors on his worksuit and lifted himself up toward the ship with a practiced, almost acrobatic grace. A calm artificial voice informed his inner ear of his progress.

Palm flexors: locked. Sole flexors: locked. Knee flexors: locked and ready. You are cleared for extra-vehicular motility, Specialist Barthes.

Each point of contact *thunked* into place with a familiar, satisfying, sucking sound.

"Thanks, Helen," he chuckled. Helen didn't care what he called her. She wasn't anything like a full VI. She wasn't even a she. No more sentient than a frying pan, his Helen. But that cool, collected, randomly generated voice was often his only friend on these long shifts, and you didn't ignore your only friend just because she was an omni-tool.

Oliver was lucky to have this gig and he knew it. The Initiative paid better than anyone, even the Alliance, and, more importantly, they paid on time. Oliver needed that. He needed the money, and he needed the reliability. He glanced down at the misty stars in Helen's gleaming surface again. One of them was Sahrabarik, and somewhere near Sahrabarik was Omega Station, and somewhere on Omega Station was an asari named Aria T'Loak to whom Oliver sent every credit he earned beyond the bare minimum he needed to keep stomach and soul together. He shuddered. He remembered her cold blue eyes. Her cold blue smile. The look on his father's face when Aria told him she'd sold his only son to a mobile work detail based out of Sigurd's Cradle. It wasn't a special tragedy. It wasn't unique. Thousands of refugees from the attack on Eden Prime (and Noveria and Virmire and so on and so forth) ended up the same way—lost and broke and bought and sold. The only thing special about Oliver Barthes was that his work detail was run by a reasonably kind elcor named Lumm, and Lumm had a policy of allowing his boys to buy their freedom, if and when they could. Oliver didn't think anyone had ever yet taken old Lumm up on it. The boys blew their meager earnings on batarian shard wine or girls or Quasar or even red sand, for the very desperate. But not him. He'd saved and scraped and starved. He didn't look at girls, even though they looked at him sometimes, even though he *wanted* to look. He drank water. He only set foot in a bar when Lumm sent him to patch some glitching Quasar machine that was paying out a little too often. Oliver was good at saving and scraping and starving. He had a talent for it, just as much as he had a talent for debugging spaceships. And when Lumm offered to ring up his liberty, he paid his price and kept his receipt.

Oliver wasn't saving or scraping or starving for himself anymore. At least, not only for himself. He was on the rent-to-own plan for his parents' freedom nowadays, and he would never, ever miss a payment. He paid Aria to keep them off hard labor and he paid her, in installments, to one day let them go.

It wasn't easy to keep up. Coding billets were usually viciously short-term. You never knew where the next one would take you. You never knew when there would *be* a next one. This was the longest contract he'd ever pulled. The other Initiative vessels had been ship-in-a-box jobs; absolutely straightforward, minimalist, nothing extra, nothing fancy. Strictly get-you-from-here-to-there action. Take your basic long-distance cruiser template, adjust for asari, human, turian, salarian. Load everyone on, put them to sleep for six hundred years, wake them up in the Andromeda galaxy where much better facilities and a healthy, balanced breakfast would be waiting for them. Quick, efficient, no mess.

But this was a quarian job, and quarians never met a boat they didn't want to mess with. They had a list of custom alterations as long as the Rift. No quarian would trust a ship built strictly to get you from here to there. *There* might never materialize. Their whole species lived on a flotilla cruising from system to system waiting for the geth to abandon their homeworld, a place most of them had never even seen. Ships were their mothers and their children. Ships were home. They would not set foot aboard unless they were confident that, if push came to shove, they could live on this thing functionally forever. And that list of alterations kept getting longer and longer, now that the Initiative had asked the soft-spoken, birdlike quarians to allow other races to buy or barter passage on their six-hundred-light-year road trip. Now they needed shipboard environments friendly to the reptilian drell, elephantine elcor, aquatic hanar, ammonia-based volus, four-eyed batarian… 20,000 leftover souls packed into one tin can like an assorted-flavor pack of ramen noodles. And they called it all not *Keelah Se'lai*, the old quarian phrase that meant "by the homeworld I hope to see one day," but *Keelah Si'yah*.

"By the homeworld I hope to *find* one day."

Oliver Barthes ran his fingertips along the belly of the *Si'yah*. What could they be like? These quarians, among all the quarians, who had given up the one thing their whole race lived and breathed: the quest for Rannoch, the quest for home. What was a quarian who didn't care about the homeworld? Were they even quarians anymore? It would be like finding a couple of thousand humans who didn't care about space at all. Or salarians who had never given one single thought to science. Or a red asari. Oliver had tried to make conversation in the Hephaestus Station bars, but he'd never been very good at that, and anyway, why would any of those beautiful aliens waste their time talking to someone who was going to be dead, from their perspective, before they woke up in the morning? It was six hundred years to Andromeda. He was already a ghost to them.

But some nights… some nights he dreamed that he was going, too. That by some miracle, one of the twenty thousand snug, identical cryopods was his. That he, too, would wake up one day staring down a new world. A world no one had screwed up yet. A world he could help turn into paradise. But then he'd wake up staring down a dented Hephaestus bulkhead. It would never be him. He was too tied to this galaxy. To Eden Prime and his parents and Helen and goddamned Aria T'Loak. Oliver Barthes was not the new world kind. He was screwed up already. Screwed up from birth.

And so he'd worked his way slowly through his portion of their endless checklist, and somehow a year in the life of Oliver Barthes had gone by with hardly a whisper. He was even beginning to feel… fond of Hephaestus Station, with all her busted vents and malfunctioning doors and total lack of architectural character. It was a rough place, like any remote station. If you turned out the lights on an argument, chances were you'd turn them back on to a body. The local cuisine was wall-to-wall freeze-dried ramen wedges and soya tablets. But at 0300, if you squinted, it could look like home. Disgusting, he thought to himself. You're like an old grandma! Next you'll be laying out doilies in your berth.

Oliver opened a fresh nodeport in the cryodeck of the *Keelah Si'yah* and paired Helen with the ship's infant systems. He sighed. Hell was other people's code. He did his best, he really did, but anything elegant or functional he managed to compile was instantly swallowed up in the hideous kludgecode of the thousand other techies sticking their clumsy fingers in the quarian pie. Someday, Oliver thought. Someday I'll get to build a boat from scratch. Just me, nobody else. Full VI interface, automations smooth as snow, self-calibrating, self-debugging. It'll be perfect. It'll be so elegant even an elcor would weep. Nobody ever made a bug-proof boat but I'll be the first. And with this beast on my résumé, it might not even be too long before I get my shot.

Oliver looked down. You weren't supposed to look down. Hephaestus Station was a glorified orbital platform. Her dry docks floated at the ends of long radials that extended from the main body of the station like the rays of a particularly ugly sun. Looking down meant looking into raw space. Nothing between you and the long drop but a bluish film of artificial atmosphere. You probably wouldn't fall—the gravity flexors took care of that, but you might throw up or pass out or freak out, and none of those things would get you another job. But Oliver had never been troubled by the yawning empty darkness of the infinite void. It just didn't bother him. He was a man, it was an infinite void; they knew each other pretty well and left it at that. His eyes slid over the black nothingness and onto the crosshatch of silver railings and ramps and mezzanines that cradled the quarian ship. Furtively, he scanned the dock for… well, for what? For someone who might see what he was about to do? Why should he care? He wasn't doing anything wrong, not really. In fact, Oliver Barthes meant to do something quite nice.

Sweet, when you thought about it. And Oliver Barthes was going to be paid very handsomely for being nice. Enough to buy his parents out from under Aria T'Loak and himself out from Lumm and set them all up for good in one mighty payoff. And maybe, just maybe, when it was all done and his family settled and he could finally dream for himself alone, enough for a one-way ticket to the future, six hundred years away.

Techies in plain worksuits ran up and down the maze of ramps and stairs. A few night owls leaned against rails, smoking or nursing a flask or just staring, staring at the enormity of the ship, at the enormity of what it meant. Anyone who set foot on this boat would never see home again, except on a long, long range scan. They'd never smell a familiar flower again.

They were an odd bunch, the *Si'yah* colonists. None of them were what you would call normal representatives of their species. Of course, they wouldn't be. The idea of even one quarian leaving the Flotilla for parts unknown, never to return, was frighteningly strange. And there were four thousand of them on this boat. It was a ship of fools: vagabonds, idealists, radicals, exiles, criminals, artists, and schemers. The quarians hadn't turned anyone away if they could pay, barter, or show their worth to a new colony. No matter who they'd been. No matter what they'd done. The Si'yah was a blank slate for everyone.

It would be madness. Oliver wished he could be there to see it.

Oliver's gaze flicked through the meandering crowd. He saw a female drell with bright markings blow a smoke ring out of her dark-green lips into the night. Some four-eyed batarian argued with a volus who glared back at him out of the mournful badger eyes that all volus suits seemed to have. A pair of quarians solved their sleeplessness with an evening walk. The worklights of the *Keelah Si'yah* flashed against the face masks of their own environmental suits. The other techies were always chattering about what a quarian really looked like inside her suit, about how they could get one to strip off and show them, about how they'd definitely bag this one quarian girl before she shipped out to god knows where, no problem. But Oliver never wondered. He'd seen their ship. He'd seen their code. He knew exactly what a quarian looked like on the inside.

Oliver didn't think anyone was watching him. He was certain they weren't. Everyone was nose-deep in their own problems. Dammit, Barthes, it's just an audio subroutine, stop being paranoid, he thought. Still, it didn't sit quite right. Oliver wasn't stupid. He was one of Lumm's boys. He knew any job that arrived facelessly through his datapad, paid so obscenely well, and demanded no questions was probably pretty far from legit work. But he'd gone over the loopcode himself. Over and over. It really did seem to be what his contact said it was: a recording of a goofy old quarian lullaby called "My Suit and Me" to be played to the sleeping colonists in their cryopods once a century until planetfall. Harmless. Sentimental to the point of cuteness. And sentiment knew no species. Things like this happened all the time with new ships, especially deep-space sleepers like *Si'yah* here. Pictures stuck up on the inside of the cryopods, a little crate of real tea smuggled on to comfort somebody's homesick uncle. One of the other techies on the same dinner cycle as Oliver had been hired by some rich fool to install a tiny perfume capsule in all the drell pods, programmed to release the scent of the usharet flower just before the big thaw. Usharet used to grow on Rakhana, their poor dead homeworld. All that effort, just so the drell could wake up on the other side of the universe to the scent of home. As if it mattered what a couple of thousand lizards sniffed first thing in the morning! Then again, Oliver supposed it was all the same. Who knew why people did the things they did, except for sentiment. When he'd asked why something so unimportant required the kind of secrecy his benefactor was paying for, Oliver had been told only that it was a kindly surprise, a gesture of unity and peace for this hodgepodge ship of fools. They were all quarians now. They were family.

What wouldn't you do for family? What wouldn't you do just to make them smile?

Oliver Barthes couldn't go to Andromeda, no matter what his dreams told him. But he could do this. He could do this for those who would go out beyond the beyond, out into the wild unknown to forge a new civilization out of raw starstuff. He could make them smile in their sleep. Maybe that wasn't much to tell the grandkids about, but it was something.

Oliver wiggled his toes inside his suit to kill the pins and needles. He instructed Helen to upload the subroutine to the cryopod maintenance matrix and erased his footsteps. It was easy, for someone like him. As easy as remembering to turn off the lights and lock the door behind you.

"Godspeed," Oliver whispered to that big, dumb, insane, beautiful ship. "Sleep tight."

All flexors in safety mode. You are cleared for Hephaestus Station re-entry, Specialist Barthes. Have a pleasant rest.

"You too, Helen. You too. Wherever well-behaved little truncated VI programs go to snooze, tuck yourself in nice and snug."

Oliver slowly climbed back down to his access platform and disengaged the gravity flexors. His feet found metal once more. He took out his datapad and sent confirmation of delivery to the address he'd been given. Then, he pulled up his account manager and watched like a kid outside a cake shop. He waited. And waited. And finally, the familiar, modest numbers of his precious savings blinked out. New numbers blinked on. Astonishing new numbers. Gorgeous new numbers. Oliver Barthes was going to a new world, all right, just like the rest of them. A world of safety and love and family. A world where what happened on Eden Prime barely mattered at all.

IIIIIIIIIIIIIIIII

Oliver walked along the main gangplank with something very like a spring in his step. He took off his helmet and ran one hand through his short brown hair. His stubble itched; time to shave. But it was done. It was done and you know what? It really was something that twenty thousand people were going to sail through the cold space between galaxies listening to Radio Free Barthes. He'd never thought he'd amount to anything special, but maybe he had, after all. Not *enormously* special, but a little. Just a little. He put his palm against the security panel. He imagined his mother's face when he told her, the quiet little sparkle of delight he remembered in her brown eyes. The elevator arrived; the door didn't open. Oliver rolled his eyes and banged on it a couple of times with his fist. Stupid things. It wouldn't take more than a day of scrubbing that almost-certainly decrepit code to fix, but no one ever bothered. He'd put in a work request in the morning. His goodbye present to old Heph. *From me to you, buddy.*

Oliver punched the slider again. It wheezed open. The elevator car was empty; he stepped inside. He wouldn't tell his mother right away, of course. He'd take them to the Citadel. Dazzle them with the green trees in the Presidium and the lights of the docking ships and the steak sandwiches at Apollo's. Then he'd show them the apartment in Zakera Ward he'd bought for them. He could practically hear his mother's voice in that dingy elevator. *Oh, Ollie, it's too much!* They'd be so happy. They'd probably cry. He'd cry, too. And then, when they were all sitting around the dinner table, stuffed senseless and drunk on the future, he'd tell them about the time he played rock-a-bye baby to a ship of aliens for six hundred years. *I wonder if you dream in cryostasis? Maybe someday we'll find out. Together.*

Tech Specialist Second Class Oliver Barthes stepped out of the elevator into the long hallway that connected the main column of Hephaestus Station to the industrial living quarters. He picked up his pace, eager to get to sleep, to get one day closer to Zakera Ward and green trees and grease shining on his father's calloused fingers from a real steak sandwich.

Oliver was still picturing his mother's laughing face when a figure in a deep gray hood stepped out from an alcove and shot him twice in the head.

The figure looked down at the techie's body for a moment, prodded it with one boot to make sure, then walked on, humming a little lullaby under its breath:

Sing me to sleep on the starry sea
And I'll dream through the night of my suit and me…

The filthy, featureless metal ceiling of Hephaestus Station reflected mutely in the dull surface of a powerless omni-tool.

I won't fear the heat of a desert breeze
Or contaminants high in the jungle trees
Even in space I shall never freeze
Because I've got my suit and my suit's got me…

KEELAH SI'YAH

1. SURFACE RECEPTORS

Sleepwalker Team Leader Senna'Nir vas Keelah Si'yah, your attention is required.

Senna groaned. A bright cascade of revival drugs sizzled through his system. The quarian second-in-command tried to roll over on his side and turn down the optics on his suit as he always did when he overslept. Nothing was ever so important it couldn't survive another five minutes' sleep. His suit did not respond. Senna's elbow hit hard iso-glass. He tried to sit up, smacked the brow ridge of his mask against the same stuff, and fell back onto a narrow bed. Pinpricks of harsh light stabbed his eyes. Readouts exploded onto his helmet display in bursts of glowing ultraviolet text.

Ship Status: Initiative ship *Keelah Si'yah* performing within normal parameters
Navigational Positioning: 1.26% behind projected itinerary
Cardiovascular Condition: good
Deviations from Endocrinal and Neurological Norms: within standard conformations
Pharmaceutical Activity: intravenous stimulants, muscular density restoratives, painkiller #4 (double dose)
Holistic Suit Feedback: all systems functional, no exterior breaches

Sleepwalker Team Sitrep: nothing significant to report
Engine Chatter: eezo conversion performing at 0.7% in excess of expected efficiency
Short-Range Scan: due to pass by binary brown dwarf star 44N81/44N82 in two weeks, two days
Communications: receiver array intact and clear, home relay communications packet download completed successfully without information loss, next scheduled packet in nineteen months, sixteen days.
Self-diagnostics from Onboard Virtual Intelligences: all performing at optimum

There was also a helpful chart showing his current rate of bone-density loss (4%) along with recommended corrective supplements. A message from his grandmother, Liat'Nir vas Achaz, blinked unread in the corner of his vision. Recorded before they left and programmed to deliver itself on arrival. It was the little things that made up a family.

Arrival.

They must be there. Here. Home.

Senna'Nir's heart raced a little whenever he thought of his grandmother. His pulse picked up now, crushingly anxious, as he had been since he was a boy, for her safety. She was so small and fragile. But then again, weren't they all? He took a deep breath, sucking in more super-saturated air from his suit to energize his lungs. Liat was fine. No harm could come to her, fast asleep with the rest of the quarians, hibernating, safe. He subvocalized to archive her message, whatever it was, recorded whenever it had been, long ago. Later. Senna would never be sorry he brought her along to Andromeda, but he couldn't take her voice just now. It was, and always had been, *piercing*.

All's well, he thought. *Strong wind and a following tide for all the ships at sea*. Senna could see his breath fog blurrily in front of his face. *Good. Fine. Back to sleep now. Sleep warm and good. Awake cold and bad.* He blinked away the onslaught of interstellar and anatomical trivia and tried to shut down his optics again. Another few minutes couldn't harm anything. All the real work was behind them. They'd be docking with the Nexus very soon, if they hadn't already. And once the captain gave the command to link airlocks and that beautiful hiss of atmosphere exchange sounded off, his responsibility for this voyage would be mercifully over.

That prim, clipped, genderless voice piped up once more.

I'm sorry, Team Leader Senna'Nir vas Keelah Si'yah, I cannot allow you to reduce your sensory input. Your attention is required.

"Unf," grunted Sleepwalker Team Leader Senna'Nir vas Keelah Si'yah as his cryopod flooded with brilliant white light. "Ow. No! What? You said all's well!"

IIIIIIIIIIIIIIII

Drell Sleepwalker Anax Therion, your attention is required.

Anax came awake instantly, her translucent reptilian lids blinking quickly over huge black eyes. Her mind raced ahead of the narcotic foam coursing through her body, organizing itself into alertness with the practice of someone who had never in their lives enjoyed the luxury of waking up in their own good time. She looked up at a note in her own handwriting, glowing on a personal display a few inches above the green blur of her nose.

Hello, Anax! You are in a cryopod on the quarian ship Keelah Si'yah bound for the Andromeda galaxy. You are thirty-one years old, 1.84 meters tall, 77.1 kilograms, and left-handed. You are a member of Sleepwalker Team Blue-7. Your favorite food is the Ataulfo mango, native to the human homeworld. The last movie you enjoyed was Blasto 8: The Jellyfish Always Stings Twice. Think about these things. Remember them. Feel them to be true. Congratulations, you are not dead! The voice in your ear is the ship's interface program. Everyone calls it K, for Keelah Si'yah, but it is not a real person, or even a real VI, so you do not have to be too bothered with keeping up niceties. You can swear at it, if you want. Insult its mother. It will still call you in the morning. Your past self has written this note in order to save us both the excruciating inefficiency of an estimated two hours and thirty-two point five minutes of post-stasis disorientation and identity confusion. You're welcome. Happy Transit Day 219,706. Welcome to Andromeda.

Anax glanced at the local time/date signature in the left corner of her note. It read: *0200 hrs Transit Day 207,113.*

"I am awake, K," Anax Therion said calmly. "Have we arrived early?"

Negative, Systems Analyst Anax Therion. Current position: 110,804.77 light years from destination. Estimated time to arrival assuming no change in speed or course: thirty years, five months, twelve days, sixteen hours and four minutes.

Anax stretched her long olive-and-black fingers and tented them over her chest. "Then why have I been revived?"

Your attention is required.

The drell took a long breath. The inside of her mouth tasted stale, medicinal, silvery. She ran her fingers over the orange frills along her jaw the way a human might slap her cheeks to wake herself up. Her mind raced to pick up its pieces and get them into some kind of useful order. But even half-thawed, that mind was faster than most—and more pessimistic.

"Just how fucked are we, K?" she sighed.

Elcor Sleepwalker Yorrik, your attention is required.

Bluish interior lighting clicked on inside a structure on Deck 8. It couldn't really be called a cryopod. Pods were small, snug, ergonomic, modular. This was more like a cryo-garage. There were thousands of them packed into the repurposed cargo bay—3,311 to be exact. Something massive and gray moved sluggishly within the layers of iso-glass, metal, and frost. It shook its colossal head mournfully from side to side. The nasal voice that emerged was completely flat and monotone.

"With great resentment," it droned, "go away."

I cannot go away, Medical Specialist Yorrik. I am installed in the ship's memory core. Please enter command-level password to uninstall.

Yorrik slammed his elephant-like foreleg into the wall of his enormous cryopod. He didn't remember that it *was* a cryopod, and he didn't remember that his name was Yorrik, and most of all, he didn't remember what a memory core was, or what *uninstall* meant, though it sounded excellent. There was an ache in his head... between... between his smelling bones and his thinking meat. Yes, that sounded right. Yorrik's thinking meat was angry and thick just now. His plodding, ancient metabolism barely noticed the whitewater rush of stimulants pummeling his nervous system.

Yorrik activated the locking plate on his massive cryopod with his huge knee. There was a hiss of depressurization. The massive creature stumbled out of the pod, tripped over the raised ledge of the thing, and crashed noisily to the deck floor. No one noticed. The other pods blinked away into oblivion. It was a nearly perfect pratfall, Yorrik thought woozily to himself, and not one person had seen it. His low, buzzing voice cut off the cheerful chirping of the ship's interface.

"With dry sarcasm: And a good morning to you, too."

Sleepwalker Yorrik, I am increasing the dosages of your revival cocktail. I have added supplementary acuity enzymes, sensory enhancements, and anti-depressants, and accelerated your metabolic rate to compensate. I apologize in advance. This will be a very unpleasant but highly addictive experience for you. I have determined that the time necessary for standard elcor revival protocols will materially worsen the developing situation. Please report to the Radial immediately. Your medical expertise is needed. Please report to the Radial immediately. Your medical expertise is needed. Please report—

Yorrik groaned, a loud, low trombone blast in the dim lighting. All his thinking meat wanted was to stomp something, preferably that damned voice. But his smelling bones were always ready for action. Yorrik scrunched up his long gray face and took a powerful whiff of his surroundings. Information flooded in. He felt immediately sharper, more grounded. Stale air, antibacterial mist, thawing frost. Plasteel, tart and tannic. His own grassy, dank sweat, hot and sour. The perfume of deep space: a cold forest lit up with the prickling, caustic smoke of a hundred million campfires burning in the dark. But underneath it all, there was something else. Far away. Not on this deck or the one above it, but on board, certainly. Something sweet and meaty and swollen, like milk just about to turn.

Death.

2. PENETRATION

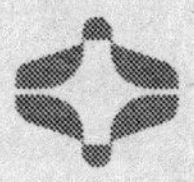

They say no one dreams in cryostasis. You aren't really sleeping in cryo at all. People just call it *sleep* because no one would do it if they called it what it is, which is technically, though ideally temporary, *death*. And the dead don't dream. Anax Therion knew that. She knew exactly how the cryopods worked, down to the icicle. What kind of person would trust their body to a machine without reading the manual back to front two or three times? All the same, when she lay down in that glass coffin back on Hephaestus Station, just before the last cool gust of atomized deep-freeze turned her green skin blue, she'd been convinced that she would. Maybe it would be different for a drell. Many things were, medically speaking. Few enough of Therion's people ever made real long-haul voyages, and if they did, they were usually one-way tickets. Like hers. Or maybe there would be a malfunction, and she alone would feel it all, all six hundred years between home and away, trapped in her body, in her memories.

The long, dark hallway between the cryodeck and the Radial stretched out before her, bending slightly with the curvature of the ship. It was all sleek, graceful glass, white metal, and bright lighting—or at least it would be. Just now, the *Keelah Si'yah* was running dark to save energy while her cargo slept the centuries away. Soft blue directional lighting ran helpfully along the floor toward her destination, but nothing else.

It was as dark and unfamiliar as an alley in a strange city. Anax Therion slumped against one unlit wall. A flood of unwelcome memory washed over her. Her milky interior eyelids slid shut. *Clouds like gunsmoke over the glass domes of Cnidaria City. Streets littered with bioluminescence. Panting, my breath like footprints running ahead in the dark. He thinks he has escaped. The krill see no pattern in their frantic swimming. But the whale sees. I am the whale. Laser targets brush the mark's shoulder blades like a swarm of summer fireflies.*

Anax wrenched herself out of her own past, the past she'd stowed safely on the other side of two and a half million light years. The drell memory was perfect and dangerous. It was as real as life. When Anax remembered, she lived it again, just as vivid, just as clear, just as pulse-poundingly immediate as the first time. She was *there*. A million miles away, on Kahje, a young data-dealer who had never given one single thought to the Andromeda galaxy, chasing an assassin through the back alleys of a hanar city, her only goal: to secure the information in his brain for the Shadow Broker. But that was long past now. Another life, another time. Yet, if Anax didn't keep her mind strapped down tight, it could come over her again without warning, without mercy. It could drown her. Her post-cryosleep mind was anything but strapped down.

And drell dreams? No vid in the galaxy could compete.

But she hadn't dreamed. Her eyes closed on Hephaestus Station and opened again on her assigned Sleepwalker cycles and it was like blinking; that fast, that seamless. Except that her joints ached and her head hurt and it tasted like a vorcha had shit in her mouth. But the Sleepwalker cycles were over now.

Team Blue-7, her team, had run the last shift, coming out of stasis to perform maintenance and systems checks one final time before docking with the Nexus in Andromeda. No more wakies till the big one. Anax Therion, and everyone else on the *Keelah Si'yah*, were supposed to be peacefully temporarily dead right now. *This had better be good*, the drell thought. But of course, it couldn't be good. The ship wouldn't wake her up off schedule for a glass of Noverian rum and a fruit salad.

"Dragging your feet won't un-fuck whatever's fucked itself," Therion said to herself. Her voice echoed in the empty deck. She put on a quick jog down the quiet corridor toward the Radial as a strange, disorienting thought popped in her mind like a bubble in wine.

The Shadow Broker was dead now. Her best client, the only one she'd never met, whose voice she'd never heard. Whoever they'd really been, wherever they'd really lived, whoever they'd really loved, whatever they liked to do on long, lonely nights, they were half a millennium in the ground. And she, *she*, little scrawny nervy Anax Therion who couldn't put two meals back to back most of the days of her youth, was still alive. Who would ever have thought it would shake out that way, all those years ago, when the rain and the neon in Cnidaria City mixed like paint in the street?

* * *

The Radial was beautiful in its own way. An industrial zen garden deep in the core of the ship, a spacious blue-black hexagon bounded on each side by thick walls of clear glass bolted into metal frames. Here, the six environmental zones of the *Keelah Si'yah* converged. Any member of any species on board could meet and communicate with any other without having to go through the time-consuming and annoying procedures necessary to keep a hanar from liquefying in the ammonia reek of the volus areas, or a drell's lungs from collapsing in the dank, moist batarian halls, or a quarian from being crushed to death by the elcor's preferred artificial-gravity settings. The six glass panels functioned as airlocks, too. From the Radial, with preparation and permission, you could freely enter or leave any zone. All the material necessary for such preparations—hyposprays, grav-bracelets, air filters, painkillers, suits and masks— were packed into a wide, low cylinder in the center of the hexagon.

None of the other Initiative ships had such meticulous arrangements. None of them had to bother, since they carried only one species each. It was one thing to vaccinate, pressurize, and suit up to suffer the mutually agreed-upon conditions of the Citadel for a year or two. But the quarians steadfastly refused to entertain the notion of forcing six species into a composite environment that wouldn't be particularly comfortable for any of them for the duration of their centuries-long voyage to a new galaxy. Andromeda was a dream they hoped to wake to. The *Si'yah* was home from the moment her main thrusters burst into life outside Hephaestus Station. Practical, solid, reliable. And home shouldn't give you gravity migraines or blood poisoning or Kepral's Syndrome. At home, you should be able to put up your tentacles and relax. Besides, if something went wrong, this great gorgeous heap of bolts might be the whole of their new colony.

The quarians always bet on something going wrong, and they rarely lost.

When they arrived at the Nexus, the full Quorum would convene here. Five of the six alcoves would contain two representatives of each species aboard the *Keelah Si'yah*, one male, one female (unless otherwise gendered), chosen by their own in a formal pre-flight election to make any decisions that would affect the ship as a whole. The Pathfinders, specialized homeworld hunters implanted with powerful new AIs called SAMs, or Simulated Adaptive Matrices, would find planets for them. The Quorum would keep these twenty thousand souls from tearing each other apart while the search was on. There were only a few hundred batarians on board, so they reluctantly shared representation—and a Pathfinder—with the quarians. The drell and the hanar, two species linked by a long history, also shared a single Pathfinder. The Quorum had been revived once at the halfway point of their journey to review operational status, and would not wake again until Andromeda, unless an emergency arose that the SAMs and ship's maintenance drones could not handle on their own.

But the glass alcoves stood empty and quiet now, washed in dim blue standby lights running up and down the deck floor. No Pathfinders, no Quorum, no eager colonists, no bustle of activity. No protocol called for the Pathfinders or the colonists to be wakened without the Quorum. Nothing moved in the Radial but time.

The Radial's only decoration was a large hydroponic flower arrangement sitting on top of the supply cylinder. Each species had lovingly carried plants from their homeworld onto the *Si'yah*, where a young volus named Irit Non had arranged them into a stunningly artful whole. Over five centuries and change the ship's botanical maintenance program had misted and clipped the bouquet as it grew. And grew. And grew. Pale bioluminescent lerian, sea ferns from the hanar world of Kahje, surrounded scarlet usharet flowers from the war-torn drell planet Rakhana. Thick purple bulbs of onuffri blossoms from the savannas of Dekuuna, where the elcor roam, wound around spiky batarian spice cones called ignac, culled from the harsh batarian plains of Khar'shan. Pungent silver kympna lobes peeked out toothily between carnivorous plants from the chemical forests of Irune, home of the volus. But the quarians had lost their homeworld to their own creations, the rogue mechanical intelligences called the geth. Only they could not contribute.

The captain, Qetsi'Olam vas Keelah Si'yah, had called the bouquet silly and sentimental.

"We made the ship," Qetsi'Olam had said. "Surely that's flower enough!"

Kholai, a hanar priest, had called the whole business ridiculous. The only people who would get to enjoy it would be the Sleepwalker teams, skeleton crews containing one skilled member of each onboard species, revived in regular rotations for equipment calibration, navigational adjustments, medical surveys of the cryopods, communications monitoring, and now, apparently, rose-pruning. Kholai had inclined its magenta head in the dim lights of Aphrodite, the only place on Hephaestus Station that could be reasonably called a bar, and proclaimed: "This one accepts that all things in the universe trend toward corruption and wishes to note that the flowers will all most probably die before the first Sleepwalker cycle, just as entropy will one day take all beings."

The hanar's followers intoned their agreement, but half the crew took deep cultural offense at the idea of not having a giant topiary in the middle of the ship. Osyat Raxios, a drell political refugee, informed Kholai that if he did not *immediately* shut the fuck up, he would stuff every one of his jellied orifices, if he could find any, with the ancient and undeniable beauty of the usharet blossom. Borbala Ferank, the retired matriarch of the Ferank crime family, claimed the only reason anyone objected was because they thought ignac cones, and by extension, batarians, were ugly and unworthy of sharing space in the "snob garden."

"With explosive fury: You can take my pretty flowers over my dead body," droned Threnno, an elcor psychiatrist.

"We need this," bellowed Irit Non, right before punching an anti-bouquet batarian in the groin. "We need something the whole ship can point to and say: We *can* grow together in peace!"

Soon enough, half of Hephaestus Station had broiled and fumed and brawled over flowers. In the end, Commander Senna'Nir, the quarian second-in-command, had presented Irit Non with six stalks of *keleven*, a breed of blooming high-protein celery developed and grown in the biovaults of his birth ship.

Thus was the first cross-species decision of the crew of the *Keelah Si'yah* made. Few subsequent ones would prove much different.

Anax Therion saw two other figures drift sleepily toward the glass airlocks. Their Sleepwalker team leader, Commander Senna'Nir vas Keelah Si'yah, stumbled forward on his birdlike, backward-kneed legs, his violet-and-gray suit reflecting in the minimal lighting. Yorrik, their medical specialist, pounded the metal deck toward the glass on four huge feet, bouncing along like the universe's clumsiest child on his triple dose of amped-up revival drugs. Anax stared. She had never seen an elcor *bounce*. She suspected she never would again. Her head throbbed in agony, but she ignored it. The pain was of no use to her, so she put it aside.

Yorrik curled and uncurled his outermost pair of lip slats. Another elcor would have understood him instantly. One twitch of his soft gray mouth would be enough to communicate an ocean of drug-induced mania, intellectual excitement, nausea, terror, and wry amusement at his own stimulant-addled behavior. An elcor's natural communication was nothing so crude as the spoken word. They used scent, infra-vocalizations, and microgestures to express a vast array of subtle meaning that was completely lost on aliens. Nothing on their homeworld of Dekuuna, or even on the Citadel, was much of a secret to the elcor. The hanar were similar. Therion had had her eyes genetically modified in order to see the bioluminescent display of the hanar language. But she had not had the foresight to get a good enough nose job to speak elcor. Elcor could communicate a symphony with a sneeze, but they could not modulate their voices to convey meaning the way the rest of the crude, chattering, squawking galaxy did, and so carefully prefaced each thought with appropriate emotional context. Yorrik intoned, "Enthusiastically: Greetings. Greetings. It is a beautiful morning. Don't you think it is a beautiful morning? With overwhelming joy: What horrible thing do you think has happened?"

Anax rubbed her long second finger against the black nail of her first, as she always did when she was trying to calculate the world around her. Back on

Kahje, men fled from that quiet little gesture. It meant she had them. It meant they were finished already.

"It's not morning," the drell answered dryly.

"Hello, Yorrik," the first officer said fondly.

"Overflowing with enthusiastic camaraderie: Hello, Senna'Nir vas Keelah Si'yah."

Therion rubbed her fingers together, but nothing came. She needed more information. The three of them revived—but no one else. Not the Quorum, not the colonists, not the Pathfinders. Not even all of Sleepwalker Team Blue-7. Just the three of them. A detective, a doctor, and a tech. Why? A ridiculous thought bubbled up in her groggy mind. *An elcor, a quarian, and a drell walk into a bar...* Anax Therion giggled, then was horrified. She did not *giggle*. Any more than an elcor bounced. She clapped her hand over her mouth to keep any other dreadful thing from coming out.

Senna'Nir spoke first. He patched his suit mic into the Radial's public audio system so the rest of them could hear him. This was a quarian ship, and the quarians ran the show.

"Situation rep—urk." Senna was clearly fighting back a bout of vomiting. His environmental suit would feed him anti-nausea meds, and not for the first time, the drell thought that maybe the quarians had the right idea with those things. "Maybe we should wait. For the rest of the team. Also for the room to stop spinning," he continued weakly.

The ship's vocal interface echoed through the empty spaces of the Radial.

The remainder of Sleepwalker Team Blue-7 are still in stasis, Commander. There may or may not have been an emergency. Due to the nature of this emergency, if it has occurred, protocol specifies limiting personnel to essential only. Please enter command-level password key to initialize additional revival sequences.

Anax Therion narrowed her huge reptilian eyes. There was an old human folktale involving a feline owned by someone by the unlikely name of Schrödinger. This feline was locked inside a sealed box with no entrance or exit. In the folktale, an impossible riddle was asked of the hero: *Can you tell whether this feline is alive or dead without breaking the box?* Anax had always liked humans. They thought everything was impossible. But the riddle was only a riddle for organics. For a computer, it was as easy as activating internal sensors. The ship should know damn well whether or not there was an emergency. And it *really* shouldn't be using personal pronouns. A drell ship's interface might, or a human ship, or an asari one. But no quarian wanted their ship talking to them like a person. It would be like genetically modifying a rabid dog so that it could tell you just how much it hated you before it ripped off your leg.

"That's fine for the moment," Senna said, shifting his weight on his slender, jack-knifed legs. "What's the potential emergency?"

The acceptable mortality threshold for cryosuspension may have been exceeded. As of 1700 hours, I think that 10.1% of the drell on board this ship are deceased.

Anax Therion's head snapped up.

Until that moment, the drell had been leaning in a rather artfully casual pose against the airlock glass. Even while her memory battered her brain, she had barely moved. She often found it advantageous to appear as though she cared about very little in the world, and paid attention to even less. That way, others could parade their cares and attentions around the room and hardly even notice the tall green woman in the corner, listening for all she was worth. When you made it your business to observe people and steal their secrets, it paid to be able to hide your own. A moment ago, Anax looked for all the world like a young punk being forced at gunpoint to attend her parents' excruciatingly boring party: long green arms crossed over her lithe chest, pointed chin sunk sullenly into her neck-frills, left hip in a posture of vaguely suggestive belligerence. But not anymore. Her heart had begun to race horribly. Her gut twisted. She stood up straight and slammed her hand against the alcove glass.

"What do you mean you *think*?" she barked. "They're either dead or they aren't!"

Your attention is required.

Senna's voice remained calm. "Give me the data from the cryopods. Port to display."

The glass alcoves in front of Anax Therion and the elcor Yorrik lit up with information, scrolling through line after line of glowing blue text as it updated.

All cryopod scans show strong life signs. I have already run three diagnostics on the pods themselves. No detectable malfunctions. No interruptions in service or connection.

"Then what's the problem?" Senna frowned.

Yorrik butted the glass wall with his head. Even a drell and a quarian could interpret that gesture. "Furious irritation: If all life signs are good and all pods are functioning you are wasting our time."

I have detected a thin layer of sublimated water vapor which has crystallized on the interior shell of 10.1% of the drell cryopods. It has been growing at the rate of approximately one nanometer a year for the last forty-four years. Very slow, but observable to my environmental scans.

"Some frost is to be expected," Senna said uncertainly, studying the illuminated readouts on the inside of his helmet. Suddenly, they changed, showing a stream of chemical symbols.

This frost contains faint traces of butanediamine, pentamethylenediamine, and herpetocrose.

Yorrik thumped the thick gray knuckles of his left foot against the deck to get their attention. "Helpfully: Butanediamine and pentamethylenediamine are also known as putrescine and cadaverine. Both are gases produced by autolysis, the initial breakdown of amino acids in fresh cadavers. Herpetocrose is a blood sugar specific to the drell. With growing understanding: 10% of the drell show signs of freezer burn, and the ice is rotting."

Affirmative.

"But the pods show all occupants alive and well?" Anax said. Who were they? Who were the 10.1%? Those were her friends sleeping away centuries in their pods. She'd gotten to know them well over the long months of waiting at Hephaestus Station. Even loved a few. Had Osyat Raxios died? Cawdor Thauma? Prokhor Rhabdo?

Affirmative.

Anax Therion's mind filled up with every corpse she'd ever seen in the streets and slums of Cnidaria City, slumped over in alleys, blown apart on docks, frozen stiff at their terminals in dingy data sweatshops, overdosed and poisoned and shot and worse. *Rotting dolls all in a row. Old blood flakes apart, flying up into the night like the ashes of a single fire. Black eyes under an eyelid of red mold.* She shoved the memories aside savagely.

"Kepral's Syndrome?" Senna'Nir asked delicately.

The poor quarian was trying to be polite. Oh yes, if it was Kepral's, then everyone could make sympathetic faces and go back to sleep with a deep sense of relief and satisfaction, the way you feel when you're resting cozy in your own quarters and hear security rushing by outside. Toward someone else. Someone who had nothing to do with you. Only the drell got Kepral's Syndrome. They were a strong enough species, but their lungs were their weakness. They had evolved on a desert world. When the hanar made first contact and evacuated the drell from poor resource-starved Rakhana, the great pink jellyfish had taken them to their own homeworld, Kahje, an ocean planet. The moist air killed drell slowly; over decades, but it killed them. Any moisture in the air was a slow poisonous rot filling them up until they finally stopped breathing. It was called Kepral's Syndrome, and Anax's parents had died of it when she was six. *Green fingers like bare tree branches, skeletal, brittle, hot with death. Coughing in the dark like gunfire. Be good, Anax. Be a good girl. But don't stay here. Find a way offworld. Find a place with no oceans. Their last breaths rise to join the sea air. They become their murderer.*

No. Anax's mind clamped down harder. The last thing she needed was to be swept away into the memory of that tiny six-year-old's misery, and everything that followed because of it.

A lot of people's parents had died of Kepral's Syndrome. But everyone who booked passage on the ark had tested clean. On the other end, they'd find a world that didn't quietly drown them. That was how it was supposed to happen. And they were so *close*.

"Have you run a *self*-diagnostic?" she snapped at the disembodied voice of the *Keelah Si'yah*'s systems.

"You said the traces were very faint. Maybe you're getting some phantom readings. A bug in the code."

Yes. I am performing at optimum.

"We didn't notice *crystallized decomposition* fogging up the glass on the last cycle?" Senna asked. "That sort of thing is the whole point of Sleepwalkers."

You would have had no reason to notice. The sublimation began after the previous Sleepwalker cycle, fifty years ago. I have revived you in order to visually inspect the affected pods. You were the last Sleepwalker team rostered for duty before Andromeda. I am not authorized to awaken the next team on the list as the list has concluded. If there is a simple scan malfunction or pod contamination, you can repair it. If the drell are indeed dead, you must decide upon a course of action. I am not authorized to make command-level decisions. You are, Commander.

Yorrik's mouth, little more than a series of triangular flaps cut deep into his gray flesh, wriggled with worry. "Suspiciously: Do you expect me to perform medical exams?"

You are the only member of this Sleepwalker team with formal medical training, Specialist Yorrik.

"Wry self-deprecation: I am a pediatric allergist. Auditory, olfactory, esophageal." Anax Therion and Senna stared at him. "In sheepish explanation: Ear, nose, and throat. I do sniffles."

Nevertheless. You are essential personnel.

"Helpless laughter: I have not touched a corpse since the battle of Viluuna. With increasing panic: You can pump me full of stims or euphoriants or children's candy, but it won't make me a drell coroner."

Senna held up his three-fingered hand. "Let's not get ahead of ourselves. We'll go down to the hibernation deck, check everything out, and proceed from there.

It's just as likely that we'll find everyone sleeping safe and sound and you won't have to do anything."

I calculate the likelihood of zero fatalities at less than 1%.

"You're not helping," Senna sighed, and disengaged from the public audio.

An hour's worth of gravity adjustments, humidity filters, airlocks, elevators, and security bypasses later, the three of them were staring down at a fully functional cryopod displaying excellent life signs.

Inside, a female drell's face contorted in frozen agony. Her eyes stared lifelessly at nothing. Frost coated small, hard sores on her neck frills and chest. Her tongue was swollen and black. Anax Therion clenched her jaw. She'd hoped, if they found a corpse, it would be one of the thousands of drell she didn't know. Connections got in the way of clear analysis. Emotions were not data. They were a kind of encryption, obscuring the information, rendering it unreadable. But Anax Therion did know that frozen girl. Not well, but well enough to drink with. She was married to Osyat Raxios, a dissident Therion might actually, at a stretch, call a friend. The two of them had kept her up late so many nights on Hephaestus, talking politics like anything in the Milky Way would matter once the ark's engines fired up in the dark.

Yorrik breathed through a humidifying mask. The air in the drell sector was so dry it would desiccate his mucus membranes in a quarter of an hour. "Deep revulsion: She smells like usharet flowers. And wet volus."

"I don't smell anything," Senna said, puzzled.

"With mild inter-species prejudice: Impossible. It reeks in here. Disdainfully: How do you even get out of bed in the morning with a nose like that?"

"Well, maybe I'm clever enough not to go snuffling around dead bodies without a suit to protect me," Senna snapped. His painkillers must be wearing off, thought Anax. Hers certainly were.

"Condescending tone: Nonsense. Cryosleep maintains the body at a temperature far too low for any harmful bacteria to replicate or spread. Appropriate solemnity: Her death is her own."

Therion looked down at the corpse. She rubbed her second finger against the nail of her first and put their connection somewhere else in her mind where it could not contaminate her analysis. "An equipment malfunction does not present with sores and blacktongue. The most likely cause of death is poison."

The elcor droned: "Leaping to conclusions: We have been sabotaged."

"*Or* there may have been a malfunction in the cryopods, a completely accidental chemical contamination. Organic tissue does not play nicely with industrial coolants or power surges. These pods utilize modest mass-effect fields, and those sores could be a reaction to topical contamination from their waste products. Or," Therion finished carefully, "it could be a pathogen. Which *could* have been acquired before stasis. Hephaestus Station was hardly a sterile environment. Of course, I'm not a doctor, but it's *far* too early to assume sabotage. We have no data except the dead. I'm surprised at you, Yorrik. I thought elcor were supposed to be slow and deliberate?"

"Uncontrollably manic: These are the most stims I've ever taken. My brain feels like a jet-fuel milkshake. Embarrassed: I will be quiet now."

Senna sighed unhappily. Anax sympathized. They had come so far in the dark without incident. They were so close. The quarian toggled his suit to broadcast again, to save time.

"K, can you detect any toxic compounds, mass-effect field byproducts, or a measurable viral load in the cadaver currently occupying cryopod number..." Senna bent down to read the serial number off the lower ridge of the pod.

"Soval Raxios," Anax said softly. "That's Soval Raxios."

"Cryopod number DL2458," Senna finished.

There is no cadaver in cryopod DL2458. The occupant, Soval Raxios, age thirty-four, shows a slightly elevated blood alcohol level. Turian brandy. She is otherwise in perfect health.

Anax, Senna, and Yorrik blinked. They looked down at the frozen corpse in its canister. Her open mouth in its rictus of death.

"Surprised understatement: She's really not," the elcor droned.

Apologies, Commander Senna'Nir. I can only report what system scans show. I am not equipped for analysis. I understand your objection; however, Soval Raxios looks fine to me.

"Soval, I am so sorry," Anax Therion whispered. Her spine suddenly went rigid with a hard punch of memory.

"Laughter like emerald bubbles," she whispered. The others stared. She hated that they stared. She hated that she couldn't stop the memory. "Eyes as clear as hope. Hephaestus; the night before. She dances in the tavern, faster, faster. Soval, who was a poet and a wife. Soval, who pours out brandy like light from one vessel to another and whispers her whiskey words: *You'll see, in Andromeda, everything will be perfect.*"

Anax's milky lids withdrew, leaving her eyes black and wet. She relaxed, shaking. The drell put one hand over her mouth so as not to breathe the air of the dead and closed her friend's eyes with the other. "May the goddess Kalahira bear you safe across the sea."

They moved down the rows of elegant rounded cryopods, but Anax no longer wondered what they would find there. The riddle was answered. The box remained sealed. The feline was dead.

Excuse the intrusion, but while you have been speaking, I have detected pentamethylenediamine sublimation in five more cryopods.

Anax Therion let out an involuntary cry of frustration.

"*Five* more drell dead?" she growled. "What is *happening*?"

Incorrect, Analyst Therion. Four drell and one hanar.

Too bad, thought Anax Therion. *Hanar can't get Kepral's Syndrome. Is that the sound of security coming back around to you, Commander? Not so cozy now.*

Senna'Nir vas Keelah Si'yah clenched and unclenched a three-fingered fist.

"Initiate revival sequence for the rest of the Sleepwalker team, K," he said. His voice only trembled a little. Anax wouldn't have thought a commander's voice would tremble at all. "Command passkey: alpha-iota-gamma-gamma-9."

The stars streamed by above them, reflecting in the glass hatches of three thousand cryopods whose displays showed identical, cheerful readings: *All's well, all's well, all's well.*

3. BINDING

Commander, the remainder of your team is revived and en route.

"Thank you, K," said Senna'Nir, as he always did, even though he knew it was unnecessary.

Senna had always felt affection toward virtual intelligences, sometimes more than he felt toward the wet, squishy, disorganized mess of organic intelligence. He could never tell anyone that, of course. Except his grandmother Liat, who never judged him. He wasn't even sure if she had it in her, the old dear. Did any grandmother have it in her to condemn her only grandson? But to call Senna's opinions on this subject blasphemy would be underselling the whole *concept* of blasphemy. Taking an ancestor's name in vain was blasphemy. This... This was far worse. It was like saying he felt affection toward the... the *thing* that attacked the Citadel two years ago. The Reaper. If it had been a reaper. If reapers were something other than a particularly ugly fairy tale. He'd been there. He'd *seen* it. And he still didn't know. All Senna could remember was a black shape as big as death itself, something part insect, part ship, part god, lasing the cool glassy corridors of the heart of civilization until they were molten slag, shattering them into corridors of fire. His Liveship, the *Chayym*, and two others, had left the Migrant Fleet in a holding pattern just outside Citadel space to dock for a month of desperately needed repairs, trade, and meetings between the Council, the Admiralty Board, and the Conclave. He'd loved every minute of it. His parents were busy all day and night, negotiating on behalf of the Conclave, the quarian civil government. He'd been completely free, and he'd taken advantage. Exploring every inch of the Lower Wards, standing in the green shade of real trees on the Presidium, haggling with hanar over whether a mint-condition Reegar Carbine was worth a tank of mindfish *and* an old set of contra-gravitic levitation packs for him to dissect in his own time. Senna had been sitting on a bench in the Presidium, outside the Embassy Lounges where his parents were in yet another closed session, debugging a complete volus enviro-suit pressurization valvework he'd gotten off a tech in Zakera Ward for hardly any of the mindfish at all. There was a keeper standing next to him, its pale-green insect body curled over a control panel, as mute and mysterious as those strange beings had always been. He looked up from his code and into the keeper's faceted eyes, lit up with the artificial sunset. And then there'd been the sound, a sound like the death of hope, and that black shape hanging in space, and his mother and father. Running. Running past him.

Running to beat the fire.

Machines were the great love of Senna's life. And that was his sin. He might as well say that he loved that *thing* that ended his world as he'd known it. But he couldn't help it. He could open up to machines, and they never laughed. Machines had never ignored or neglected him because there was so much more important work to be done. Machines had never left him alone for days while they shouted and argued in the Conclave. Machines had never lied to him. Machines had never told him he was wasting his potential. Whenever he wanted to talk to a machine, the machine answered. Right away. Like they wanted to talk back. Late at night, with his emergency induction port sunk into a glass of turian brandy, he could even understand the geth. Yes, they had destroyed his people and stolen their homeworld, but they had their moments, their beauty, their logic. After all, what being anywhere wanted to be a slave?

He envied the quarian Pathfinder, a stellar cartography specialist he'd known for years named Telem'Yered. It had been down to just the two of them in the end. He still didn't know why the captain had chosen Telem, a lower-ranking officer. He didn't think it was personal. All that business between them had been years ago, before the Citadel, and long before the Initiative. The captain had loved Senna once. He loved her still. She had done her Pilgrimage with the salarians, he with the elcor, and afterward, they'd been assigned to the same ship, a mid-range freighter called the *Pallu'Kaziel*. He'd always liked that, since he first saw his name next to it on the Great Roster. *Pallu'Kaziel: Nevertheless, Justice Comes*. It had pained him somewhat to remove it from his name when they finally committed to the Initiative project. To never again be Senna'Nir vas Pallu'Kaziel, and now and forever be Senna'Nir vas Keelah Si'yah. Senna and Qetsi had been happy on the *Pallu'Kaziel*. His grandmother had approved of her. At least, he thought she had. It was always hard to get much out of her when it came to that sort of thing. They'd been young and hormonal and political. They'd joined the Nedas movement together, a group of radical quarians who believed the endless quest to recapture Rannoch had doomed their species to an eternal hardscrabble homelessness, without a future, without a past, without a voice in the hallways of galactic power, for who bothered listening to a people without a planet? Nedas wanted to give up the battle and simply find a new world to settle on. Start over. Create something new. Senna remembered their initiation, in a tiny clean room on the *Pallu'Kaziel* that their friends in the movement had prepared for weeks so that they could share environments, the greatest intimacy possible among quarians. Side by side, giddy with ambition and rebelliousness and a frizz of fear at being outside their suits, their friend Malak'Rafa had tattooed the motto of the Nedas movement onto Qetsi'Olam's and Senna'Nir's biceps with a thrice-sanitized holo-gun: "Mered'vai Rannoch." *Forget Rannoch.* No one else would ever see it under their protective patchwork suits, but they would always know it was there. She'd been so beautiful, behind her faceplate.

But Qetsi'Olam had always been more serious than he. About everything. About nutrient paste, let alone the destiny of their race. She always saw the big picture, and the picture was always biggest when she described it. Details never mattered as much as the dream. And before the Citadel attack, he just couldn't feel the same urgency she did. He could be happy on the Fleet, or on Rannoch, or on a new world. He'd drifted away from politics. She had not. Their unequal feelings had found a natural equilibrium. Until the Initiative had given her, and the Nedas movement, a way to achieve all their dreams with one gorgeous ship and one gorgeous pinprick on a star chart, six hundred light years away. Qetsi'Olam was finally a captain. And she would finally get her way, for the sake of any quarian who would follow her.

After the Citadel, that ability to be happy in the sky or on a homeworld or in a clean room the size of a closet, asking a young punk quarian exactly how many times he had sanitized that holo-tattoo gun, was gone. And once it was gone, into what dark unknown would Senna'Nir not follow Qetsi'Olam?

But it wasn't like Qetsi to let emotional considerations, to let *history*, however complicated, get in the way of her decisions. And she must have known that for Senna, having the SAM installed would be a secret dream come true. Such an advanced synthetic intelligence coupled with him forever? Even if he'd only been allowed to carry the implant in his suit instead of in his skull like the others. Even if his SAM had to be shackled, hobbled, hard-coded never to become a true intelligence. No quarian would fly with a full, unshackled AI. Not after Rannoch. Not after everything. Not even Qetsi'Olam. As radical as she fancied herself, she was not *that* progressive. He did understand that, even if he didn't agree. A true machine mind was like any other sentient creature: some were kind and good. Some were monsters. It was all in how they were raised. The quarians had been bad parents, there was really no denying that.

Still. It would have been like having a new best friend. One who could never leave like everyone else did.

And maybe, just maybe, those thoughts were *exactly* why the quarian Pathfinder was good, solid, upstanding, anti-geth hardliner Telem'Yered, sound asleep as he should be at 0517, thirty years before arrival, while Commander Senna'Nir was wide awake with the mother of all headaches and something terrible happening, quietly, slowly, all around him.

His throat was dry. His suit immediately increased the humidity of his air supply, but it didn't help at all. He took in fluid from the pipette near his mouth. The others were coming in. It would not impress anyone to have his voice cracking like a teenager.

The hanar apothecary Ysses drifted up into its alcove, its huge wedge-shaped head nodding gracefully, long pink tentacles floating above the deck. Slowly, the squat, round volus design engineer called Irit Non trundled up and leaned against the glass for support. The eyes of her brown-and-white environmental suit flashed yellow in the ammonia fog of their zone. A confused batarian female took a seat near the clear glass barrier. She was old, but wiry. Three of her enormous black eyes were unfocused and bleary with the lingering effects of cryosleep. The fourth, her lower right, had been gouged out and badly healed. Her chartreuse skin had a sour teal slick to it in the dim running lights. She looked angry. But then, batarians always looked angry, and Borbala Ferank was the most perfect specimen of her species who ever lived. The ship's manifest listed her as a former security officer. She was not, Senna knew, but it amused her to be listed as such. The irony was as endless as the voyage to Andromeda. Borbala had once been the matriarch of the greatest crime family on Khar'shan, the Queen of Smugglers, the Knife in the Dark. She was now, theoretically, retired. Though that ruined eye made it a bit more than theoretical.

Sleepwalker Team Blue-7 was fully awake and assembled. It was no longer quiet in the Radial.

A buzz of annoyed bewilderment filled the room. The three newcomers got busy sorting through the emotions Senna, Anax, and Yorrik had already processed. They were not due to arrive for another thirty years. The viewports conspicuously failed to show the cool white docking terminals of the Nexus, the massive station already built by the Initiative and waiting for them in the Andromeda galaxy. Yet here they were. Senna found himself unreasonably irritated by their slowness. *Yes, yes, come on, catch up.* All anyone was really saying or mumbling or growling or sneering, in various ways and combinations and with varying levels of profanity, was: *What the hell is going on?* And Senna had no time for a repeat performance of this particular pantomime.

"Good morning, everyone," announced Commander Senna'Nir.

"Still not morning," Anax Therion sighed.

The quarian commander ignored her. "I hope you all slept well."

"Wry rejoinder: It is not the sleeping but the waking up that is hard," Yorrik droned.

On a ship of strangers, they were old friends. Senna had met the ancient, enormous Yorrik on his Pilgrimage on Ekuna, learning the elcor combat tech. Those great creatures carried sophisticated, backhump-mounted mobile VI systems into battle that ran constant simulations of every possible action-reaction-outcome triad. Before an elcor fought once, he fought a thousand times. As his final test, Senna'Nir had built one from scratch. Compared to the top-of-the-line models it was about as fast and lethal as a large hat, but it worked. Yorrik had taken him to see a live performance of their favorite play to celebrate, and afterwards, they'd gone on a bar crawl through New Elfaas City that would go down in the annals of inter-species history. He'd taken immuno-supplements and antivirals for weeks beforehand to prepare for just what exactly a shot of krogan ryncol would do to his insides. Senna had rather liked what it did to his insides in the end. Made him feel like he was made out of stained glass.

When Qetsi'Olam had told Senna about Andromeda and the *Keelah Si'yah*, he'd contacted Yorrik at once and made the offer. *Come with me. Let's make that crawl stretch between galaxies.* Yorrik had always had a sadness about him. Senna had known this long trip into the wild was just what his elephantine friend needed.

Ysses pointed its soft triangular head toward the flower arrangement in the center of the Radial. The hanar, a massive, genderless jellyfish-like creature whose light home-zone gravity kept it floating upright without levitation packs, seemed displeased that the flowers had not died. Its long magenta tentacles quivered slightly.

"This one does not feel good," said Ysses shakily, in the peculiar musical voice common to the hanar. No hanar would ever be so arrogant as to refer to itself as *I* or *me*. They believed that an ancient race called the Protheans had created all things, and would one day return to lead them to glory. Beside the Protheans, all species were as simple bacteria, and bacteria were not worthy of personal pronouns. "This one's filter glands proclaim the end of all things."

The elcor medic Yorrik intoned: "With deep sympathy: The psychological effects of cryosleep vary in severity and duration individually as well as from species to species. Rueful amusement: Some patience may be necessary."

"I feel fine," snorted Borbala Ferank. She crossed

one black leather-wrapped leg over the other and leaned back, scratching the complex bony ridges in her long skull with greenish-yellow fingers. "Only the poor get hangovers."

"No one asked you, Khar'shan-clan," wheezed Irit Non. Volus always sounded like they had a bad cold. They wore protective suits, like the quarians, but not because their immune systems were compromised from centuries of living on the Flotilla. Volus were an ammonia-based species, accustomed to the intense gravity and high-pressure greenhouse atmosphere of their homeworld, Irune. Yet even in the heavy stench of their custom environmental zone aboard the *Keelah Si'yah*, Irit Non kept her suit on. But then again, Senna supposed, so did he, despite the safe, near-complete sterility of the quarian sector. His suit was a part of him, and he was a part of it, like the old lullaby. *Sing me to sleep on the starry sea and I'll dream through the night of my suit and me…*

Maybe volus felt the same way. Who knew with aliens?

Anyway, no one ever went out to a bar determined to find out what a volus really looked like under all that. On the outside, they looked more or less like large, fat, tailless badgers walking upright. The muzzles of their masks, like old radio speakers, filtered their voices into a nasal, metallic whine. But Irit's suit was not like other volus suits. It was sleek and stylish. It gave off an air of power, of mystery. The patterns of brown, black, gray, and white mesh were as elegant as a raloi's feathers. Senna'Nir could not stop staring at it. There were many vastly more important matters at hand, but he had never seen a volus suit look *beautiful* before. He hadn't even known they *could*. But, of course, it would be. That was what Irit Non was famous for. She was a tailor, in a manner of speaking. The wealthiest volus in the galaxy withered and died on her waiting list without complaint, on the mere hope of receiving one of her custom environmental suits. That wheezy volus was the closest thing to a celebrity on the *Keelah Si'yah*.

"Remind me why we let batarians on board again?" the volus hissed.

Senna, for whom the Battle of the Flower Arrangement had happened only a few days ago, and not nearly six hundred years in the past, rolled his eyes inside his helmet and pounded twice on the glass with his gloved fist.

"Shut up, all of you, thanks. I know you're all confused and sick and irritable, but we have a serious problem, and you need to focus on what I'm saying, because time may be a factor here. If you need to throw up, try not to get any on the glass. Do hanar vomit? Never mind. Not important. All right. Approximately four hours ago, Yorrik, Anax Therion, and myself were revived to deal with an apparent malfunction in the hibernation systems."

Ysses's pink skin rippled. Irit Non came to attention. Even Borbala uncrossed her legs and sat up straight. They might come to blows over flowers and hangovers and whether or not the Andromeda galaxy really deserved to have batarians inflicted on it, but the hibernation systems were a grim equalizer. Anything that affected the cryopods affected them all. Anax Therion visibly seethed in her alcove, but said nothing. Senna went on: "What we found is considerably worse than a malfunction. As of 0530 hours, we have visual confirmation that four hundred and sixty-one drell and two hanar have died in their pods of unknown causes."

Anax rubbed her second finger against the top of her first. Senna wondered about that. She'd done it on the cryodeck, too. He knew little about her, except that she'd been some kind of detective on the hanar homeworld, which was, presumably, why the ship had deemed her essential personnel. Would they have a problem? Detectives often took poorly to not being in charge. But for now, she seemed to be keeping her peace.

"They did not revive; they did not suffer," Senna said, though they were not entirely sure about that. Soval Raxios's dead, open, horrified eyes floated up into his mind. Shouldn't they have stayed closed in deep freeze? "In fact, their pods still report their status as alive and in perfect health. Which presents us with a number of grave questions."

Irit Non cut in. "Do you mean to say there's still a bunch of frozen sides of dead drell beef just lying down there among all the others? No burial rites? No quarantine? Savage!"

Borbala Ferank tilted her head to the right. Senna had met a batarian or two on his Pilgrimage on the elcor homeworld. He knew this meant she considered herself far superior to the person who'd dared to speak to her. The commander saw Therion clock the gesture as well. In her line of work, Anax had probably met a lot more batarians than he had. He needed to talk to her. Alone.

"Their souls have already risen through their eyes and left their bodies," Borbala said dismissively. "What is left is unimportant. Chuck them out an airlock like empty cargo containers. That is what they are."

"With great delicacy and hesitation: We may need those bodies," Yorrik answered.

The quarian commander cleared his throat. "We may indeed. And either you're not listening or you're still too groggy to put one logical foot in front of the other here. The *Si'yah*'s scans can't actually 'see' any problems with the pods. Of course, they don't *see* at all, strictly speaking, that's merely a convenience of language. What we mean when we say a ship *sees* is a complex data relay of input, output, and throughput return—"

"Now is not the time for a technical lecture, Commander," the drell said softly.

"Yes, sorry. So, the problem is, all systems read each and every one of the four hundred and sixty-three deceased as alive and well. I can assure you they are the opposite. Even when we removed one of the bodies from its pod, the ship's medical scan reported that they were *completely* healthy, ready to jump up and run a couple of laps around the physio-maintenance deck. The scans are *useless*."

"This one inquires into the status of the other VI on board," hummed the hanar. "There are several independent virtual intelligence systems on the *Keelah Si'yah*: the diagnostic VI in medbay, the navigational VI on the bridge, the calibration VI in engineering, the educational VI in the children's areas. This one also presents a subject no one else wishes to discuss: what its family on the homeworld would call 'the unenlightened heathen in the room'—the SAMs. This one would feel great peace if this team were simply to awaken the Pathfinders and allow them to resolve the dilemma."

"Now *that's* a good idea," said the batarian, clapping her hands. "That jelly's the only one of you with a brain. Problem solved."

"Problem *not* solved," Senna insisted.

The night he took her offer to serve as second in command, Senna and the captain had sworn to each other over plates of nutrient paste that they'd treat every species aboard equally, no matter what bad experiences they might have had with their people in the past. They were a one-ship Migrant Fleet now. They were all quarians. So why, when he meant to be open-minded, did batarians always have to be so terrible? Presumably one or two existed who were not slavers, dealers, pirates, or worse, but Senna had never met or heard of one. "The other VIs are just as bricked as the *Si'yah*'s internals. They're hardwired into the ship's array in the first place; their scans use the same mechanisms. If the well is poisoned, so are the villagers, so to speak. Convenience of language or not, the Keelah Si'yah is blind. As for the SAMs, I thought of that. Pathfinders aren't assigned to Sleepwalker teams for a reason. They're just plain more important than us. We're interchangeable. They're not. They have one job—find us homeworlds. This is pretty far off their duty roster. And right now, we could just be looking at a technical glitch—a tragic one, Anax, I'm not trying to downplay it. But it's probably a glitch we can repair in a few hours. In which case, I'm not willing to break Pathfinder protocol because it's annoying to have to be the one to fix it. And if it's not... Ferank, if it's not, if we're talking about a disease here, we can't risk exposing the Pathfinders to it, or the SAMs to whatever is infecting the ships' computer systems. If these deaths are intentional—"

"Intentional?" interrupted Borbala Ferank. Her tone had a vicious edge. "Am I to understand that we are under attack?"

"We?" Anax said icily. "The drell have lost over four hundred. If there is an attack, it was clearly targeted at my people. Sit down, merchant."

Hate boiled in Borbala's three good eyes. You could not insult a batarian by disparaging her looks or her parentage or even her intelligence. But to imply a lower socio-economic class was fighting talk. Senna would have thought Anax had a cooler temper than that. At least she hadn't called her a beggar.

"If it is intentional," Senna shouted over them, trying to keep it calm and professional and utterly failing, "we must know before we arrive. With the ship's internals doing whatever it is they're doing, or not doing, our investigative legs have been cut out from under us. The only reason we even know about it now is that the *Si'yah* found a slight chemical discrepancy between an environmental report and a medical report. We are here because those 'sides of drell beef,' as you so diplomatically put it, turned up a bad case of freezer burn. Otherwise we might have docked at the Nexus as a ghost ship. Now, Anax, Yorrik, and myself have drawn up a plan of action. Don't worry. There's plenty of work for everyone."

The hanar's soft voice slid through the Radial's audio. "This one wonders why we must be awakened. You are fully capable of performing funerary rites and retaining a statistically relevant number of the deceased for diagnostic purposes. Allow the dead their peace in the embrace of the Enkindlers. This one humbly suggests that if a mechanical accident has occurred, nothing can be done about it now. If a murderer has done his work within our sanctuary, that vicious sin is accomplished, and no others are in danger. This one is certain that the Nexus will have many experts and devices to separate the wicked from the good. What is this one expected to do?"

Senna sighed and spoke to his ship directly.

"K, since we have been discussing this, how many more pods have shown necrotic freezer burn?"

Two drell and one hanar.

"It's not over," Senna said grimly. "It's spreading."

"This one would inquire as to the nature of this it you speak of with such certainty," the hanar thrummed. Pale bioluminescence slid up and down its tentacles.

"No certainty at all," Anax Therion spoke up, and Senna found himself relieved to let her take the helm. He had accepted Qetsi'Olam's request that he serve as second-in-command because he'd accept her request to shove himself out an airlock if she made one, but at heart, Senna had been and always would be a tech. Telling machines what to do was so much more straightforward than telling people what to do. Machines did exactly as instructed. People always thought they knew better.

The drell detective stood in her alcove with military-grade posture. "As of right now, the probabilities are fairly evenly split between accidental poison, such as a toxic malfunction or leak in the pod itself, deliberate poison, which would obviously require a poisoner, whether on board or back at the station, or a communicable disease, again, acquired on board or on Hephaestus. Soval was a member of Sleepwalker Team Yellow-9, so we cannot rule out her encountering something else on the *Keelah Si'yah* and carrying it into the cryopod system when she resumed her hibernation some fifty years ago."

"But the cryopods are not linked," protested Irit Non with a strangled wheeze. "They're designed as self-contained systems, precisely to avoid this kind of cascade effect in case of a malfunction. Someone would have to interfere with every pod individually in order to kill the occupants. That seems incredibly unlikely."

"Why?" answered Therion. "Be careful of ruling out possibilities just because they seem improbable. People are improbable. Technology is improbable. We are riding in a bullet fired six hundred years into the future. That is improbable. At this stage, it is criminal to dismiss any theory. Consider: Whatever happened began after the last Yellow-9 cycle. Is it impossible that someone programmed a single pod to revive after they completed their shift and spent the last fifty years at liberty on the Keelah Si'yah, working on pod after pod? Some of us are very long-lived. Fifty years would be nothing to an elcor—"

Yorrik's broken-trombone voice blared over Therion's. "Offended protestation: No elcor would do such a thing. Proudly quoting in expectation of warm mutual recognition and acknowledgement of source material: 'In form and moving how express and admirable, in action how like an angel, in apprehension how like a god. The beauty of the world. The paragon of animals.'"

"I'm sorry, are you quoting *Hamlet* right now?" Senna'Nir cut in, laughing despite himself.

"Defensively masking wounded self-esteem: Elcor *Hamlet*."

"You know that bit's about humans, don't you?" Borbala Ferank barked laughter. "And it's a load of dung either way. I've always known you elcor weren't so big and cuddly and innocent as everyone thinks."

Anax Therion went on calmly. "You're all thinking of this far too simply. This is one possibility. There are many others. We are trying to determine causality from a desert of data. Think of the possibilities like a forking river. The largest fork is this: on purpose or by accident? From there, infinite possibilities split off. If: then. If by accident, then we need fear nothing, and must only control the damage. If we are dealing with a single point of failure, an individual saboteur, then fifty years is not an entirely unreasonable commitment for a hanar, either. If they were willing to sacrifice themselves for the work, any drell, quarian, volus, or batarian could be our man, if a single person, or any person, is responsible at all. It would be a simple thing for us to miss one empty cryopod among the thousands. It could even be one of us. Who were the last people we can be absolutely certain were awake before everything went wrong? I'm looking at them."

"Who the fuck do you think you are?" the batarian Borbala Ferank snarled. "I will not be accused by some eyeball-licking lizard who thinks it's people."

Anax took a deep, calming breath. "I am but a simple servant of the god Amonkira, Lord of Hunters. But I do not hunt for meat. I hunt for data. And I am not accusing anyone. I'm trying to show you that *we don't even know what we don't know*. For example, none of what I just said takes into account the possibility of an asari or krogan stowaway, for whom fifty years would be a hilarious joke. If it was an asari or krogan, it's as easy to imagine they did their work a hundred years ago or more. What matters a century to a krogan? And naturally, a percentage must always be set aside for something I have not yet thought of, something I have missed. But it could be more than one person. It could have been an accident. And knowing *who* did it, if there even is a who, is less useful to us than curtains on a salarian dreadnought if we do not know *what* they did, or *how* it happened without the ship shutting it down."

"The pods have more sophisticated scrubber systems than a quarian suit," Irit rasped through her own air filter. "There is just no possibility that poison or a disease would not be discovered and immediately purged. It has never happened before in the history of cryotech!"

Ysses's tentacles rippled. "This one regretfully interjects that no being has departed their mortal form in a cryopod in the history of cryotech, and yet, it seems to have occurred. Nearly five hundred times. This one additionally humbly begs to understand why the quarians do not remove their suits when they enter stasis if the pods are proof against all infection."

Senna started to answer, but he didn't get a chance.

"I don't think you understand what I'm talking about," protested the volus. "You are not an engineer, you're an apothecary, which we all know means booze smuggler, not scientist. You don't understand how things *work*. Even *if* you entered stasis sick, *and* somehow the initial medical scan didn't find the problem and patch you up, even *if* you somehow got injected with a tube full of the goddamned genophage in transit, cryostasis stores the body at a temperature far, far too low for any viral or bacterial replication. Nothing *happens* when tissue gets that cold. That's why we don't age. There simply are no physical processes taking place. If you fall asleep with a sniffle, you'll wake up with one. It can't be an infection, because people are dead, and you only die when a pathogen can get its trousers on in the morning! No harm can come to a person in cryostasis. That's the whole *point*."

"Regretfully: Any disease that would kill a drell would have a very hard time jumping to a hanar. Your anatomy is not compatible. Helpfully sharing: Viruses and bacteria are fine-tuned to the species they infect. Only an extremely small percentage is even capable of cross-species contamination. Brightly: For example, while drell live in close proximity to the hanar on Kahje, Kepral's Syndrome cannot infect the hanar, because it is a degenerative lung disease, and the hanar do not have lungs."

"Maybe we got a bad batch of pods at the outset," Senna said doubtfully. The Initiative wouldn't skimp on something like that. "The sores could have been chemical burns, or mass effect field runoff, like you said."

Irit Non had gotten herself so worked up she was pacing in her alcove like a trapped animal. She seemed somehow offended on the pods' behalf. "Senna, you're a code man. I respect that, but expecting you to know the first thing about the hardware is like expecting a psychiatrist to cure the Blood Plague. If it was a problem on the fabrication end, they'd all have failed at the same time, and you'd see failures all over the ship, not just Rakhana-clan and a few Khar'shan-clan."

Anax Therion's green browline lifted in amusement. "Well, congratulations, Sleepwalker Team Blue-7! In less than ten minutes, you seem to have ruled out poison, disease, or equipment malfunction, as well as sabotage, and accident. You're about as helpful as the *Si'yah*'s scans. It must not have happened, then! What a relief for all those drell. Back to your pod, then, volus. Back to your 100% safe, completely uncompromised, flawlessly functioning pod. We won't even check it over, since you're so sure. And obviously, since it's perfectly capable of adjusting pressurization and gravity, and no harm can come to a person in cryostasis, you won't need your environmental suit, either. In you go, naked as a newborn yahg."

"You do love to hear yourself talk, don't you?" chuckled the batarian. "If you're so smart, why don't you figure it out for us and we'll see you at the Nexus."

Senna could see the drell beginning to lose her patience. "I *told* you, we need more *data*."

Irit Non wheezed and coughed. She stopped pacing. She curled her chubby shoulders in, as if to defend herself from their reaction before she said whatever was about to come out. "I'm not drell. Or hanar. And nothing can get past my suit's filters. So it's… not my problem."

Anax Therion and Borbala Ferank stared at the volus with five black reptilian eyes between them.

"Sorry," the volus mumbled. "Sorry."

"This is what's going to happen," Senna announced, a little too loudly. But it did the trick. Not a person on this ship hadn't served aboard another one at some point. They came to attention eventually, if you sounded like you were giving a command, not asking for an opinion. "Suit up for common environmental conditions. We're going to split into three teams. Yorrik and Ysses will be Team What. You'll take three of the corpses into medbay and perform autopsies, figure out a real, solid cause of death we can build a theory on. Anax and Borbala, you'll be Team Who. Scour the ship for your theoretical stowaway—"

The volus Irit Non wheezed and sucked at the air through her filter. "You want them to secure the ship on foot? This ship? The *Keelah Si'yah*? We're a kilometer and a half long and weigh seventeen million tons. Surely the ship's computer isn't a *complete* paperweight."

Senna'Nir was grateful that his helmet made it impossible for anyone else to see the sarcastic curl his lips always took on when someone blathered on at him about a totally simple solution he must not have thought of.

"K, please run a scan for any life signs on board. Exclude the six of us and all entities currently in cryostasis."

The voice of the ship's interface came back cool and calm as ever.

No life signs detected, Commander.

"Any empty pods in the cryobays?" The quarian continued.

Negative, Commander.

"See? A lot of work saved," said Irit with a modest cough. The yellow-green lights of her eyes even seemed to shine a little brighter with self-satisfaction.

"Yes, and we'll definitely believe her, because she was so right about everything else. She literally can't tell the difference between a corpse and a living person at the moment. What makes you think she can see a living person if they don't want to be seen?"

The tall, lithe drell blinked both sets of eyelids at him with a slow sensuality he always found unsettling among her kind. They never *meant* to look at anyone like that. It was just how they were built. "She?" said Anax curiously.

A helmet covered a multitude of sins, and this time it covered his flush of shame. Shame, and very slight pride. Of course the ship's computer interface had no gender. The voice he'd selected from the audiobank was slightly more on the female side of the slider than male, but no more than slightly. But he was the quarian he was, and he'd worked so closely with K. He thought of her as her. *This is why you're not Pathfinder,* he told himself ruefully. *Telem'Yered didn't teach the ship interface to use the pronoun* I *because he thought it sounded friendlier. Telem'Yered never installed three separate conversational matrices so that the ship could talk to him at night. Telem'Yered never talked to the ship at all if he could help it. That's what a real quarian is. You're just a freak.*

"It. Whatever you like. The point is, Analyst Therion, access the small arms locker on the bridge, and check the Sleepwalker logs for anything unusual that might have fallen through the cracks in the *Si'yah*'s diagnostics, as they are obviously taking a very long lunch break. And if there's time, sweep the ship as best you can, at least the cryodecks."

"Six hundred years of Sleepwalker logs," the batarian repeated sourly. "With *her*. Lieutenant I'm Smarter Than You."

"I'll be gentle," said Anax Therion.

Senna ignored them. "Irit Non and I will be Team How. Hardware and software. We'll take the pods and the scans, pinpoint the blockage, and fix up any damage. With a little luck, we'll have this locked down within forty-eight hours. Just another Sleepwalker shift. Yorrik, how long will it take to run the autopsies?"

"Anxious distress: Normally, three autopsies would take no more than an hour, but—"

"That's fine, let's meet in medbay in three hours to report findings," said Senna, in the tone of voice his mother used to use when she wanted to move to a vote in the Conclave.

The metal rings on the elcor's blue-and-purple

head covering jangled as the creature shook his head violently. "With stubborn but necessary resistance: It will not take an hour. It will not take three hours. Without medical scans or a diagnostic VI, there is no useable equipment in medbay. All medbay devices are networked with the ship's computer. If we cannot use the *Keelah*'s datacore, medbay is functionally empty. What we need is there, but, to use the vernacular, it is all bricked. Resentful rhetorical question: What do you expect me to do an autopsy with, a shotgun and some omni-gel?"

Silence returned to the Radial. As they all thought it over, several red usharet petals fell from the flower arrangement to the clean floor of the ship.

The drell leaned carefully against one wall of her alcove. Her pale interior eyelids slid closed. Senna heard her whisper through the glass: "In a steel cavern, a shipment of shadows. Chests of treasure stand everywhere like lonely walls on a battlefield. Like a school of bright fish people move around me: pink, green, brown, yellow, gray, violet. A little bird calls to its mother: a quarian child runs in. Quick, darting. Her suit the color of storms. What does she cry out? 'Mummy, Mummy, I can't go to sleep without my friends! They're stuck in there!' Mother bird swoops down. Her fingers move like light on water over the surface of one treasure chest among thousands. Its true name graven on its flank: NN1469P/R. Out of the darkness within, the mother plucks two soft dolls, beloved, worn as memory: a plush green keeper with plastic claws. A toy volus with glowing eyes. 'Pick one, Raya'Zufi vas Keelah Si'yah,' says the mother bird. 'Only one.' Little bird sings, clutches her keeper to her chest. The volus vanishes back into the chest. Curious:

Mother bird ignores what lies beneath. But the volus hides the true treasure: a black statue with a heart of silver and glass."

Anax Therion's eyes cleared. She raised her green three-fingered hand. "I think I saw a kid's toy microscope in the cargo hold when I came on board. Crate NN1469P/R. Does that help?"

4. SUSCEPTIBILITY

Yorrik and Ysses stood side by side in the freezing, shadowy medbay. The dead hanar on the slab before them looked almost purple in the steady blue running lights that glowed all along the floor and out of the wall recesses. Scabbed, frosted blisters ringed the upper third of its tentacles, where the arms joined its body. In the cold, the living pink jellyfish hanging in the air next to Yorrik smelled like seawater and ozone with a touch of nervous herbal greenery somewhere deep within the waves of personal scent. The elcor inhaled deeply, trying not to look like he was inhaling deeply, hoping to get a sense of who his new lab partner was beneath all those tentacles and softly shifting lights playing over its slick skin. He had never really known a hanar. Perhaps he was misinterpreting the tense, fearful wafts of astringent plants in its body odor. Perhaps that's how a hanar smelled when they were fully at peace.

Senna had promised to bypass the energy-saving protocols as soon as he and the volus could image the ship's run state at the time of the initial malfunction. Yorrik wasn't a tech. He didn't know what that meant, except vaguely that since the lights were out when everything went sour on them, they had to stay off for a while longer. No different than any other autopsy, he supposed. It only did any good if the poor bastard was in more or less the same condition they had been in when they died. Not that it mattered much.

An elcor's sense of smell was far more powerful than all four batarian eyes put together. As for the hanar, they communicated amongst themselves by pulsing with elaborate patterns of bioluminescence. Their entire culture relied on being able to see the slightest flicker in the dark. The lights were not the problem.

The problem was, Yorrik wasn't much of a doctor, and this wasn't much of a medbay. In the end, no matter how prepared the quarians wanted to be, the *Keelah Si'yah* was never meant to be anything more than an intergalactic tram service. Here to there. Nothing more. Frozen people didn't need complicated medical procedures. If anything went seriously wrong with a Sleepwalker, standard operating procedure was simply to put them back to sleep and wake them up on the Nexus for a quick patch-and-go. There had simply been no need to waste time, space, and money on very much more than medi-gel, a couple of bandages, and a few vials of vitamin and calcium supplements. After all, the quarians themselves had their suits, which was almost as good as walking around inside of a fashionably cut medbay all your own. And in Yorrik's experience, the quarians were not a thoughtful people when it came to races other than their own. Except Senna. But then, Senna was an exception to so many things. Nevertheless, Yorrik would probably have agreed with the decision if he were not currently being punished by it. Why splash out for state-of-the-art? The medbays on the Nexus would have every luxury. They'd be able to sort all this out in half a minute, tops. Here… Here it was going to take longer. The lab was spacious enough, but Yorrik had seen better-stocked field hospitals. *After* the battle. Everything was gleaming and clean and brand new, the hypodermic injectors and readout displays still factory-sealed. But of course, they couldn't use the readout displays. And without one measly scan online, essentially, this medbay was a very fancy closet with one shoe left inside it. And that shoe was a very poor fit for an elcor allergist.

Yorrik had never wanted to be a doctor in the first place. His father had been one, and his grandfather. He'd done what was expected, when he was a young elcor. Served honorably in the military as a medic in this war and that. But he'd wanted so much more out of the Milky Way than staring down stuffed-up slats and infected olfactory canals his whole life. He wanted excitement, adventure, artistic fulfillment! He wanted *applause*. That was why he was here, hurtling toward some absurd unknown galaxy. To escape a tedious lifetime of telling frightened little elcor, "Say ahhhh." Yet here he was. Back in a medbay looking down another goddamned sore throat.

These particular sore throats were, admittedly, somewhat *more* sore, and a lot more interesting than any young calf with a cough.

Three corpses were laid out neatly and ready to go in the operating area. They were still frozen beneath a hard, clear environmental control hob that would keep them that way. The hob, at least, seemed to be in working order. Frost glittered on the drells' swollen black tongues. A male, a female, and whichever or both or neither of the two a hanar was. Anax Therion and Borbala Ferank had hauled them up from the cryodeck before heading down into the cargo hold and crate NN1469P/R to retrieve, hopefully, Baby's First Electron Microscope. Leaving them to wait. Alone. In the dark, with three dead bodies. Yorrik looked out the observation window at the stars beyond, then down at the horrible death popsicles before him and sighed. "Glumly: I was almost Polonius, you know," he said flatly.

The hanar hung in the air, shining faintly. After a long, awkward moment, it murmured: "This one cannot formulate a socially appropriate response to that statement."

"Melancholy nostalgia: They auditioned hundreds of elcor. I made it all the way through the auditions, callback after callback. Seeking praise: I look the part, don't I? I'm properly big and imposing, old but not frail, warm and fatherly. I've got it all. Mr. Francis Kitt went with a younger actor in the end. Jaded bitterness: Don't they always? But I was assured by the studio that I was absolutely their second choice. With defiant certainty: He might have been younger, but he didn't love *Hamlet* more. No one does. Conspiratorially: I do not believe that Shakespeare wrote it. I do not believe any human wrote it." Yorrik was not accustomed to speaking or thinking this quickly. An elcor's life was large and long. They could afford to consider. And reconsider. And reconsider their reconsiderations. They did not share with outsiders. They did not make small talk. But now, fueled by revival drugs, Yorrik's intellect moved at the speed of an overstimulated salarian. He could not stop himself. "With disdain: I have met many humans. They move fast, shoot quickly, speak carelessly. Withheld revelation: Hamlet has the soul of an elcor. He cannot decide. He must deliberate for a long, long time. With excitement: Do you not think the famous line, 'Accusatory: Eyes without feeling, feeling without sight, ears without hands or eyes, smelling sans all' could describe the sensory organs of my people? We have four feet but no hands," Yorrik lifted one massive foreleg and flexed his long, thick, soft gray three-fingered toes to demonstrate, "and our eyes are weak in comparison to our sense of smell. Why else would Hamlet say, 'Wry awareness of double meaning: You shall nose him as you go up the stairs?' Humans cannot even tell their mothers from a batarian war beast with their puny noses. Additionally, *Dennmaark* sounds far more elcor than human. Some have theorized it is a bastardized form of *Dekuuna*. Bashful admission: By some, I mean me. I have theorized that. With deep spiritual certainty: There is no possibility that it was written on Earth. Thoughtful speculation: Perhaps, if Hamlet had had an elcor combat VI system, he could have run a simulation, and been more confident of the correct choice. Confidential whisper: Yorrik is not my real name. I was born Naumm, in New Elfaas on the planet of Ekuna, a very respectable, very serviceable, very plain name. I changed it, to honor the greatest play ever written. Quiet desperation: To remind myself of my dream. In Andromeda, there will be no Francis Kitt to cast a younger elcor. There will be Yorrik, and many people thirsty for entertainment. With fierce ambition: I spent my time on Hephaestus Station writing elcor *Macbeth,* which is not quite as good as *Hamlet* but has a higher kill count among the *dramatis personae*. It is sixteen hours long. The Nexus will love it, I am certain."

"Yorrik is your soul name," the hanar agreed musically. It seemed relieved to have understood something in the elcor's story, anything at all. "This one also possesses a soul name. Ysses is but this one's face name. But this one strongly suggests that it is unseemly to tell your soul name to a stranger."

The elcor snorted. "With great annoyance: It is unseemly to stand around in the dark with corpses with nothing to do and not make conversation."

Ysses pointedly said nothing.

"Regretful addendum: I am sorry. Did you know… that one?"

Ysses pulsed in time to the low hum of the ship. It stared down, if they could stare, at the dead hanar. Its third longest tentacle twitched. Yorrik noticed and tried not to read anything into it. It was always very hard to remember that other species did not encode their every gesture with vast banks of personal information. On an elcor, that tiny movement would have meant: *You're an idiot, I hate you, and if there were any justice in the universe, I would be in command of this entire vessel.* But sometimes a tentacle was just a tentacle.

"This one accepts the fundamental truth of the universe that all things decay and become corrupted. The ambitions of mortals are especially vulnerable to the forces of chaos in the universe. That one's face name was Kholai. This one did not know it well, but it is the reason this hanar came to Andromeda. Though of course all save the Enkindlers are as weak and degenerate as insects devouring the remains of a log, Kholai was… a great insect. It would appear that its ambition… was vulnerable. This one cannot believe the death of this particular being among all the hanar on board could be an accident."

"Curiosity: Was Kholai a government official? A magnate? An actor?"

Ysses's voice grew thick and watery. "It was a priest. This one does not wish to discuss it. This one mourns." The hanar seemed to compose itself. "This one wonders if an elcor cannot simply *smell* the cause of death and save a great deal of trouble."

"Patiently: It is possible, but we cannot thaw the bodies yet. If an infectious agent is at work, it would be very dangerous to work with chemically live tissue. The volus was correct—cryostasis reduces the body's temperature far below the lee at which any physical process can take place. When Senna and Irit Non restore full power, we can activate a biostasis shield to protect ourselves. Until then, they must stay cold, and while they stay cold, their scents are stunted. I am limited much as the ship is limited. In hopeful friendship: Do you want to tell me your soul name, since you know mine? Then we will not be strangers, and everything will be seemly."

"No," the hanar said quickly.

The voice of the batarian woman burst into the room over the comm system, so loud in the large, empty hospital bay that both Yorrik and Ysses jumped.

"All right, you big dumb peasants, we've located crate NNwhotheshitcares and got the damn thing open. In what will be news to no one, quarians *really* love garbage. Whoever belongs to this crate stuffed it full of junk, most of it not even quarian junk. And, good news! We can all rest easy knowing that the Andromeda galaxy will not have to suffer without little girls' tea parties, because there's a whole set of cups and saucers and crap in here, as blue as an Afterlife dancer's ass. Oh, and a case of Horosk straight out of Palaven's cellars. Naughty, *naughty* mummy and daddy!"

The emotional context of Borbala Ferank's voice was extremely clear, even to Yorrik. Batarians were a very trying people. It was very trying for Yorrik to believe the best of them, even though he tried to believe the best of everyone, no matter how many eyes they had. As the indecisive Dane himself said: "Depressive utterance: There is nothing either good or bad but thinking makes it so." And no one, either. When you had to preface every phrase with such careful emotional exposition every day of your life among aliens, you learned empathy quickly and well. It was probably very trying for the batarian to go so long without stealing anything, snorting red sand, or enslaving anyone. Everyone had trials.

The drell's voice somehow managed to roll its eyes. "I cannot imagine they would have been allowed to take much from the Migrant Fleet, Borbala. Bad enough they permanently reduced quarian manpower. No one would have let them carry off any tech useful to the Flotilla. Besides, you must know the quarians do not generally believe in belongings."

"Yes," chuckled Borbala Ferank over the comm. "It's a very convenient belief for those of us who *do*. Everyone should adopt it."

They could hear Anax rummaging in NN1469P/R. Her voice was muffled by the crate, while the batarian's echoed in the cavernous cargo hold. She did not seem to be helping. "We're lucky they brought luggage at all," the drell said. "Ah! Here! Microscope achieved, medbay. It is not much of a microscope, I fear. I believe it was designed to interest small children in the wonders of science. Small krogan children, by the maker's mark. That's... optimistic of them." Decades ago, krogans had been infected with a disease called the genophage by the salarians to control their overactive fertility. Their fetal mortality rate was over 99%. There would be krogans on the Nexus, Anax knew. She would be very interested to find out how they expected to get a civilization going in Andromeda. "I suppose salarians don't need to be encouraged to go into microbiology instead of blood sports. I hope they got a good trade from the quarians for it, whoever they were. It is old. It is heavy. It 'comes with a detailed full-color manual and pre-packaged slides of sixteen different kinds of exotic plant and animal tissue from around the Milky Way to capture the imagination.' But it is something."

"In despair," Yorrik droned. "Wonderful."

Anax's stifled voice came back: "Is there anything else you can think of that might be useful?"

As the last of his personalized stim cocktail worked its way through his bloodstream, Yorrik lost his patience, which is to say, he spoke as evenly and without intonation as he ever did, but much louder, and medbay suddenly smelled like a vicious grease fire on a lake of cheap black coffee as his pheromonal glands pumped his frustration into the air.

"With helpless fury: A MEDICAL SCAN. A MEDICAL SCAN WOULD BE USEFUL. IS THERE A MEDICAL SCAN IN THERE, ANAX THERION? Is there a diagnostic VI in that crate? What about a blood analyzer? Perhaps a full cellular regeneration cart?"

The hanar rippled with concern. "This one worries at this level of agitation and whether it is conducive to science. Although this one is greatly ignorant in the field of medicine—"

"Aren't you supposed to be an apothecary?" Borbala interrupted over the open comm line.

"May the Enkindlers forgive the arrogance of this one in using such an august word to describe its profession. The words of the volus in the Radial came nearer to the truth of this one's insignificant existence. This one possesses more experience in the provision of pleasant toxins than the expulsion of unpleasant ones, and in the holy realms of pharmaceutical medicine, can only make the gift of knowledge of such tonics and serums which confer side effects desirable to paying customers. However, this one does not wish to discuss its personal history, but to propose an alternate—"

"By the Pillars of Strength, is it still *talking*?" The batarian's gravelly voice rolled through the empty medbay again. "I swear that we could all die and turn to dust before a hanar can get around to the damn point. Yorrik, my dear and darling member of the intellectual class." Yorrik knew enough of batarian society to realize this was not a compliment to his intelligence, or a compliment at all. On Khar'shan, you were aristocracy, or you were meat. "With impatient emphasis: Is. There. Anything. Else. We. Can. Get. You."

Yorrik stamped his left foot against the spotless, glassy medbay floor. "Explosive resentment: You do not understand. When there is something wrong with a patient, the doctor runs a scan. I am well trained to run a scan and prescribe treatment and say, 'There's a good boy or girl, here is a candy for being so brave.' I am not well trained in communicating telepathically with blood cells, which is what you seem to expect me to do. Sarcastically: Hello, little blood cells, what seems to be the trouble today? Do you have a bit of a nasty cold? Poor little blood cells. Growing anger: Do you think Ekuna is some kind of backwater where we treat our sick and dying with sticks and the juices of berries?"

Anax Therion said, "Of course not," but not loudly enough to drown out Borbala Ferank saying, "Is is not?" or Ysses meekly pleading, "Yes, but this one would like to point out—"

"None of us have a lot of options here, Yorrik," the drell said gently. "But people are dying."

"Stubborn resentment: Then you come up here and do it. Desperation: This medbay does not even have any petri dishes. Am I just supposed to grow cell cultures between my toes?" But even as the dull, emotionless words left his mouth flaps, his revved-up memory dredged up decades-old field medic training from the kindly ancient landfill of his mind. It was a deep landfill. Yorrik was three hundred and ninety-eight years old. Cell cultures. His grandfather Varlaam had grown cell cultures. During what New Elfassians called the Little Invasion. It hadn't been enough of a crisis for the rest of Ekuna to call it anything. Gangs of outsiders overran the city defenses, and then the power arrays.

Not outsiders. Not *just* outsiders. Quarians. Yorrik did not like to remember it. He loved Senna'Nir vas Keelah Si'yah, and had loved him when he'd been Senna'Nir vas Chayyam. The great, gentle elcor tried to put those memories back, but they would not go. All those helmets like mirrors where you only ever saw your own face, never theirs. Those strong, quick legs bounding through ancient streets, sacred gardens. Those gray-and-purple figures in the night. They'd gone dark for weeks, then. Under siege. He understood now that they were not proper quarians. Fleet quarians. They were criminals, gangs of undesirables and anti-socials the Fleet could not adequately contain. They had been dumped on Ekuna, a harmless outlying world. A Fleet problem had been solved. An elcor problem had been created.

He'd been terribly young, only a hundred and twelve, and terribly sick. If Grandfather Varlaam had not known the old ways, he would have died. The old elcor had tried to teach his grandson, of course. With every twitch of his long toes and pulse of his musky, smoky, rich forest scent, Varlaam had told him how to heal without a medbay. *You can't call yourself a doctor if you need fancy machines to do the work for you, my boy. The machine can call itself a doctor, but not you.*

But Yorrik had only half listened. He had never wanted to be a doctor in the first place.

Borbala's gritty voice cut through his memories on the comm. "Uh, did you say dishes?"

"Hopelessly: Yes."

"I can make dishes happen. May I interest you in the little girl's tea party set? There's at least… service for six here. Cups, bowls, saucers, and I think this is a Thessalian spice pot? Does it matter if they match? Because one of the cups is clearly from a human set. It has hearts and Earth butterflies on it. Gods, I can't stand humans. So obsessed with their stupid world they even draw their insects on their belongings."

"Why would it matter if they match?" the drell said, dumbfounded.

"Well, *I don't know*, Anax, I'm not a scientist, that's why I'm asking *questions*."

Ysses interrupted in its friendly alto tone, only slightly strained by not being listened to in the slightest. Yorrik noted the change in smell: a tang of blood in the seawater, coppery and rich. "This one thanks the Enkindlers for their miraculous gifts of a microscope and petri dishes, as well as inspiring, in their wisdom, the quarians to equip this medbay with working laser scalpels which do not seem to be affected by the present technical difficulties. This one inquires with great love and respect for all beings who seek knowledge whether this is not enough to begin a rudimentary analysis." The hanar seemed surprised that it managed to get through more than one sentence and pressed its luck. "Furthermore, this one deeply wishes to illuminate something—"

Yorrik, still half-sunk in his memories of the Little Invasion, ignored Ysses. "Pessimistically: Please remember that we do not know what we are looking for. We are merely hoping the most basic tests provide a result because we have no capability to pursue anything more than the minimum baseline analysis. Deferential callback: Anax, as you said, we are still at the first fork of the river. If; then. We must run a full-spectrum toxicology scan, in case it is chemical contamination or deliberate poisoning, and *also* analyze blood and tissue samples for the presence of any foreign virus, bacterial infection, or at least the presence of antibodies, in case a pathogen is responsible. If we are very, very lucky, it will be a bacterial infection, because we could see that with your baby krogan microscope. If we are not lucky, it will be a virus or a poison. Viruses are too small to be seen without real equipment. Experimental joke: And while toxins are perfectly visible, they do not wear nametags."

How had Grandfather done it? Yorrik tried to remember their old house in the working-class district of New Elfaas, the warm clinic full of helpful substances and devices he did not have now. He tried to remember the smell of Varlaam's lessons, not unlike the current smell of Ysses's fickle body—saltwater, ozone, the ripe clean sweetness of fish ready to be eaten...

"Sudden realization: Anax Therion, is there anything in your quarian crate that glows in the dark?"

"Um… a few things, I suppose. Why?"

"Excited explanation: A long time ago, my home city had some trouble with… embittered euphemism: tourists. With growing confidence: While the battle raged on, my grandfather made us test whether our food was safe to eat. There are certain fluorescent dyes which undergo a chemical reaction in the presence of a wide variety of toxins. If the poison is there, they will glow. One color for this poison, another for that one. It will be very faint, even under the microscope, and they cannot detect every possible toxic compound like a proper scan would, but it would cover a lot of ground. Ashamed: I am foolish not to think of it sooner. Additionally, while viruses are too small to be seen under a microscope, they cannot absorb dye through the surface membrane, and therefore, in any given sample, the *absence* of dye should be very obvious."

"Excellent, Yorrik, walk me through it. What am I looking for?"

"Self-denigrating frustration: I cannot remember. My grandfather told me to pay attention but my fever was very high and… and… miserable confession: I did not care. I thought I would be something more than Varlaam when I grew up. I thought I was too good for the family business."

The bioluminescent film that hugged Ysses's magenta body brightened in a series of quick pulses. "Please, friend Naumm, this one begs you to listen—"

Yorrik let out a small trumpeting squawk of indignation. Three of his stomachs curdled. Had the hanar a nose, it would have gagged from the stench of hot soup and rotting fruit that flooded the room as the elcor's humiliation reached his scent glands.

"Naumm?" said Borbala Ferank.

"Is someone else there with you?" the drell asked sharply.

"Deeply insulted: Naumm? My name is Yorrik. Betrayed: Why would you call me that? I told you that in confidence."

"This one meant no offense. Yorrik is your soul name, chosen to match the true nature of your holistic being. This one did not wish to enter into intimacy with you, nevertheless, you intemperately shared both your names with this hanar, and thus by the law of the Enkindlers a bond exists where this one desired none. It is this one's duty to protect those with whom it shares a bond. You should not use your soul name so casually, among workplace colleagues and batarians. This one calls you by your face name to honor and protect—"

"With hurt and anger: Don't."

The hanar dipped its shell-like head in shame. "This one begs all those present to allow it to present a simple solution—"

"Embarrassed determination: No, I will remember. I can remember. I am not better than Grandfather Varlaam and I will not let my ancestors down. Speculative response: Anything phosphorescent is likely to have usable compounds, however..." It *was* coming back to him now. The labels on Varlaam's bottles, the little mnemonics his grandfather learned from the chattering traders who sold him those bottles by the crate. He'd loved them. He'd been so charmed by the idea of needing words to remember something when you could just give it a sniff and know everything about it. "Reciting from memory: A minimum of six dyes are necessary to perform a broad-spectrum screen. Impatience with the effects of aging on the mind: What was it Grandfather used to say? What was it? He thought it was the funniest thing he'd ever heard, a mnemonic of infinite jest..." Yorrik's lip slates flared stubbornly.

"This one must insist that this mental effort is—"

"Triumphant roar: I've got it! *Happy Turians Treat Raloi and Rachni to Dinner.* Proudly: We specifically need hydroxypyrene, trisulfonic acid, thionin acetate, rhodamine, ruthenium dichloride, and... delicately: the commercial dye known as Drell Belly Green no. 15."

"Is that what it is known as?" came Anax's dry voice on the comm.

"Regretful reply: I am sorry, I did not name it."

The hanar's skin flashed a furious blue. The smell of clean fish and seawater coming off Ysses had turned to rotting fish and sopping mold.

"Who does this one have to strangle to get a word in edgewise in this Enkindler-forsaken place? Listen, unbelievers!" Ysses tilted its head upward. Its tentacles fell straight and relaxed to the floor. "This one wishes to speak with the computer interface of the ship *Keelah Si'yah.*"

Hello, Sleepwalker Ysses.

"Greetings, *Keelah Si'yah.* This one entreats you to list the ways in which blood may be analyzed without the use of a medical scan."

In case of power malfunctions, please access the data hub on Deck 14. In the meantime, limited results may be achieved using a microscope, electron microscope, quantum microscope, cell cultures, hemagglutination assay, gene sequencing, injection of artificial antibodies in order to bind with any antigens present, enzymatic catalyzation, chemical reactivity tests, or the introduction of fluorescent dyes into the sample.

"Forgive this one's further intrusion, but what are the names of these fluorescent dyes?"

Hydroxypyrene, trisulfonic acid, thionin acetate, rhodamine, ruthenium dichloride, and veridium tricupridase, known commercially as Drell Belly Green no. 15.

Ysses's satisfaction smelled like sunlight on warm water and boiling sugar. Yorrik usually liked it when people smelled happy. He didn't like it now.

"This one has been attempting to inform its companions that there is no need to reinvent the submersible. The *Keelah Si'yah* may be blind, but it is not yet stupid. Though all living beings are but savages beside the grace of the Enkindlers, no one has yet been reduced to utter barbarians. The gifts of the gods still abound. *Keelah Si'yah*, this one respectfully wonders where these dyes may be most commonly found?"

"Well, I'll be fucked by a turian with a grudge," laughed Borbala. "Shoulda listened to the jelly."

Hydroxypyrene is used frequently to amplify the output of industrial and domestic worklights by applying a thick coating to all reflective surfaces. Trisulfonic acid—

Anax yelled suddenly from the innards of crate NN1469P/R. "Wait! Wait a second, I'm certain I saw—yes! I've got a bedside lightdome here. It is shaped like a miniature omni-tool. One down! All right, K, what follows hydroxypyrene on our glow-in-the-dark grocery list?"

Trisulfonic acid is an important component in small to mid-size batteries and power packs as well as cosmetics suitable for dextro-protein species.

"There must be some quarian make-up in there. Check the mother's stuff," Borbala advised, and by the clarity of her voice on the comm, she was still advising while lounging comfortably outside the crate.

"Belaboring the obvious: Do you think quarians live their whole lives in suits only to open them up every morning and put on lipstick?" Yorrik droned.

"Actually, the microscope 'comes ready-to-learn with four supplementary power packs to satisfy even the needs of your little scientist.' Batteries secured. Next, K." The drell was actually beginning to sound cheerful.

Thionin acetate is used primarily by weapons manufacturers to illuminate power indicators, overheat displays, night-scopes, and decorative flourishes without draining the main fuel supply of the weapon, as well as in the payload of certain flare guns.

Ysses and Yorrik listened patiently to a long rummage and several loud crashes.

"Would an Adas Anti-Synthetic Rifle work?" asked Anax finally, slightly out of breath.

Affirmative, Analyst Therion. The safety indicator, scope light, and ammunition gauge all utilize thionin acetate.

"I must admit, I'm positively *invested* in this family," mused Borbala Ferank. "Guns, booze, toys, and a junior science fair."

"Dry wit: Sounds like a quarian to me," said Yorrik, who was beginning to worry that this was taking so long. They had to report back to Senna'Nir in a few hours. He glanced down at the frozen corpses nervously. He did not like the look of those sores on the drell neck-frills. He did not like them at all. There were so *many* of them.

"Amonkira walks by my side on this morning," said the drell with a raspy, rather pretty laugh. She corrected herself. "Still not morning. Once more unto the hunting grounds, K?"

Ruthenium dichloride is most often used together in commercial canning, preserving, bottling, and labeling, though it is toxic to asari, humans, and salarians.

"Quarian nutrient paste doesn't require much in the way of preservation," Anax said doubtfully. "I don't think we're going to find any jars of jam in here. Most of our food stores were meant to be supplied by the Nexus and the Pathfinder worlds. Maybe in the other cargo holds. I did not want to go through the luggage records if we did not have to. There are twenty thousand of us. We'll be in the Andromeda galaxy before we finish paging through every copy of *Fornix* someone just had to bring along."

They heard Borbala Ferank's phlegmy chuckle coming through loud and clear. "Yeah, we don't need to. My favorite mummy brought herself that crate of Horosk, even though she's a naughty little war beast who knew it wasn't allowed. I've bought and sold more Horosk bottles than you want to know about. You can see the cork from space. Try something harder next time, you great hulking boat."

Veridium tricupridase, or Drell Belly Green no. 15, is widely used in toy and jewelry fabrication.

"Taken care of. The easiest one yet. Rhodamine is the last, yes? Honestly, my dear Yorrik, when you said fluorescent dyes, I thought there was no hope. Perhaps there is a rough luck in this universe, after all. Where can we scavenge our rhodamine, K?"

Yorrik marveled at how expressive the drell's voice was. He had no trouble understanding her, as he often did with aliens who insisted on speaking to communicate. The elcor could hear her smile through six decks between them.

Rhodamine was once a popular choice for laser etching and engraving, but is no longer favored by contemporary artists, due to its rarity. I am not aware of any mercantile exchange that advertises rhodamine in its inventory. It cannot be "commonly found."

Yorrik fumed. He'd known *at least* half of those. He'd have remembered in another minute or two. Of course the computer could come up with the answer. But the *Keelah Si'yah* didn't need an audience to thrive. A computer didn't need *applause*. And it didn't matter in the end. The ship didn't have the final answer any more than he did.

"And where," came the rough, velvet, unbothered voice of the drell detective, "might it be *uncommonly* found?"

Rhodamine can be found in mineral deposits on the moons of Xathorron in the Attican Beta system, in several outdated salarian vaccines, and was briefly popular as a lip stain among the asari. It can also be extracted from some species of bioluminescent deep-sea fish, such as the belan jellyfish, khar'shan snapping eel, and thessian sunfish, Analyst Therion.

"Wounded sarcasm: Good thing the Initiative built an ark for all those Thessian Sunfish who longed to leave it all behind and start their lives over again. I imagine it's right behind us."

The hanar chimed in. "This one knows you are all aware that all pets were classified as contraband by the Quorum."

"Disgruntled response: What kind of fool takes pet fish to space? They'd be dead before the first week was out. Dismissive pessimism: I assure you, there are no little cryo fishbowls full of iced eels on board. With insincere warmth: Unless you want to show us how the ship's computer can make tropical fish appear out of nothing, Ysses."

There was a long uncomfortable silence. The hanar glimmered. The elcor loomed.

Then the lights came on.

Medbay was flooded with blinding white light as Senna'Nir and Irit Non shut down the energy-saving program and fired up the power of the *Keelah Si'yah*.

The light flickered. Medbay went completely black. No calming blue running lights. Utter darkness.

The commander's voice joined the already crowded comm channel.

"How's that, Yorrik, better?" Senna said warmly.

"Weary sarcasm: Perfect."

Irit Non's phlegmy voice came through the comm. "Command node reports all power restored to medbay."

"This antechamber is as dark as the end of hope," mused Ysses.

Non growled. "I'm looking right at the sensors. It says full power restored. K, status report: lighting and temperature control, Deck Nine."

Hibernation-setting power protocols revoked for Deck 14. Temperature increasing. Full habitat lighting in use.

"See?" said the volus.

The darkness in medbay continued to be absolute.

"Growing realization: The sensors also say the cryopods are full of live drell." Yorrik looked down at the decidedly-not-live drell on his examination table.

"Shit," said Senna. "Inventory says there are some worklights in the supply locker. Do the best you can while we figure out what the hell is going on. Meet you in medbay in four hours. Senna out," crackled his friend's familiar voice.

Silence returned, somehow deeper and more awkward than before.

Finally, Borbala Ferank spoke into the comm. She no longer sounded quite so amused by everything that was happening, or convinced of her own untouchable superiority.

"Listen." The retired crime boss spoke as if each word was being dragged out of her. "I'm going to regret this, I just know it. You say we need fish? I can make fish happen. Just… sit tight. Ferank out."

The comm went quiet. Yorrik and Ysses were left once more alone in the dark with the dead.

Yorrik waited two full minutes before trying to make friends with the hanar again. He turned to the tall pink jellyfish and droned: "Hopefully: Do you want to hear the beginning of elcor *Macbeth*? I can do all three witches…"

5. PERMISSIBILITY

Anax Therion stood in the dark surrounded by frozen fish.

Crate ZB3301T/V was full of them. Any kind of fish you could ask for. Illium skald fish, prejek paddle fish, koi, striped dartfish, khar'shan snapping eels, even a massive Earth bluefin tuna, which, as far as Anax knew, was profoundly extinct. Dead to the world, they all floated in, by her guess, about fifteen hundred glass globes white with frost and capped with black plasteel instrument panels. Crate ZB3301T/V looked like it was crammed full of marbles. But they weren't marbles. They were contraband. Miniaturized cryopods. Less than a quarter of the energy required for theirs, keeping the fish special on ice for the big day. Anax Therion had never cared much about money beyond where it could get her, but she didn't even want to try to calculate how much profit she was looking at. What people on the Nexus would pay for a taste, figuratively or literally, of home.

Borbala Ferank shrugged. Her three good eyes shone in the dark of the cargo hold. "Old habits die hard, eh? You won't begrudge me my little nest egg, will you? My bastard sons drilled my accounts along with my fucking eye when they decided it was time for old Mama Bala to retire. Don't you just *love* the young? Ah, well, that is their right. Nothing made me happier than listening to the pitter-pat of little feet as my offspring schemed behind my back to take everything

I had. But they let me live! What a bunch of sniveling cowards. I should have turned them out on the street as infants. What was I supposed to do in Andromeda, take up an honest living? Ha! I am what I am. And what I am is a Ferank, and a Ferank is a smuggler and a schemer who ends up on top. And credits are credits, even in another galaxy. You gonna rat me out?"

Anax ran her hand along the top of a bright orange koi. She had seen one just like it on Earth, once, long ago. The day she heard the folktale of the cat that might or might not be dead in its box. The memory threatened to roar up inside her, but she sidestepped it. Her post-stasis disorientation was gone. She didn't want to think about Earth, or golden fish, or what she had done there for the sake of the hanar. So she didn't. She turned back to the batarian. She wasn't any more thrilled to be working with this unpleasant creature than Borbala was to work with her. Batarians didn't do *data*. They did *guns*. And Anax Therion felt quite confident that no gun would blow a hole in this situation large enough for the truth to bleed through. But at least she could keep an eye on the old warhorse.

"I do not know what else I expected," Anax said. "Is this it? Did you smuggle *anything* else on board?"

Borbala's red chin markings looked almost as black as her clothes in this light. She grinned, her chubby chartreuse cheeks dimpling. "Absolutely not."

The drell sighed. "Fine, pick us out a nice fat snapping eel and a couple of sunfish for our supper and let's go. We've still got our own assignment ahead of us, now that we're done supplying Ysses and Yorrik's mad science experiment. At least we will get to stretch our legs. And who knows? Perhaps we will find ourselves a rogue asari and get some real exercise."

"Sounds good to me," Borbala snorted. "Shove it all in the cargo elevator and hit medbay. They'll figure it out. Command and control is between here and the security hub, so we can load out there for a long, thrilling night of… watching vidscreens. Wanna snatch a couple of bottles of that Horosk? Because this is going to be excruciating and I don't get the feeling you're a very colorful conversation companion."

The two of them carried the cryofish back across the hold to the quarian area and began boxing up the rest of the haphazard collection of items the elcor doctor needed to save them all from whatever was happening. The drell's mind logged input and adjusted output so instinctually she hardly had to try anymore. Right now, the only available suspects were the other Sleepwalkers, and Borbala Ferank was the first to fall into Therion's analytical crosshairs. She was a likely enough prospect. There was a saying among deep-space merchants: *When something goes wrong, look for the simplest solution. When something goes* really *wrong, look for a batarian.*

You gonna rat me out? Borbala had included her in a small, but significant, conspiracy, the conspiracy of fish. That was how a batarian indicated trust and fellowship. She had made the effort to frame smuggling as a nest egg, something any outsider could understand and sympathize with. And now an offer of alcohol. It stank of an attempt to get the drell's guard down. Or friendship. In Anax's life, she had learned to view friendship as a very attractively wrapped grenade. It was always a trap. The minute you met someone, the pin was half-pulled.

Colorful conversation. Anax adjusted her posture, her voice, her vocabulary to become something closer to what the target wanted. What the target expected. There was no better way to investigate than by becoming the kind of person any given suspect most wanted to encounter in that moment. Anax Therion constantly calibrated her personality and behavior to illicit intimacy from anyone who had something she needed. Intimacy was the breeding ground of data. She was good at many things. But this had always been her great gift. The drell had evolved from reptiles, but Anax was a true chameleon. Micro-expressions, gestures, vocal tone, dialect, personal anecdotes, each of them infinitely variable to the needs of the millisecond. She had only been truly herself for one person, for one day, years and years ago. It had been a deeply unpleasant experience, one which Therion had sworn never to repeat.

Colorful conversation. Comrades of the bottle in the dead of night. Data points received. Calibrating.

"I spent a decade in the service of the most powerful member of the Illuminated Primacy, traveling the diplomatic road from world to world, party to party, gala to gala. I wielded my intellect with one hand and an M-6 Carnifex with the other. Oleon always said it valued me for my conversational skills nearly as much as for my marksmanship. I can sparkle when I need to. You need have no fear of a tedious vidscreen, Borbala Ferank."

"I didn't ask about your intellect, you bourgeois little scamp. I said *colorful*. How many languages can you swear in?"

Calibrating. Anax Therion laughed, a laugh designed in a laboratory to indicate both self-awareness and a roguish rough-and-tumble past. "How many are there?"

Anax grabbed two bottles of Horosk and tucked them in beside the omni-tool nightlight. She put the stuffed volus on top of it all, the toy young Raya'Zufi vas Keelah Si'yah had not chosen to take into her cryopod with her. The toy with glowing yellow eyes, just like a real volus. *When you wake up, all will be well, Raya'Zufi,* she thought. *You will examine every one of those sixteen slides with your krogan microscope and keep your omni-tool lamp on at night to scare away the things that move in the dark. And then you and I will have a tea party on a new world. I promise.*

Something caught Therion's eye as she was sealing crate NN1469P/R closed again for the duration of its long shipping and handling. She hadn't noticed it before, somehow, even though she'd been up to her eyeballs in this family's personal effects. It was folded up tight and small, but as she swung the lid over, the blue running lights flashed on its surface like a magnifying glass in the sun.

Anax activated her comm line to medbay.

"Hey, Yorrik," she said, to show Borbala that she could speak casually if it pleased her, "would a quarian suit help?"

A pause, and then: "Overwhelming relief: Yes, yes, absolutely. Enthusiastic cultural reference: A suit, a suit, my kingdom for an immuno-environmental suit. Uncertainty: But not if there is a quarian in it."

"No, it is an adolescent suit, most likely waiting for our young friend Raya to grow into it while suit fabrication spins up in Andromeda. I don't think she would mind if we borrowed it."

"With sincere gratitude: I will replace all of her things that I am about to break."

"Standby, medbay," the drell said as they pushed

their box of hope and backdoor science into the cargo elevator. Anax ran her hand over the young girl's environmental suit. They did love their suits. More like a friend than a piece of clothing to a quarian. Therion's eyelids slicked closed and she was back in the hold on packing day, surrounded by twenty thousand souls stowing their entire lives in chest-high crates, hoping to open them again on new lives.

She whispered: "Little bird hops along the steel, her mother's gray fingers like fog in one hand, her plush toy keeper green as new life in the other. The song of the little bird drifts through the cavern like snow falling into shadow:

Oh, I love my mother who holds me tight
And I love my father taught me right
Oh, I love my ship sailing strong through the night
And I love the homeworld for which we fight
But what do I love like a lock loves a key?
What holds fast my heart, head, shoulders and knees?
I love my suit and my suit loves me.

"May Amonkira walk beside you in your quest and secure your prey with swiftness, friend elcor," Anax said, and opened an access pad on the wall to return the elevator to medbay, key the directional lighting toward command and control, and make damn sure the infamous Queen of Smugglers didn't see her command code as she entered it.

IIIIIIIIIIIIIIII

"*Now* we're getting to the good stuff," Borbala said, rubbing her arms to keep warm outside the bridge hatch. "Small arms locker. Whaddaya think they got in there? Reegar Carbine? Terminator Assault Rifle? Maybe a Banshee or Hurricane IV?"

"Those are hardly small," Anax answered evenly, turning her body to shield her command code again as she opened the hatch for them. She didn't trust batarians and she certainly didn't trust this one. Yes, they were in this together, but that was no reason to get sloppy. "How can you be so cheerful?"

"Should I not be?"

"People have died. Many people. My people. The hanar. Maybe yours next. And I will tell you that while the commander says he believes the crisis will turn out to be minor, he does not really believe that at all. Neither do I."

"Many people always die. All the time. Every day. Do you know how many times I have personally witnessed the souls leaving the eyes of my own offspring? How many of those I helped along myself? I have no phobia of death, and anyone in my household who did I would invite to cure it by the only effective means: exposure therapy. If Borbala Ferank meets her end out here in the black, so be it. I will have no regrets, except that I did not drown my youngest nephew Ignac at birth. Death is the greatest pirate of us all. He will raid even our best ships, drag us off by the hair, and he will ransom not a single one of us. The only defeat is to let him enslave you before his cannons even begin to fire on your starboard flank. So *I* will not tremble like the hanar up there. *I* will not exhaust myself tracking the mystery of the thing like that old elcor war beast put out to pasture. *I* will drink old Mummy Quarian's turian Horosk on the bridge of the most magnificent ship I've ever met, and tell a dirty joke about that time a vorcha and a pyjak walked into a bar. *You* can do as you like."

The hatch irised open. The sleek, almost untouched bridge spread out before them, gleaming black and blue, and the whole of space outside the observation window, stretching on into nothing and everything. The drell headed straight for the small arms locker. Her fingers flew over the security panel. *Calibrating. More casual. More contractions. Flattery. She wouldn't make a speech like that if she didn't think it made her look good.*

"That was a really excellent bit of bravado, Bala. I imagine I'll be quoting it in the future." She pulled an Arc Pistol, an M-3 Predator pistol, a Reegar Carbine shotgun, and a Lancer III rifle out of the canister, along with a modest bandolier of ammunition. She held one pistol out reluctantly to the batarian, strapping on the rest.

"You did say you were retired, didn't you?" Therion said.

"Oh, just give me the weapon, you great racist iguana." Borbala snatched the Arc Pistol out of Anax's hand.

"All I ask is that you *try* not to shoot me in the back. I know it'll be hard to resist the temptation, but just… see how it feels."

"Oh, it's to be stereotypes, is it? I'll tell you what. I'll try to overcome my inherent batarian nature and not shoot you in the back if you promise to keep the spoken-word poetry fugue-state stuff to a minimum. Metaphors give me a headache. And maybe don't *sigh* too hard and keel over and die when those lacy lungs of yours give out, you fancy, fainting princess from a race of fainting princesses."

Any other time, Anax would have laughed. She knew she *should* laugh. It was the most advisable response to incite feelings of camaraderie in the target.

Batarians were criminals; drell died young. It was all in a good day's space prejudice. But there were four hundred drell down there in the hold, and they had fainted dead away. And if you were already smuggling fish across galaxies, what else might you sneak on board? She wouldn't ask, of course. Borbala would just say she had nothing to do with it, and the batarian would have gained a reason to be on guard, while Anax gained nothing. Asking was pointless. It was blunt-force trauma. Real, usable information rarely came from a direct hit.

"Too far," the drell said quietly.

"No such thing," Borbala answered, but, in the interests of an efficient working relationship, the grizzled batarian softened her voice. Very slightly.

Borbala Ferank cleared her throat and walked up the ramp to the navigator's station, frowning. "You know, I don't think we need to walk all the way back to the security hub. I think I can port the vid footage to the bridge. Put it up on the big screen. Save us some time."

Anax shrugged. It made no difference to her where they worked. Soval's dead eyes flashed before her. Her eyes, her bursting tongue, her throat choked by that necklace of blisters. She shook her head to clear it and settled into Captain Qetsi'Olam's chair. The leather squeaked, it was so new. Borbala lounged next to her in First Officer Senna's seat. The viewscreen flickered and filled with slowly cycling images of the cryodecks, date-stamped in glowing numbers.

"Do you know what those sores on Soval Raxios's neck are?" Anax said after they had watched a century of nothing happening to a lot of frozen aliens. "Little dark-blue lumps all over her frills? Have you seen that before?" *What do you know about the ways drell can die?*

"I can't say I have. There's a poison or two on Khar'shan that will give you a nice suppurating scarf, but not a blue one. Mother's Milk is so caustic the victim's throat dissolves mid-swallow. So that would be red. Pauper's Pleasure makes you break out in purple hives before your saliva boils and you slowly braise in your own fluids. There's one called the Final Jest that basically turns your blood to lighter fluid and uses your own brain's electro-chemical pain response as ignition to set you on fire on the inside, so those poor bastards *definitely* end up with sores all over the place, big fat orange heat blisters, and they can be blue if the venom sacs weren't too fresh, but… uh… they explode pretty quickly, so it's probably not that." Borbala leaned over, chuckling. "Hey, one time I shorted my niece Gyula on a shipment of red sand and geth scrap so she dipped my paintbrushes in Pauper's Pleasure—such a clever girl. I imagine she thought that when I licked my brush tip to give it a nice, defined point, I'd know what she thought of me. Of course, I've been poisoned so many times by so many people no little girl's snit could so much as dent my auto-immune response. Poor, dumb Gyula. She's at the bottom of a swamp now." Borbala suddenly seemed to notice that Anax had stopped looking at the vidscreen and was staring at her. "What? I didn't put her there. That was Ignac. Oh, but I did put *Ignac* at the bottom of a swamp. Different swamp. And he got out eventually. Never liked girls, Ignac. Ignac liked knives. Where did I go wrong? By my *eyes*, woman, why are you *gawping* at me?"

Anax shook her head. She tried to imagine a batarian in an artist's smock, holding a palette full of watercolors and painting lilies in a pond. She had spent her life imagining the very worst and very best that people were capable of. But she couldn't picture it. "Nothing."

"What? I like to paint. I'm a complex individual, Anax Therion. You should try expressing yourself artistically. It might loosen that steel pylon from your spine."

Anax smiled, a precise smile, the prelude to a swaggering boast. "I was the first drell to win a hanar poetry duel on Nyahir and see my name inscribed in fire on Mount Vassla. I am sufficiently expressed, Borbala Ferank."

"Gods, that sounds terrible. Please don't recite it. This morning is bad enough as it is."

"Still not morning," Anax corrected her.

Therion glanced back at the viewscreen. Sleepwalker Team Green-5 was going about their rounds, one hundred and sixty years after launch. She saw her friend Osyat checking instrument panels. Osyat Raxios. Would she have to be the one to tell him about Soval? They watched as the team finished their work four hundred and seven years ago and returned to their cryopods.

"Are you hot? It's getting really hot in here," Borbala complained, loosening the leather straps on her chestpiece. "I'm sweating like a beast."

"I feel fine." Anax shrugged. She liked the heat. She was meant to live in a scorching desert. The universe had just… never arranged one for her. But it did seem much warmer on the bridge than it had been when they arrived.

The datestamp in the corner of the footage began to speed up again now that there was no motion on camera, moving through decades at a quick clip.

"Have *you* seen those sores before?" Ferank asked

after a few minutes. "They looked... they looked sort of *dusty*, didn't they? It was strange. You would expect frozen blisters to be shiny. Strange."

The images of the *Keelah Si'yah* sleeping through time and space reflected in Anax's reptilian eyes like second screens. "I may have."

"Then why don't you haul your pretty green ass up to the lab and tell them?"

"Because I may be wrong. I hope I am wrong. I long for nothing in this universe but to be wrong. Because if I am not wrong, something extraordinarily bad must have happened to put that boil on a drell throat. If I am not wrong, this may be the last pleasant night of my life. Or at least the last uneventful one. And I am spending it in front of a holomonitor with a batarian pensioner."

"We really should have a bowl of vacuum-popped Kharlak eggs. Doesn't feel right watching vids without Kharlak eggs." The batarian raised one bony yellow-green brow muscle. "Oh, am I being too cheerful again? I'll try to keep an eye on that." She tapped the horrible scar tissue where her lower-right eye used to be with one finger. "Get it?" Borbala Ferank barked laughter. She laughed like a biotic misfire: short, messy, and devastating.

"Did your own sons really do that to you?"

"Erno, Kelemen, Tiborc, and Muz. Four children turned against you out of seventeen is not a bad score for one lifetime. Afterward, they dumped me in a crate of nutrient paste and traded me, and the paste, to the quarians for a couple of old terminals and a shoe, just to add insult to injury. One shoe, mind you. Not even a pair. Because I am worthless, you see. They are very subtle, my boys. Don't feel bad if it takes some time to grasp the complexity of their attempt at humor."

Anax handed Borbala one of the Horosk bottles. Turian liquor went down like plasma fire, but both of them had led lives to steel the digestive tract. She was getting somewhere. Anax pushed slightly against the new data.

"But *why*? And why didn't you have it replaced with a synthetic one?"

The batarian spun the first officer's chair toward Anax. The shadows on the bridge looked ghoulish on her skull ridges. "That's personal, day laborer. I know those frozen fish back there better than I know you. Mutilation is between a son and his mother. Unless you have children yourself you can't possibly understand. Do you have offspring, drell?"

"I do not."

"Then shut up."

Sleepwalker Team Blue-7 woke up on the screen before them. Three hundred years post-launch. The two of them sat back and watched themselves go about a happier Sleepwalker cycle in which nothing out of the ordinary occurred. Fifteen minutes of stony, unpleasant silence later, the halfway point in the *Keelah Si'yah*'s journey arrived. The Quorum and all the Sleepwalker teams revived briefly for a mission update, status updates sent ahead to the Nexus and back to the Initiative, and a historically excellent drinking binge in the mess hall. Anax leaned forward, observing everyone she could in the cheaply recorded image. She saw herself, meditating on a food crate. But she didn't need to see herself. She could run through that night in her mind as perfectly as the vidscreen could show it to her. But she could only remember what she actually witnessed. She needed to see *now* what she hadn't seen *then*.

"I am roasting *alive*," Borbala groaned. "Can you not feel that? It's like a jungle in here!" The batarian pulled more of the black straps from her chest to give her room to breathe. Therion couldn't waste time paying attention to something as irrelevant as ambient temperature.

Anax watched the footage in real time. She saw the volus political radical called Gaffno Yap, who had somehow been elected to the Quorum to the surprise of all, jump up onto a table and insist that everyone praise his singing voice. Irit Non begged her shipmate to come down, seething with anger. Anax watched Threnno and Nebbu, the elcor Quorum members, discussing something angrily in a corner of the room, but the footage had no sound, and certainly no smell. A batarian Sleepwalker, a male Anax did not know, drank bottle after bottle of shard wine and started trying to balance one on top of the other. The drell Quorum representatives, Kral Thauma and Glamys Azios, and the hanar representative Chabod watched on, impressed. Evidently, Borbala did know him. She hooted derisively at the screen.

"Ha! Zoli Haj'nalka, you old fraud! That's Zoli. He thinks he is a philosopher, but he is a drunk. It's a common mistake among the upper middle class. Do you know what his most famous koan is? *I kill, therefore I am*. Ha! I piss deeper than the great Zoli Haj'nalka! Kiss up to them all you like, Haj, they'll never let us on the Quorum. As in the Milky Way, so in Andromeda. No representation, no consideration. Someone's always gotta be on top, whether they call it a council or a quorum or a gaggle of geese. And it's not gonna be us. Stick that in your ethical framework and light it on fire."

Anax said nothing. She took it all in. Borbala's ranting beside her and the images in front of her.

She could review everything later in her memory if she needed to. In the upper-left corner of the screen, Senna'Nir took the captain's hand and disappeared out the hatch to the mess hall. *Interesting*. Several hanar congregated near the food dispensers, including Ysses. The one called Kholai, the one dead in medbay upstairs, gesticulated at them with his tentacles, more animated than Therion had ever seen a jelly. Yorrik took the volus's place at the center of attention. She couldn't hear him on the soundless footage, but she remembered. He'd done them a bit of his elcor *Macbeth* and then passed out with a thunderous crash to the mess hall floor halfway through "Murderous frenzy: Come, thick night, and pall thee in the dunnest smoke of hell, that my keen knife see not the wound it makes, nor heaven peep through the blanket of the dark to cry, 'Hold, hold!'" Soval and Osyat sat in a circle, playing some sort of drinking game with the other Sleepwalkers. Soval put her head on her husband's shoulder. The party was winding down.

One by one, the midpoint crew dispersed silently. The datestamp began to pick up speed once more.

To get data, it is sometimes necessary to bait it out, Anax thought, *and data loves nothing so well as more data. The batarian has shared a history, you have shared nothing. There is a conversational debt. She'll give nothing else until it is paid.*

"After my parents died," she began.

"Lungs too fancy for this world?" Borbala said.

Anax clenched her green jaw. "Indeed. After they died, I lived alone under the dome of Cnidaria City on Kahje. It is the only place drell can live without immediately succumbing to Kepral's Syndrome. We were crowded there, packed in like cords of firewood.

I was a child. I begged and stole so that I could eat. I brawled with other children, with grown beggars, with dogs for a place to sleep. I became one of the *drala'fa*, the ignored. I was eleven before a hanar called Oleon found me, hiding in an alley with a man rich enough to buy and sell me and the street we both stood on, an arms dealer who had been places I could never dream of. I was selling him my prize possession, the only thing I owned with any value at all. He paid me practically nothing for it. But it seemed like riches to me then. Oleon watched the deal transpire, and saw talent in me. I had spent months tracking the arms dealer, memorizing his contacts, his prices, his suppliers' names and their contacts. I held it all in my head as easily as a coin in the hand. I could have exposed him and put him on a prison colony for the natural life of a krogan. But more importantly, I had seen, in all my spying, where his wife went one night a week with his business partner. Not bad for my first job as a freelance data-dealer. I knew that information was more valuable than any weapon or drug when I was eleven years old. What I did not know was that the giant hanar that suddenly towered above me was Oleon, a chief member of the Illuminated Primacy, the hanar government. It saw my talent. It saw my *potential*. It offered to take me into the Compact, make me a part of its household, pay for my biotic implants, to educate and employ me to do whatever work it asked of me without question."

"Sounds like slavery."

"I suppose it would, to you. But a ranking member of the Illuminated Primacy does not need its floors scrubbed. It needs secrets. Everyone's secrets. That was what the hanar trained me to find, to erase if it could harm them, to bring it home if it had value. And years later, when I was older, Oleon sent me on a mission."

The century turned over onscreen. Only a hundred and fifty years from the present day, now. Click, click, click, the security cameras cycled through the ship.

"'Go to Talis Fia in the Shrike Abyssal,' it ordered me. 'It is a volus world, and like many volus worlds, the little fools banker-ed themselves into a depression there. It is overrun with criminals, brothels, assassins, and advantage-seekers. You will feel right at home. There is a volus there called Pinda Kem who has stolen from this one. Discover this Kem's worst deed and bring it back to Kahje, where this one will use it to teach a virtuous lesson on the subject of respect, and revenge.' And there, on Talis Fia, was where I saw blue sores like the ones on Soval Raxios's neck—"

Anax Therion sat bolt upright in the captain's chair. "What was that?" she snapped. "Run the footage back. I saw something."

"What? I didn't see anything. I was listening to you talk about yourself."

"Run it back two years, I'm sure it was there."

Ferank frowned. She ran a hand around the fine black hairs that bristled all over her skin. "Wait, but what were the blue sores? On Talis Fia. Where did you see them?"

"*Run it back.*"

Borbala keyed the command into the console that curved around Senna'Nir's station. The footage blacked out and came on again. The volus cryobay. *Click*. The elcor cryobay. *Click*. The batarian cryobay. *Click*. The drell cryobay.

"Stop!" yelled Anax, far too loudly on the empty bridge. "I saw it. I know I saw it."

"There's nothing *there*. Everyone's frozen. You're imagining things."

"Run it back again."

"Remember when we made a deal concerning whether or not I can shoot you? I might like to revisit that."

Anax walked up to the enormous viewscreen. The image of the empty cryobay dwarfed her, washed out her skin to almost black. It went dark, and then flashed on again, an identically boring, nearly motionless image, somewhat further in the past.

"There," Anax said suddenly. Borbala froze the image.

"*What*, you mad serf?"

Anax Therion turned back to the batarian. She lifted one arm and pointed at a space in the cryobay, too far to the left for the first camera to see, too far to the right for the second camera. Perfectly placed in the blind spot between the ship's eyes. But not completely invisible.

"A shadow," the drell whispered. "Something moving when all the house is fast asleep."

Ferank saw it then. Flickering across the cryobay floor, caught in the blue running lights for half a second before it was gone. The datestamp crawled forward while they stared until their eyes ached, watching for that flicker, that motion in the blind spot. They found it twice more, three times more. They ran the film backward and forward again, from its first appearance to the present day, searching for any appearance they'd missed. Sleepwalker Team Yellow-9 revived onscreen, one hundred years ago. Soval was on that cycle. She walked by the camera on her way to her station at the communications array, stopping to speak briefly to a hanar. She smiled, untroubled. Her eyes very nearly met the camera. Anax watched her as she spoke and held up one green hand as if to touch the dead woman's holographic face.

"I saw those sores on a volus child," Anax said, slinging the Lancer rifle over one shoulder. They had what they needed. Time to become a search party. Time to hunt. "The favorite son of Pinda Kem."

Borbala checked her sidearm and rubbed her three good eyes. "Did he die?"

"Not in the least. As far as I know, after I ruined his father, he went on to live a long and happy life. Happy for a volus, anyway."

"If the little brat didn't die, why are you so afraid they're the same sores?"

"Because Soval Raxios *did*, and she shouldn't have. And I do not yet know why Irit Non had nothing to say on the subject herself. Until I do, I palm the card until it is my play."

The drell balanced the Reeger Carbine in one hand and looked appraisingly at the batarian. An Arc Pistol was one thing. Could she risk the two of them being equally armed?

"Whatever happened to your hanar friend?" Borbala asked. "Did it come with you? Pay your fare? Off to the great unknown together to spy on new and interesting people?"

"Oleon was assassinated. I was a freelancer before I met it. I was a freelancer after it died." Anax allowed a certain percentage of the grief she carried with her to show in her posture. "I worked for the Shadow Broker for a long time afterward."

"Never heard of him."

Anax didn't believe that for a second. The Shadow Broker was well known to the entire criminal element of the Milky Way. "Nevertheless, now I am here. Alone."

"Sad. Who got the old jellyfish?"

Anax Therion locked eyes with the batarian. Her eyelids slicked shut, but she kept to her word and did not speak the memory that rushed over her. *The color of roses. The smell of the sea. Trusting. Gentle. That one's head rests heavy in the grotto of sleep. Blood follows. Blood everywhere like a world of oceans.*

"Some things are between a drell and their hanar," she said evenly, knowing the implication in her words, using it to her advantage. "Unless you have made the Compact yourself you can't possibly understand. Do you know one single hanar's soul name, batarian?"

"I do not."

Anax smiled softly. "Then shut up."

As they headed toward the hatch at the rear of the bridge, the voice of the *Keelah Si'yah*'s interface filled the room. The blue running lights along the floor turned an ugly yellow.

Emergency lockdown procedures initiated. Safe zones are indicated in yellow. Prohibited areas are indicated in red. Please proceed to the nearest safe zone. Emergency lockdown procedures initiated. Please proceed in an orderly fashion to the nearest yellow zone.

Yorrik's heavy, monotonous voice came through on their comm lines.

"Barely controlled panic: Senna, I am afraid the rendezvous at medbay at 0330 hours will not be possible. Formal announcement: By my authority as the medical specialist on Sleepwalker Team Blue-7, I have triggered lockdown. You may approach the observation glass, but you will not be able to come inside."

"Nor will the elcor or this one be able to depart," Ysses's musical voice added.

"Pervasive dread: I am so sorry. Medbay is now under quarantine. Please come as soon as you can. Futile advice: Try not to touch anything."

The drell handed the shotgun to Borbala Ferank. A calculated risk. She hoped she wouldn't regret it.

"I guess our stowaway sweep will have to wait," said Ferank. "I was looking forward to the chase. At least we can get the hell out of this sauna."

"You may get your wish. Take point," Therion said grimly. "And be careful. Whatever is happening in medbay, one thing is certain: There's someone else awake on this ship."

6. FUSION

Senna'Nir vas Keelah Si'yah turned a corner toward medbay and stopped dead in his tracks.

"Wait," wheezed Irit Non, running up the hall behind him on her short, stout legs. She was no match for a long-legged quarian with bad news.

There was a quarian girl in there. Behind the glass. Sealed up inside the quarantine zone with Yorrik and Ysses. He could see the top of her purple hood through the glass walls. It was impossible. No one else should be awake. Who the *hell* was that? He couldn't see clearly. It was still dark in there, except in the pool of ghostly white-and-orange mobile worklights around the operating station, and the great gray bulk of the elcor was in the way.

The volus and the quarian approached the clear glass medbay walls, tinged red for quarantine. Every thirty seconds, a soft alarm tone chimed throughout the ship. Loud enough to remind you of an emergency, but not so loud that it burned out your ability to think. Senna pounded on the glass. Yorrik turned toward him, revealing a scene of wanton and nonsensical destruction. Both the elcor and the hanar were wearing sterilizing collars, large metal torques that projected a thin sanitizing forcefield in front of their mucus membranes like ancient doctors' masks.

The frozen drell and hanar corpses were surrounded by piles of smashed, gouged out, torn apart, shattered, oozing garbage. Punctured glass globes, a cracked nightlight shaped like an omni-tool, a large anti-synthetic rifle with the scope snapped off and the gauges pried loose, bottles of booze, peeled-apart battery packs, a huge black microscope that looked about as advanced as a stone wheel. Some kind of stuffed child's toy lay next to the dead hanar's frozen skull, its glowing eyes punched out and drained dry, its stuffing pulled free of what looked like a cute, fat version of a volus. The autopsy slabs were splattered with glowing fluid and a slurry of liquefied fish guts. Yorrik and Ysses were covered in the stuff, half-dried, half-dripping. It looked like a murder scene in an Afterlife dumpster in there.

The quarian girl looked down on it all, her spine bent at an awkward angle, her faceplate ripped out of the helmet and fastened on backwards with surgical staples so that the heads-up display faced outward. Two eyes, a nose, and a mouth were drawn crudely on the glass in fluorescent green paint. It was an empty suit, hung up on the swinging arm of a laser scalpel, arms and legs swinging limp at its sides. Senna felt sick. It was just an empty environmental suit, but it looked for all the world like someone had flayed a child alive and hung their skin up to dry.

"What the *fuck* is going on in here?" Irit Non wheezed. "Where did you get that… that thing? Those dolls are offensive, you know. They're exaggerated, *bigoted* representations of my people—"

"Non, that is hardly the most important issue right now," Senna protested, but the soft bonging quarantine alarm seemed to be the last thing on the enraged volus's mind.

A guilty ultraviolet aura ran up and down Ysses's

tentacles. "The doll does not belong to this one. Only the eyes were needed. This one does not even know where such a doll may be purchased."

"Get rid of it, get rid of it immediately!" Irit rasped.

Senna pointed at the ghastly face drawn on the quarian helmet. "Yorrik?" he said. "Who is that?"

"Gallows humor: Senna'Nir vas Keelah Si'yah, right now that is my best friend in the world. With growing defensiveness: It has been hours. I was lonely. Ysses does not like me. Ysses does not have a face. Ysses does not know anything about cell replication or surface proteins. Horatio knows a great deal. With growing guilt concerning the appearance of recent actions: I named him Horatio. Exhausted defiance: Do you like him? You should like him. He is the one with the answers."

In all the time Senna'Nir and Yorrik had spent together, apparently the elcor had never noticed that only female quarians wore those patterned lavender hoods. "Horatio" was not a *he*. But Senna saw no purpose in pointing that out just now. You couldn't talk the old doctor out of anything once he had his mind made up.

"Where the hell did you get it?" Senna hated not being able to be in there with his friend. He felt useless out here in the hall, trapped away from what mattered most in this moment. Were they safe out here? They must be. That was the function of an emergency lockdown.

"Shifting blame: Anax found it," Yorrik droned. "Urgent query: Is this really what you want to talk about right now?"

The hanar bobbed up and down on its levitation pack. "This one wishes to assure the commander that the Enkindlers have provided a miracle in our hour of need. If Analyst Therion had not secured this clothing, the autopsies would have concluded poorly."

"You couldn't use a microscope?" the volus grumbled. "It's a kid's toy. Surely the two of you intellectual giants can figure it out."

Ysses lifted one rosy tentacle and activated the power on the massive blocky microscope sitting on a pile of spare parts. A foot-high hologram of a krogan drill sergeant flickered to life on top of the machine.

"Greetings, young warrior!" the krogan educational VI bellowed. "Ambush slide A and overwhelm its defenses, soldier! Go! Go! Go! Seize Slide A in your mighty fist and spill the blood of the immersion oil onto its miserable flesh! Did you hear me, young champion? I said make a mighty fist! Now puncture the staging clips with the enemy carcass of Slide A and interrogate it for information! That is the sorriest excuse for science I've ever seen, grunt! Do it again!"

The hanar switched the microscope off again. "This device is extremely stressful to use," it said. "It also lacks in-depth analytical capability. It could only reveal the presence of the problem, not its nature. Additionally, this one has argued many times that attempts to control the tendency of nature toward entropy are by *their* nature futile. This one accepts the end of days. It has no need to know the name of its killer."

Yorrik grunted and said to Senna: "Plea for sympathy: Do you see what I have been dealing with?"

Anax Therion and Borbala Ferank arrived at medbay as the hanar finished speaking, loaded out with the contents of the small arms locker.

"Senna," Anax said, and nodded at him.

"Anax," Senna answered, and nodded back.

"The guests are all here," Ferank said in her habitual half-growl. "Let's get the orgy started. I presume we're all going to die?"

The batarian looked expectantly at the commander, then into the quarantined medbay clinic. Yorrik said nothing. He shifted uncomfortably on his long toe knuckles. Ysses hung in the air with a vaguely nihilistic sheen to it. The color drained from Borbala's face.

"Oh, fuck, we are," she said.

"Half-hearted attempt to cheer: You are not going to die, Borbala."

Ferank breathed a sigh of relief. "Excellent news. Don't scare an old woman like that. You had me thinking there was a real problem for a minute there. By my eyes, it's *freezing* in here. You all should try the bridge. It's hot enough to boil your spit. Turn up the heat, will you, Senna?"

"K, increase ambient temperature on Deck Nine," Senna said impatiently. His suit regulated his own temperature, but not everyone was so lucky.

Ambient temperature on Deck 9 is already at maximum, Commander Senna'Nir. I cannot increase it without immediate damage to organic tissue.

Borbala Ferank's teeth were starting to chatter. A thin sheen of frost gleamed at the corners of the medbay glass.

That made three, Senna thought. Three systems failing that the ship could not even tell *were* failing. The cryopods, the lighting, and temperature control. Something else, too, was spreading.

"Hesitant awkwardness: I am also not going to die. Nor will you, Commander, or Irit Non." The elcor turned his kindly face toward Anax Therion.

"Ah," the drell said. "But I am. And the hanar, perhaps."

"How are you feeling, Analyst Therion?"

"I feel fine."

"Genuine relief: That is good. That means there is a possibility that not all the drell pods were compromised."

Therion: "It is a virus, is it not, Yorrik?"

Senna'Nir's stomach curdled. Any quarian's would have. They lived in fear of infection, even in clean rooms where no virus dared to tread, even in their suits. Centuries on the Migrant Fleet had left their race with immune systems about as effective as holding an old handkerchief to your mouth. What were the chances of this happening at the same time as the ship's systems suddenly going haywire? This was bad. This was horrendously bad. And on his watch. What had he done to deserve this? They were almost to Andromeda. Why couldn't that lizard have waited another couple of decades to drop dead?

"Depressed: Affirmative, Anax Therion." Yorrik turned to the quarian suit hanging next to the male drell body and intoned flatly: "Affectionate entreaty: 'O good Horatio, absent thee from felicity awhile, and in this harsh world draw thy breath in pain to tell my story.'"

The painted fluorescent smiley face stared back at them. Yorrik made a small, embarrassed sound through his slats and keyed something into the arm. The flipped faceplate lit up with information, readable to all of them instead of only to the dark interior of the suit. Words and numbers scrolled up and down, framing the visual field, a crawl of data monitoring and status updates cycling along the chinline, just like Senna's own interior display. He felt oddly naked with the others peering in at the view quarians saw every day. It felt private.

"Report, Medical Specialist," he said gruffly. This was getting disorganized. He needed to take command of the situation, and he was tired of waiting. "Then Team Who, then Team How. Go."

Yorrik inclined his elephantine head toward the mess of hollowed-out trash on the autopsy tables. "Informative address: Chemical Specialist Ysses and I took blood and tissue samples from each subject using the lab's native equipment. This concluded our use of the lab's native equipment. Using a broad-spectrum fluorescent dye test, we were able to determine fairly quickly that none of the three victims suffered from any appreciable blood toxicity."

"This one spared us the task of listening to the microscope. This one witnessed the illumination of the blood and was able to interpret the gradations of color necessary for diagnosis with its naked eye," Ysses hummed with a tinge of pride. "As vain as all such efforts to preserve order must always be," it added quickly.

"Irritated: Yes, you did very well. Anxiously moving on: The krogan microscope called us miserable piles of klixen dung and ordered us to do one hundred pull-ups, but we were able to use it, barely, to rule out bacterial infection, again through visual confirmation. This left few possibilities. I affirmed the presence of a virus through a dye injection test. As I have explained to the others, viruses are too small to be seen under a normal microscope; however, they cannot absorb dye through the surface membrane, and therefore it is possible to verify the presence of viral cells when there are undyed structures in the tissue sample. Translation: To see what is there by seeing what is not there.

It was at this point that I instructed the ship to initiate quarantine procedures. It was also at this point that a more efficient method of diagnosis occurred to me. I had only intended to use Horatio as a virtual test subject to synthesize possible treatments from the curative capabilities of the suit. Apologetic: I am not overly familiar with the specifications of this technology. We then injected Horatio with a blood sample from the drell female. The hydraulics were immediately overwhelmed with an antibody flood; however, it has not been effective so far. More importantly, in order to manufacture antibodies, the suit had to recognize the virus. It did. Dramatic revelation: The cause of death was a highly contagious infection called Yoqtan."

Irit Non coughed and spluttered. "Impossible! You are lying in order to implicate the volus. Yoqtan has never killed anyone! The treatment is a couple of soothing baths and a mother's love!"

Anax Therion interjected: "Yoqtan is volus chickenpox. Their species all get it when they are juveniles. It is almost a rite of passage. The symptoms match up: a rash of dark-blue sores, swollen tongue, high fever, chills, and in severe cases, persistent nausea. Only the weakest of children do not survive Yoqtan. It should not have killed a thirty-year-old drell."

"It should not even be possible for her to *have* it," snarled Irit Non. "She doesn't have the right glands. And anything that could thrive in our blood should turn hers into a half-frozen milkshake. This isn't a quarian ensemble," the volus gestured at the elegant fiber mesh covering her body. "We don't wear them because our immune systems are too precious to withstand a strong gust of wind. Our normal body temperatures are nothing like yours. Outside of Irune's high-pressure jungles or my suit, our bodies would blow up like a balloon, split open and whatever was left would desiccate immediately in your toxic goddamned atmosphere. And if the completely insufficient pressure didn't get us, we are allergic to oxygen. Your blood is full of it. Yoqtan just could not survive in a drell. It needs the same things volus do to live and replicate. Why are you *lying*, elcor? I didn't think elcor could lie!"

"Insulted: We can act, can't we? Furious indignance: Look at Horatio. You can see I am telling the truth. Or do you think I can program this damnable tuxedo to do anything it doesn't want to do? Attempted explanation: Please look for yourself. You can see the electron analysis and RNA sequencing. It *is* Yoqtan."

Anax Therion glanced at the concave faceplate. "91% Yoqtan," she observed.

"Acknowledgment of mutual understanding: Correct. The rest I cannot positively identify without proper equipment, but it seems to be an assortment of junk RNA. Presumably, this is what allowed it to infect a drell in the first place. It clearly began in the drell, and runs its course much more quickly in a drell host. Disconcerting implications: However, as I said before, drell and hanar physiology bears almost no comparison. Very few viruses mutate sufficiently to jump between species. It is rare enough that the names of those that do are well known: measles, Ebola, Marburg virus, Sangelian hemorrhagic fever, Teukrian flu. I cannot think of one that commonly afflicts both drell and hanar, and neither can the ship's computer." Yorrik paused. The poor man was clearly deeply disturbed. "Inevitable conclusion: Either we are witnessing the birth of a new life form, or this is a manufactured virus, deliberately engineered."

"Who could hate the drell so much?" Senna said softly. They didn't conquer other races, they didn't outbreed or outgun anyone. And thanks to Kepral's Syndrome, fewer and fewer of them were left each generation.

"Regretful admission: I have no explanation as to how multiple drell came to be infected to begin with, or how hanar could contract the Yoqtan pathogen when the cryopods are self-contained systems. We have no patient zero. We have no model for the progression of the disease, only its end stage, and we are unlikely to develop one, since we can only detect new infections when the victims have already died, by the telltale 'freezer burn.' We have only a name. Yoqtan. Hollow optimism: The good news is there is no reason to think any other species will be affected. If we follow standard quarantine procedures, we should still be able to dock with the Nexus and let them find a cure." The elcor's enormous shoulders relaxed. He settled back slightly on his haunches. "Authoritative command: Airlock these bodies immediately. We have all the samples we need. Do not open the remaining cryopods under any circumstances. Deep fatigue: This completes our report to date. The rest is silence."

Senna'Nir, first officer of the *Keelah Si'yah*, clenched his jaw. "How many of those sanitary collars did we stock in medbay, Yorrik?"

"With full knowledge that the answer will not satisfy: two."

Senna rested one long arm against the glass and buried his face in his elbow. Everything hurt. He hadn't known *eyelashes* could hurt. The universe was truly full of wonders. He shut his eyes and frowned beneath his mask. He happened to know, because he had told K to pin the information to his display, that in the seven hours since the Radial, six more hanar and thirty-four more drell had expired in their pods. *Keelah Se'lai, will there be any drell left by the time we reach the Nexus?*

"Yorrik, if what you're saying is true, this is a fatal virus—"

"It *isn't*," insisted Non.

"—an apparently very fatal virus and you are trapped in a confined space with it." All elcor hated confined spaces. It was the reason so few of them took to interstellar travel. But Yorrik was an exception, as he was to many things elcor. "Why aren't you panicking?"

The elcor droned emotionlessly: "Panic: I am panicking."

"There is no need for panic. This one is serene, despite the knowledge that the elcor is safe, while this one will almost certainly die in this very room," crooned Ysses soothingly.

"That's *quite* enough out of you, you overgrown flashlight," Borbala cut in, fingering the firing mechanism on her shotgun thoughtfully. "Keep talking sweet to that superbug and I'm going to start thinking you had something to do with it."

"This one respires and excretes innocence. This one would rather both galaxies burned from end to end than see the slightest harm done to the one called Kholai, who lies rotting before you. This one merely admires the tools the Enkindlers use to achieve their holy purpose."

The batarian grimaced. "Right," she said slowly. "Well, that's just spectacular, Ysses, thank you *so* much for opening up to us and sharing your insight and unique point of view. Please never do it again." She blew into her hands and rubbed them together to stay warm. "Listen up, you filthy farmers. Team Who makes it two for two on results."

The drell stirred and snapped into an authoritative tone and posture. Senna had never seen anyone listen more vibrantly than she did. Anax explained about the shadow they had found on the cryobay footage. "It appears first about one hundred and fifty years ago. Whatever is happening has been happening much longer than we initially theorized. Similar shadows turned up on other parts of the ship: the mess hall, briefly, once on the bridge, a few times in engineering, twice on the residential decks. Never more than a shadow. A flicker. We almost missed it. We did miss it. We had to run back through years of recordings to find the other shadows once we saw the first one." Her green brow furrowed.

"What is it, Therion?" Senna coaxed.

"Something has been bothering me since I first saw it. Commander, it is *always* a shadow. We never saw so much as the back of a heel or the top of a head. It's as though whoever it was knew *exactly* how to move and where to stand so the camera sweep would miss them every time. And we went through centuries of cams. They never made a mistake. They never had a chance to practice." The drell's breath fogged in the icy air. "Someone *knew*. They knew when they came on board. There was a plan."

Senna began to pace back and forth in front of the sealed door to medbay. "Where is this shadow now?" he asked.

"We don't know," answered the batarian. "We didn't have time to start a real security sweep before this one hit the apocalypse button."

"Are you still thinking it could be one of us?" he said, half not wanting to know the answer.

Anax shook her head slowly. "A hundred and fifty years is a long time. And even if they slept through some of that, bringing yourself in and out of cryostasis would be brutal. They'd be in terrible shape by now."

"So asari or krogan," the volus said eagerly.

The drell rubbed her longest finger over her index finger. That curious gesture again. She said nothing for a long moment.

"Most likely," she said finally. "To survive long enough to see it through." Her large black eyes fixed on something far down the darkened hallway. "Most likely," she repeated. "What did you find in the datacore?" Therion asked suddenly. She leaned back against the glass, still pulsing red with the lockdown alarm.

"Nothing," Senna said, straightening up. He rubbed the mesh of his skullcap with one hand. He was going to have to wake up the captain. This was so far above his pay grade. She would know what to do. Qetsi'Olam was born knowing what to do. Her contingency plans had contingency plans, and those contingency plans had fallback positions. This ark was her baby. She would nurse it back to health. He could fix the code; she could fix the people. Proper division of labor was what defined a team. Relief settled over him as he made the decision. Now he could focus. The beautiful soup of the *Keelah Si'yah*'s base code decompiled and recompiled in his mind all over again. It had been flawless. All systems go.

"Nothing?" Borbala snapped. "You had almost seven hours and you found nothing."

"Nothing," repeated the volus, still obviously furious. "No bugs, no bad command lines, no fragged drives, no invasive programs, no unscheduled reboots, no spaghetti code, no run errors, nothing. The hardware is fine. The software is *perfect*. Except that things keep *breaking* and the ship keeps insisting they're not."

A network of fine frost crept slowly over the red, pulsing quarantine glass.

Perfect, Senna'Nir thought. *Perfect. But nothing is perfect. Even if everything is running at optimum,* no *code is that perfect at the baseline. There is always something buggy in there, something left over from previous versions, something inelegant in the guts of the program.*

"We see what is there by seeing what is not there," he said to himself.

"What? Speak up, homeless," the batarian sneered.

"I have an idea," Senna said. He couldn't help the excitement creeping into his voice. Everything was just horrifying at the moment, but it was a horrifying puzzle, and he might be able to solve it. That was part of why he loved machines so dearly—they were an endless supply of puzzles for his mind to devour like meat. And after nearly six hundred years asleep, he was *starving*. "I have an idea of where to start, anyway." He needed to talk to his grandmother. Liat'Nir had been a tech genius in her day. She had fought against the geth. She had programmed some of the geth trying to kill her and everyone she loved. When he talked to Liat, he never had to slow down or explain anything, he could just run out his mind. The old lady might be a relic, but she could still keep up. His greatest breakthroughs had come from bouncing contingencies off of her. He turned back to his team. "I need to go to my quarters and get some things." Command staff had assigned quarters on the *Keelah Si'yah* before departure. Their belongings were stowed there, not in the main cargo hold. "I won't be long. Borbala and Anax, start your security sweep. Yorrik and Ysses, continue your analysis, try to get an idea of how much time we have, and whether or not this is a natural mutation." *Wishful thinking*, he thought to himself. He did not believe in accidents, not really. Not big ones. Not like this. "Irit?"

"What?" the volus breathed gutturally. "It's not fucking Yoqtan," she finished weakly.

"Help them get Horatio optimized for the next phase. You can direct them from this side of the glass. Turn him into the next best thing to a mobile virological lab. And, Irit..." Senna resisted the urge to pat the short alien on the head. "I presume you brought the tools of your trade along with you?"

"Don't be stupid," the volus snapped. Of course, Irit Non would never leave it all behind without grabbing everything that wasn't nailed down so that she could set up shop again wherever they landed.

He gestured at Anax Therion. "Make her a suit. We can't have you dying on us, Anax." She was the only one of them who was vulnerable. The only one with no protection from the invisible killer that could be anywhere, all around them. "And somebody grab a terminal port and see if there's anyone we can revive who would be more useful than the six of us poor *bosh'tets*. A geneticist, a scientist, a xenobiologist, anything." He took a deep, rattled breath. "K, initiate revival sequence for Captain Qetsi'Olam vas Keelah Si'yah, authorization passkey indigo-9-9-white-architect-4-1-1-6-nedas."

Passkey accepted. Revival sequence initiated, Commander.

Yorrik butted his knee lightly against the medbay wall to get the commander's attention. "Warning," the elcor said. "The more people you revive, the more chance the infection has to spread to fully thawed and active hosts. We are keeping the bodies as near cryo-temperature as possible. But there is still a risk. We do not yet know how it spreads, and several hours passed before we took any countermeasures at all. Simplistic explanation: It may be on the walls or in the air or in the water supply. There is no way to tell."

"Commander," whispered Anax Therion suddenly. "We are not alone."

The batarian checked the thermal clip in her shotgun and dropped into cover behind one of the terminal nodes across the corridor from medbay. The drell took up a flanking position, rifle already up on one shoulder. Senna saw the blue crackle of biotic implants sizzle along her arms. She tossed him an M-3 Predator. Borbala Ferank seemed to at least consider giving her sidearm to the volus to protect herself.

Senna'Nir heard footsteps. Footsteps far off in the dark. He strained to hear. Heavy? Light? Krogan or asari? Wounded? Malevolent?

"Identify yourself!" Borbala roared into the shadows.

"Oh, good work, you fool," sneered Non. "They'll run now. You've warned them off. Maybe it is one of us after all. Is that your friend creeping around down there? Give me that pistol, you yellow bitch!"

Borbala ignored her. Anax was silent. Senna could feel his heart hammering in his eardrums. The footsteps were getting closer. Closer.

A shape lunged toward them out of the blue-lit passage to the lower decks.

"Are we there?" it panted. "Is this Andromeda?"

A batarian male stumbled directly into their line of fire. He looked around at the weapons trained on him. The man smelled strange. Sweet, soft, like perfume. It wasn't right. Nobody sweating like that could smell so good.

"Jalosk?" Borbala Ferank whispered, lowering her weapon. "Jalosk Dal'Virra?"

His eyes seemed to focus when he heard his name. Jalosk rolled his head blearily toward her voice, then took in the whole of Sleepwalker Team Blue-7. The batarian went ashen, turned, and explosively vomited reeking bile, blood, and the blackened remains of his own intestinal lining against the clean medbay glass like a river of hell.

7. CONTROL

Yorrik watched them all helplessly through the quarantine glass. It was painful. For a creature whose language was mostly scent and microgesture, watching a mob of aliens turn on each other while pungent vomit slid down the wall in front of him was like being bombarded with a deafening crash of sound. The newcomer had collapsed in a trembling heap against the sealed door of the medbay.

"I *knew* it. I knew it was a batarian!" Irit Non seethed.

"Dal'Virra. Don't listen to them," barked Borbala Ferank, not lowering her pistol. No one, in fact, had lowered their weapon. They'd only leapt backward to avoid the splatter of his insides against the glass. "Don't say anything. You know how they are." She turned on the rest of them, the scar tissue in her ruined eye socket throbbing. "Can't you stow your provincial pitchforks for half a second? Can't you see he's sick?"

"Increasing concern: Perhaps it is unwise to get too close," Yorrik said. No cryopod hangover was this bad. No matter how many times you froze and thawed, you didn't sick up anything that color. And so *much* of it.

No one listened to him.

The man glared malevolently at her out of all four eyes. "Stay away from me, mother of worms," he snarled. Saliva pooled on one side of his mouth and spilled out. One side of his face wasn't moving quite right.

"K, identify the batarian *bosh'tet* on the med deck!" shouted Senna'Nir.

There are no batarian males currently present on the med deck.

"God *dammit*," the commander said. He leveled his weapon at the man's head. "What's your cryopod number, sir?" The batarian groaned and stared listlessly out of his four eyes. "*Sir!*" Senna barked.

"BT566," he moaned.

"I told you, that's Jalosk Dal'Virra," insisted Borbala Ferank.

"K, what is the status of cryopod BT566?"

Cryopod BT566 contains the batarian male Jalosk Dal'Virra, forty-six years of age. Homeworld: Camala. Berth type: Family. Guardian of Zofi Dal'Virra, age nine, and Grozik Dal'Virra, age four.

"What did I say?" Borbala rolled her eyes.

Senna waved his hand at her. "Forget about that part, K. Who authorized a revival cascade for cryopod BT566? Are any other pods open?"

Cryopod BT566 has not undergone a revival cascade since transit day 164,250. It is currently in active stasis mode, temperature seventy-seven degrees Kelvin. Occupant's life signs are optimal. No cryopod breaches reported. All passengers in stasis with the exception of Commander Senna'Nir nar—

"Enough!" Senna cut the ship's interface off. Yorrik had never seen him so upset, even on the day he'd left Ekuna to end his Pilgrimage. Even when Yorrik had told him what happened to New Elfaas all those years ago. He wanted to comfort his friend. But quarantine made no exception for emotion. On the other hand, Yorrik thought, looking down at the putrid slime that covered the hallway, was there any use left for quarantine protocols now?

The former occupant of cryopod BT566 dry heaved onto the floor of the corridor. He clawed at his neck, grunting. In the shadows cast by the worklights inside medbay, the dark circles under all four of his eyes looked ghostly.

"Thank you, K, that's just... just *fantastic.*" Senna'Nir shook his head.

The volus was livid. "All that talk about damned Yoqtan, trying to pin this on us, and it's the same old monsters it always is. *There's* your stowaway, Anax. Not some fanciful asari or krogan. Didn't you say they'd be in terrible shape by now? Just *look* at him!"

"Look at him?" Senna'Nir bellowed. "I'm looking right at him, and he's obviously got whatever the others had!"

"Probably," Anax said calmly, adjusting the scope of her weapon. "I said probably."

Jalosk had begun to scratch his arms viciously. His fingernails were useless against his black leather sleeves, so he tried to tear them off. This would normally be no trouble for a batarian. Yorrik himself had seen one tear a Quasar machine apart with his bare hands. Jalosk must be very weak indeed to be sitting there clumsily pulling at the fabric of his clothes like a child. The medbay glass was thick by design. Scent particles would not pass through. But his slats flared anyway, trying to catch the smell of the man, of the horrifying fluids that had burst out of him.

"It's your right to dispose of him as you wish, Anax Therion," Non wheezed solemnly. "His crime was against Rakhana-clan. Rakhana-clan should determine his punishment."

"What an astonishing number of assumptions," Anax answered softly.

"*Dispose* of me? What do you mean *dispose* of me? Where the fuck am I? Have we docked? Why is everything dark?" The presumed Jalosk Dal'Virra had teal markings all over his face. The skin on the concave sides of his skull ridges was starting to peel. "I demand to be taken to the chief security officer of the Nexus," he said.

At least, he tried to say *I demand to be taken to the chief security officer of the Nexus.* A bout of coughing so intense he nearly passed out choked off most of it. He had the decency to put his yellowish-green hands over his mouth. The sad little useless gesture touched Yorrik, somehow. More than touched him. Why would a saboteur bent on infecting the poor drell of the *Keelah Si'yah* with that Yoqtan monstrosity care about keeping his germs to himself? He turned to ask the hanar, but Ysses merely hung in the air beside him, watching with interest, as if concerned only with what might happen next.

"Authoritative interjection: I do not think it is him," the elcor droned.

"What do you *mean* it's not him?" Non snapped. "Why else would this Khar'shan-clan toad be skulking around the ship? Why else would he be awake at all? Airlock that *thing* and be done with it!"

"You don't know what you're talking about," sneered Borbala. "You see a batarian and all of a sudden it's just so *simple*, isn't it? Put him in an airlock, no trial, no interrogation, just a bit of laughter and a champagne toast to the universe being exactly as your tiny little brain always thought it was. He's clearly sick, you *fucking peasant*."

The volus's air filter made that sucking, gulping sound they always did. "You know him," she rasped.

"Oh, so we all know each other now, is that it?" roared Borbala. "Do we all look alike, too?"

"Yes, *obviously you do*!" shouted Irit Non. "The two of you were in on it together, admit it! And you meant to frame the volus for your crimes!"

"You did say his name," said Anax gently, slinging her rifle over one shoulder, finally. "You recognized him."

"Yes, well, I only met him on Hephaestus. Dal'Virra is scum. His family is only half a generation out of the slave caste. He is a small-time weapons dealer, on the run from his debt and his third wife with two of his offspring, he is judgmental, rude, unpleasant, conservative, and he cannot hold his shard wine."

"Die prostrate on a burning pyre of all you hold dear, mother of worms," Dal'Virra said matter-of-factly, and sunk his head in his hands.

"He doesn't seem to care much for you, either," observed Senna'Nir.

"And in that, he has much company and always will. But despite—"

"You are a traitor to our people," Dal'Virra hissed.

"But *despite* being unworthy to pick up the leavings of my least virile war beast, he is not half smart enough to do something like this. I drank with him for three nights on the station before he realized who he was talking to and started in with *that* charming patter."

Dal'Virra scratched his neck furiously, his face a rictus of pain. But he still had energy for Borbala, it seemed. "No wonder you tucked your pyjak tail between your legs and ran away to Andromeda like a coward. Like a *slave*."

The batarian matriarch sighed and tilted her head to the right, a sign of how far above Jalosk she considered herself. She chuckled. "Given that I am the only one on your side, you landless craven pustule, I would say you are not half smart enough to wash yourself in the morning, let alone sabotage an Initiative cruiser."

The drell took a step to approach what Yorrik already found himself thinking of as his patient. The elcor had not often found it frustrating that he could not make his voice carry all the panic, desperation, and fear of their situation. He could not bellow a command at them like Senna could. Like he badly needed to. But he felt it now. He had to make them understand.

"Urgent scream: Do not go near him. Do not touch him. Do not allow his fluids to come in contact with you. Especially you, Anax Therion."

But for once, that deep monotone was frightening enough. All four of them stopped in their tracks. They retreated slowly. Anax understood instantly. Her arm flared blue as she threw a biotic barrier toward Jalosk. It hissed where it touched the wet, black, sour mess on the floor of the hall. The batarian groaned miserably and vomited again; the barrier held. Yorrik found himself wondering how many biotics were on the ship. A simple barrier would not stop a virus, but it could stop almost anything or anyone else.

"Stern admonishment: What is wrong with you? There is an infection on this ship and you want to go splashing around in the vomit of a sick man? Imperative: He must be isolated immediately. There is an iso-chamber in the medbay, Senna'Nir. It is accessible through the cleanlock vestibule at the end of the hall." However poorly supplied, the medbay was logically constructed. The iso-chamber was segregated from both the main deck and the rest of medbay by a series of disinfecting fields. A patient could enter from the outside without air exchange between the corridor and the rest of the clinic.

The elcor glanced meaningfully at the blast pattern of the batarian's bodily fluids. Black globules dripped from the ceiling. Quarantine protocol might well be a sad joke now. But it was all he had.

The quarian commander keyed something into his portable node and released the locks separating the *Keelah Si'yah*'s sole iso-chamber from the vestibule connecting it to the main deck. The first glass door slid aside. "Sir, would you mind escorting yourself in there?" he said, politely enough.

"*Please* tell me what's going on," the batarian begged, bile crusting on his lips. "I haven't done anything. I don't want to go in there. I won't put myself in your prison cell, son of scavengers. I'll never leave it. Not when the volus wants my head. Wants my head for *nothing*. For the vicious crime of waking up. That's all I did. I woke up. My pod released its seal. I thought I was the first one revived. But I felt *terrible*, just… just terrible. And it's so dark. What happened to the lights? I tried to go down to the cargo hold but—" Another bout of nausea hit Anax's barrier. This time it was full of bright, oxygenated blood. "I was just looking for medbay, you bootlickers. To find some medi-gel for my… my everything. I found you instead. And *her*. And I'm not going to be locked up for it!"

"If one word of that is true I'm a turian beauty queen," scoffed Irit Non. "Why didn't you go check on your precious babies before sneaking around six decks above them? What was so important that you went straight for the cargo hold on an empty ship? *What did you do to the datacore, you piece of varren shit?*"

Borbala snorted. "Oh please," she said. "He can't even spell it. Show that man a datacore and at *best* he'll just start looking for a place to stick his meat into it."

Jalosk Dal'Virra was soaked in sweat and shaking. But not from fear, Yorrik thought. At least, not only from fear. What batarian before this very second would let a volus see him tremble? He started babbling hysterically. "Shut *up*, you vile bitch! Mother of worms! Mother of dung!" He turned his head toward Senna, pleading. "You can't force me in there! Quarians have *ethics*. I've heard. So do drell and elcor and hanar. You won't force me. You won't. That fat space elephant said not to touch me! He said! He said!"

Anax rolled her eyes and dropped her barrier. Dal'Virra gave a ragged sigh of relief. Then, without a word or even so much as shifting her stance, the drell's elbow went rigid and she snapped him up in the turquoise bubble of a biotic throw, lifting the miserable weapons dealer off the deck floor and depositing him roughly inside the cleanlock. The door slid closed again. A forcefield inside vanished, allowing him to shuffle into the iso-chamber and collapse on the cot.

Yorrik thumped his head against the glass to get her attention. "Fierce emphasis: Anax Therion, get out of here. You are susceptible. You cannot risk exposure."

"Who is going to interrogate him if not me?" The drell raised her hand to her mouth, but did not move to leave. Nor did she step through the liquid biohazard between her and the iso-chamber. "What do you know of criminality that you did not learn from a human playwright, Yorrik? He is not a terminal node for Senna'Nir to hack. Non already assumes his guilt. Any information achieved through Borbala's... methods... cannot be relied upon. And a hanar would always prefer a drell to do such work."

"This one does not know what the servant of Kahje implies with her barbed words," Ysses hummed.

"My words have no barb unless you bring your own to bear upon them," Anax said with stiff formality. "And besides, it would be illogical to assume that because he is sick, he must be sick with the same thing that killed the others. He has no Yoqtan sores. No one else left their cryopods alive. More importantly, Jalosk Dal'Virra is unmistakably batarian, not drell or hanar. If you look closely, you can tell by the number of eyes."

"With great distress and need to be obeyed: Anax, you must leave this deck until we can know for certain."

"Surely if I have been exposed the damage is done," Therion ventured.

"Strained patience: That is not how any of this works. Not everyone exposed to a virus will contract it. Not everyone who contracts it will die from it. There are always variations in susceptibility across a population. We do not even know its main transmission vector. If it requires direct bloodstream-to-bloodstream contact, such as the human disease known as HIV or the Asari Cyanophage, you are perfectly safe. Wry sarcasm: If it is airborne, I suggest at least putting something over your mouth and nose. And prayer. Imploring: Take the volus and do as Senna asked. Assemble a protective suit so you do not die."

"I'm not going anywhere," Irit Non whined. "I am staying here, with that murderer, until you all admit the volus had nothing to do with this."

"Pleading: We have only the six of us to discover what has happened here. We cannot afford to lose you. Soft reflection: 'On Fortune's cap we are not the very button.'"

There was silence for a moment. No one moved.

"Seven, I should think," came a lilting, rather lovely accent from the shadows down the left-hand corridor. Captain Qetsi'Olam vas Keelah Si'yah emerged, her violet hood almost black in the harsh working lights. Senna'Nir reached out and squeezed her shoulder, overcome with relief at her presence.

Yorrik knew they had a history. A *long* one. *I met her before I knew how not to fall in love with a woman like that*, Senna had told him that last night, both drunk, stumbling down Dekaano Street toward the lights on the river. *I was a child, and what do children do when they find something that fascinates them? Humorous jest: Put it in their mouth?* Yorrik had suggested. *Never let it go*, Senna had answered, and he hadn't been joking at all. *Poor quarian*, the elcor thought. *They live such short lives, and with so much regret. You can't really call anything love that hasn't lasted two hundred years.* As Yorrik thought these thoughts, his eyes met those of the terribly sick batarian through two barriers, one of glass and one of mass effect fields. The man's eyes looked already empty. Yorrik made a mental note to revise the contextualization of Lady Macbeth's final monologue so that, in some small way, his elcor Macbeth would recall all this when it was finally performed. His friend on the riverbank years ago, his friend in and out of love now, the mortality of that yellow beast in his shimmering cell. "Wishing it were otherwise: 'Out, out brief candle! Life's but a walking shadow, a poor player that struts and frets his hour upon the stage and then is heard no more.'"

Qetsi'Olam pressed one three-fingered hand, encased in the gray mesh of her suit, to her visor. "*Keelah se'lai*, my *head*," she moaned.

"Allow me to ask one question, and I will go," said Therion quickly, rubbing her longest finger against her index. She stared down at the miserable Jalosk, those dark, enormous eyes as empty of emotion as Yorrik's own voice. "Jalosk, were you assigned to a Sleepwalker team?"

"What the *hell* is going on on my ship?" said the captain sharply. Anax ignored her.

"Yes," the sick man mumbled into his trembling hands.

"Which one?"

"Yellow-9," he coughed.

Anax looked over at Senna'Nir and tilted her head to one side.

"K," she addressed the ship interface, "who else was assigned to Sleepwalker Team Yellow-9 besides Soval Raxios, Kholai, and Jalosk Dal'Virra?"

Elcor team member: Analyst Threnno. Quarian team member: Medical Specialist Malak'Rafa vas Keelah Si'yah. Volus team member: Security Specialist Goz Kympna.

"Please revive Specialist Malak'Rafa and instruct him that he is to be confined to my quarters. You'll need to light us both a path through the quarantine," the drell said. She nodded to the volus. "I will meet him there after I… dress for dinner."

"Permission granted," said Qetsi'Olam archly. "And what quarters would those be?"

"Designate something, Captain," Therion said over her shoulder as she walked away. "I need a place to work."

Qetsi's three thick fingers curled into a fist. She was not accustomed to being spoken to that way. But she said nothing.

After a moment, Irit Non let out something between a grunt and a shout in their general direction and followed the drell down the hall, back toward the cargo hold.

Captain Qetsi'Olam looked around at everything. All of it. The dead drell and hanar on the autopsy slabs, the torn-apart objects leaking fluorescent dye, Horatio, the empty quarian suit hanging there with its grotesque smiling face painted on the faceplate, the ropes of batarian bodily fluids staining the deck and the gently flashing medbay glass like sprays of horrible paint, the very awake Sleepwalker Team Blue-7, the drawn weapons, the quarantine lights, the prisoner-patient in the iso-chamber.

She shook her head. And then she laughed. What else, Yorrik supposed, could anyone possibly do?

"Will someone please explain to me what is happening before I lose my mind?" Qetsi said, calmly and sweetly.

"Certainly," Borbala Ferank sighed. "This ship is well and truly fucked. That is what is happening."

"With grim determination: No," Yorrik said. His low, buzzing voice echoed in the quiet. "What is happening now is that everyone not wearing a containment suit is going to leave. Then you, Mr. Dal'Virra, are going to stand against the rear wall of the iso-chamber and allow the remote diagnostic array to collect samples from you and put them in the hazmat capsule on your side." The elcor indicated a circle cut out of the medbay wall, sealed with a glass bubble, that terminated in a shallow, empty drawer where whatever was being passed between the safe zone and the unsafe zone could be collected. "Or I will instruct the iso-chamber to release the mother of all sedatives and take what I need anyway."

"And what is it you need, Specialist?" the captain said grimly.

"Vomit, blood, tissue, saliva, lacrimal fluid, hair, fingernails, everything. Grim determination: Then, what is 'happening' is that I am going to watch over a batarian weapons dealer with three ex-wives, financial trouble, and two young children. I am going to watch him while he either recovers from the worst cryosickness in recorded medical history, or, more likely, while he slowly dies behind that forcefield. I am going to take copious notes. And I am going to try to think of a way to save us." If Dal'Virra had Yoqtan, the virus had achieved spillover: crossing between species. And it had done it *twice*. If he could record the progression of the disease, they would at least have somewhere to begin. He would at least be able to tell if any of the others started to show symptoms. "Fond yet trepidatious quotation: 'Murder, though it have no tongue, will speak with most miraculous organ.'"

"That's barbaric," said Senna'Nir. "It's completely unethical."

"Guilty rejoinder: So is dying alone in space, Senna. You have a suit. We do not. Do not lecture us on the ethics of a pathogen."

"This one is filled with fascination, but will not be able to bear witness. This one must prepare the body of Kholai for its eternal rest among the stars," Ysses sang. "This one cannot allow the corporeal form of the Enkindled to be 'airlocked' with those who did not serve it."

"That sounds *spectacular*," said Borbala, checking the charge on her pistol. "It really does. And you should definitely do that, after you call the janitorial drones to clean up... let us call it the last failure of Jalosk Dal'Virra. But we have another problem."

"You mean other than that we've all been running for almost twenty-four hours without food or sleep, we're all exhausted, the ship's systems are as useful and responsive as a krogan with a head injury, and there are almost six hundred infectious corpses on ice in the lower hold?" asked Senna'Nir. "Other than that, what care could we have in the world, Borbala Ferank?"

The batarian matriarch lifted one long green-yellow finger into the air. "Listen," she said.

Yorrik strained to hear what she meant. He could hear the unsettling, bubbling respiration of Ysses beside him. The hum of the laser scalpels on standby. The ragged, tortured breathing of Jalosk Dal'Virra in his makeshift specimen cage.

But the rest was silence.

Then.

Plink. Plink. Thunk. Thunk-SLAM.

Borbala's three good eyes blinked at them in succession. "That's debris," she said. "Just the normal little tiny bits of dust and dead rock floating around in space. You know, the kind of junk we have a huge array of biotic shields to keep from slamming into us at faster-than-light speeds."

Plink. Plink. Knock. CLUNK.

"That's the sound of it hitting the ship, new friends," Ferank said. "It's been happening every nine minutes and forty-one seconds. That is *not* a good sound."

Plink. Plink. Plink.

8. INCUBATION

Anax Therion stood on an overturned trunk, her arms held out to the side like an aristocrat's wife being fitted for a ballgown.

"It is not my best work," Irit Non muttered as she strained to seal two slabs of flexible, elegant chocolate-brown and bone-white nano-mesh fibers around the drell's long green thigh.

It was quiet in the cargo hold. Quiet and cold. Their voices echoed against the high concave ceiling. Irit had already decided it was "creepy down here" and wanted to be done with this whole business as quickly as possible. But Therion found it oddly comforting. She had been here before. They had solved problems in the cargo hold, she and Borbala Ferank, whom she had rather begun to miss. The two of them had been given puzzles with gaps in the picture, and they'd filled them in here. She had been successful with Borbala, and that was the same as liking her. The cargo hold was a place of solutions. Being surrounded by all those tens of thousands of people's futures packed into shipping crates was almost like being surrounded by the people themselves. To Anax Therion, the shadowy, cavernous cargo bay was as crowded as a party.

Irit's personal crate was massive, roomy enough for them both to stand up comfortably inside—though that was far easier for the short, round volus than the lanky drell. Far bigger than the quarian family's allotment; sweet, useful little Raya'Zufi with her ancient krogan microscope and her stuffed dolls. Anax wondered what the volus had paid for the excess.

"You are too thin," the volus designer complained. "It is extremely unattractive."

There were probably comedy vids in the archives that involved drell in volus suits, Anax thought, without embarrassment. Anax Therion had never seen the purpose of embarrassment. Or comedy. Both seemed inconvenient afflictions. Though useful enough to incite in others. She had not yet been able to get much of anything out of the volus, even during the long fitting. She had some sort of resentment toward males, and the usual volus paranoia of being the most hated species in any given room, even one with a batarian in it. But Therion could not yet decide what the creature wanted, other than for them to stop using the word *Yoqtan*. She had always found the time between meeting a person and understanding fully what role was most advantageous to play for them highly uncomfortable. She could take a guess, but it would only be a guess. And a risk. Therion despised risk.

The suit was a patchwork job, sewn together with astonishing skill from pieces of a thousand other suits that Irit Non had packed away in the cargo hold to stock her new shop on the Nexus, modified for a body that bore no resemblance to a volus whatsoever. The long pale flaps that hung on either side of a volus's muzzle to protect the air-exchange mechanism instead hung down on either side of Anax's small, muzzleless head like white hair. The famous glowing eye gaskets shone against the brown ridged skullcap. To her surprise, the tinted glass did not color the world yellow. She could see normally, and with the benefit of a visual display not unlike a quarian's, it was able to show her the status of the various suit seals, filters, pressurization zones, hygienic sieves, and exterior conditions, as well as her own vital signs.

"It'll never be as good as a Fleet-clan suit," Non sighed. "That's just not what we make them for. They wear suits so nothing gets *in*. We wear them so *we* don't get *out*. But I can install some basic medical shields, prophylactic reservoirs, contaminant stopgaps, and... hey, look, this is the best part." Irit snapped her short fingers in Anax's face. She had been putting the readout display through its paces, memorizing the facial tics that controlled the various options and menus. "Pay attention. I might start offering it as a featured upgrade when I open for business. If the suit detects aggressive foreign cell structures, like a virus, a virus which is most certainly not Yoqtan, you'll see a little icon flash in the bottom-right corner of your corneal display. Like this." And a bright-red circle with a cross inside had appeared in the gasket glass, blinking on and off. "It might also detect cigarette smoke or amorous pheromones or eezo or an oncoming thunderstorm, as well; I don't exactly have time to make the sensor precise."

"Can we be sure its scans are working?" Anax asked. "Scans are proving unreliable around here."

Irit Non made a truly revolting half-snorting, half-gargling noise in the back of her throat, opened a heretofore-invisible sluice gate the size of a fingernail under her chin, and flung a spray of coppery-blue volus spit into Anax Therion's face. The red icon flared up right where it should have. "None of my processors were ever connected to the *Si'yah*'s systems, and they aren't now. Computer problems can't just magically hop from machine to machine like organic problems.

There has to be a packet exchange of some kind." Non paused. "Still, probably best if you test it once in a while."

There was no ego in the statement. Neither shame nor arrogance. In everything else, Irit was proud. To an already irritating fault. But when it came to her suits, her only concern was that they did their work. Anax admired that. She felt the same. The volus opened a forearm cuff and jammed several wafer-thin discs between the layers of copper-brown mesh. She sealed it around Therion's left wrist, which went numb for a moment as the gauntlet accessed her bloodstream.

Irit spoke softly. She didn't meet Anax's eyes. "Yorrik said all this could still be an accident. The birth of a new life form. But you don't think so, do you?"

Anax Therion looked down at the volus. "Irit Non, I will tell you what the hanar who raised me told me. *One misfortune may be chance; two might be divine punishment. Three is a plan.*" She ticked them off on her fingers. "The virus and the system malfunctions leave us somewhere between divine punishment and a plan. Do you really think we will be spared a third?"

"Ah. No. But then, I am a committed pessimist."

"I knew we would find common ground somewhere, Non," Anax said with a soft smile, half concealed by her unfinished helmet.

A long silence. Irit was clearly famous for good reason. Even now, under stress that would break a Spectre's sense of professionalism, the volus had added flourishes and touches of style without even seeming to be conscious of doing it. "It wasn't us," she whispered. "I'm not angry at you for suspecting so. It's natural to think of the ones in the suits, the ones with an immunity to Yoqtan from childhood, the ones who even know what Yoqtan is. But it wasn't the volus."

"You can't know that. There are three thousand of you on board."

The volus wheezed heavily and sat back on a box of eye-lenses. "Look," she gulped through her air filter, "I know my people, just like you know yours. When you rise to the top of a society, you have an excellent vantage point on the people in it. Would you grant me that?"

"Certainly," Therion said. She wouldn't, not really. In her experience, a seat at the top of a society afforded a view of nothing more than the top of that society. But the best way to get someone to keep talking was to agree with them, and that transcended species. Everyone wanted people to agree with them. It was, perhaps, all anyone wanted.

Irit leaned forward, her elbows resting on her knees, her large belly hanging between them. She did look up then.

"This just isn't our style, Anax. First of all, we have no quarrel with the Rakhana-clan. Or Kahje-clan, except that preachers are always extremely annoying, when they preach anything other than your own religion. In fact, we have a certain sympathy for you. The client relationship between turians and volus is not so different than the one between hanar and drell. Secondly… let me put it this way. If the volus were to strike out at the drell, we would much prefer to simply buy out their Compact with the hanar and take their place. To have a client species of our own would greatly increase our standing in the new galaxy. Forgive me for putting it bluntly, but if we wanted to get rid of you, we would far rather absorb you into the volus culture and benefit as the hanar have done for so long, or finesse the Fleet-clan or the Khar'shan-clan into declaring war on you. We long ago did away with waging war ourselves, of course. Wasteful. But we are very interested in *other* people's wars. There is more money in war than anything save entertainment. We would never deny our munitions manufacturers such an opportunity. But this? There is no profit in a simple death, only expense. In disposing of bodies, in extra work to make up the lack of laborers, in concealing our involvement so as to avoid retaliation. No, a volus might shoot you directly in the face for money, but at least it will be direct. Biological weapons are messy. Unpredictable. We volus dislike unpredictability, in both markets and life." Irit made a disgusted sound. "My father would say that is our great weakness as a people."

Irit Non stood up with a grunt and rummaged through her stock for more piecework. She strode around behind Therion and began the final lacing of the torso section.

Target acquired. When in doubt, it's always daddy issues. Therion trod carefully. "Your father?"

Non yanked on a structural panel with unnecessary brutality. Therion gasped. She let herself gasp. It was what the suit designer wanted. To express a small domination over her. It cost Anax nothing to let her have it.

"My father says a lot of things. In fact, you could say that all the fat old bastard does is say things. Professionally. My father is an invasive fungus in volus form. We do not get along. And yet…" Non fastened the other half of Therion's faceplate into place. "And yet I am here. The miserable gasbag pissed off so many people so many times that the Vol Protectorate forced him into exile. Do you know how many writs of exile the Protectorate has issued in the history of civilization? Three, and two were for my father."

"Your father is Gaffno Yap? The terrorist?" She knew of Yap, of course. It was hardly possible not to. He was a regular feature in political satires across half the galaxy, a cartoonish villain among the volus, a violent criminal among the courts, a tragic figure among others. But this she had not known. A volus's second name was not a surname; it indicated no genetic relationship, as they disliked the implication of families owning their offspring. Between this and the identical suits, it was very hard to piece together the shape of relationships between individual volus. She remembered Irit hissing furiously at Yap on the security vids.

"Never proven!" snapped Non. "As if my father would lift a finger to do his own work. He is radical, yes. He is an agitator, yes. He is an anarcho-communist who preaches the abolition of currency and personal property to the *volus*, for fuck's sake, yes. But he had nothing to do with those bombings. He just... inspires people. It's not his fault those people invariably run off holding hands and skipping through the flowers to blow up banks and treasuries and any place where there might be a lot of money or influence or money and influence all together in one spot."

"People like your mother."

Irit did not take that bait. "I had to grow up with that voice whining in my ear, singing *all property is theft, all money is blood money* as a lullaby. He thought we should emulate the quarians, and give up the whole notion, not just of capital, but of trade itself. Revolting. To isolate us that way. To take away the lump of sugar that coaxes any species to take the risk of interacting with any other. And when I made a success of myself, he took it as a personal insult."

"Yet you came with him. You left your success behind."

Irit Non's shoulders slumped a little. "He is old. He is not well. All his life he has had followers to manage his affairs. Now he is in disgrace. He has no one. They abandoned him once there was no more profit in writing tell-alls about spending a bit of their youths rubbing elbows with the intellectually dangerous. But Gaffno is an optimist to my pessimist. He actually thinks he can convince the volus on board to join him in creating a new society on whatever world the Pathfinders discover for us. I could not… let him be alone when he finally understands that they will not. I am weak, in that way. And that pill will be all the more bitter for him, now that his only other friend is dead."

"Oh?"

"Kholai, the hanar. You must have heard it on Hephaestus. It was preaching day and night, with a throng of hanar hanging on every word. Kholai was the leader of a cult of some kind, or at least a sect. He and my father had much in common. There's a group of hanar, fifty or so, who believe that only in Andromeda will they be able to practice their religion freely. The one with Yorrik in medbay is one of them."

"All hanar practice the same religion. There is no religious conflict on Kahje."

"Oh, they still worship the Enkindlers. They just think Kholai is their only true prophet. They call it the Enkindled One. They believe that the Enkindlers made a mistake in uplifting primitive life in the Milky Way.

That we should not be. Because they erred in directing our evolution, all present organic life is tainted and trends toward chaos and wickedness." Non sighed, as if she were reciting from a particularly annoying book. "The Enkindlers will one day return to punish the children of the galaxy for their impure way of life, for using their blessings improperly, for polluting themselves by intermixing with the cultures of others. On the 'Day of Extinguishment' the Enkindlers will return to destroy all those who have sinned against them and raise up those who have lived an immaculate life into a new paradise. The usual doomsday song. The Illuminated Primacy objected to their missionary work, spreading the idea that the Enkindlers were capable of error. So they hope for a new world where they can wait for the Day of Extinguishment without the temptation of outsiders. Sounds delightful, I know. Kholai is a very persuasive speaker. It has a beautiful voice. Had. There. I think you're settled. I have a mirror, give me a moment."

The volus hauled out a mobile dressing-room unit from the rear of her cavernous crate. Therion looked herself over. The suit flowed naturally around the curves of her body as though drell had been wearing habitat suits for centuries. Stripes of white-and-brown titanium mesh divided by flexible structural boning defined her waist and conformed to the shape of Therion's muscular legs, her arms, even her feet. The large round central processing unit rode on her solar plexus, blinking softly, all systems online. The air-exchange nozzle that gave the volus's voices that trademark wheeze-and-suck sound covered her mouth and nose, breathing for her, with no effort of her own expended. The gloves transmitted textural information directly into her cerebral cortex and newly augmented visual display. She couldn't *feel* things through the fabric, but she could instantly *compute* them, without the irritating inefficiency of physical contact. The drell hadn't even known how badly she'd always wanted that until now.

Anax Therion looked… disturbingly good. She had to admit it. The whole effect was utterly alien, extremely formidable, and wholly unsettling, even frightening. It was entirely possible that no one in the history of either galaxy had ever looked the way she looked standing in the hallway of a stranded ghost ship a hundred light years from anywhere.

"I'm not going to sound like you, am I?" Anax said experimentally.

She didn't, not exactly. Her voice was suddenly very gravelly and rough and breathy, a nightclub singer after a three-day bender voice, but not quite as hard a wheeze as Irit's. The air exchange didn't actually have to exchange air for a drell, nor did the pressure panels have to hold her lungs together in an intolerably low-pressure environment.

"Ungrateful," the volus puffed. "Do you know what this kind of bespoke job would cost you back in the Milky Way? Your firstborn child wouldn't even cover the down payment. I honestly don't know why Rakhana-clan don't suit up like the rest of us. You don't see us stuffing the hospitals with Kepral's corpses." Her snout lifted thoughtfully. "I can feel a new profit vector in my kneecaps. By the gods, I hope we survive this." Non reached up and gave Anax's stomach a solid whack below the central processor unit. A dark stain in the shape of her fist spread over the mesh.

"Feel that?"

"Not a thing," Anax answered.

"Good. Unlike mass-produced ensembles, Irit suits all come standard with a patented pain-response dampening matrix. Your nervous system is shaped like an idiot child's drawing compared to mine, but it seems to work." The volus sucked in a long, bubbling swallow of air. "Your display will record impacts or breaches, but if you start feeling anything, you're probably already dying." The stain was fading as the matrix did its work, but slowly.

Therion inclined her head. "You are an artist, Irit Non. I am grateful."

"Gah. Don't say that word. You sound like my father."

"Grateful?"

The volus shook her head. "Artist."

Therion smoothed the long white flaps that hung down slightly past her shoulders. "My people are reptilian," she explained. "Our skin secretes a toxic compound that I am sure you know other species find highly intoxicating and even hallucinogenic. Normally, our sweat evaporates harmlessly. I estimate I can wear this suit for approximately thirty-five to forty-eight hours before my bloodstream has absorbed enough of my own venom to have degenerative cognitive effects. We could never live inside such suits for long periods, as you do. We would go quite, *quite* mad and suffocate in our own subcutaneous oils. For the next two days or so, however, it is an acceptable alternative to dying of your mutant volus pox."

Non scowled. Anax could tell, even in the suit. "It is not our pox, I told you. But your body makes it, how can it harm you?"

"Your body makes many things," Therion said

with some amusement. "I doubt you would enjoy ingesting them." A soft chime sounded in her ear. The suit was wired into all her personal devices. "The captain has transmitted directions to my shiny new quarters and interrogation room. Shall we?"

"Right. Shall we discuss what you hope to beat out of this dumb quarian?" Irit wheezed as she moved about, re-securing the mess she had made of her cargo.

Anax Therion placed her gloved palm against the wall of the crate. Her visual display immediately scrolled a metallurgic analysis, structural weak points, factory origin, and installation date across her peripheral field. Touching without touching. It was positively addictive. "Of the six members of Sleepwalker Team Yellow-9," she mused, "two are dead and one is looking extremely poorly. Malak'Rafa is not."

"But only drell and hanar can get sick. So wake them all up. We'll have a party. Why this one?"

"Of the three remaining members of Yellow-9, he is the only one I can be certain poses no danger to us, nor we to him, because, even in cryostasis, he was wearing his own personal quarantine zone. And I suspect whatever happened on board our little ark happened first to Sleepwalker Team Yellow-9. The quarian on the other side of that door could be behind everything that's happened. Or he could be the unluckiest *bosh'tet* this side of Rannoch."

"*Him*? A quarian? I know you're meant to be some kind of detective, but only a brainless oddskull would think a quarian would voluntarily come within a thousand kilometers of a *weaponized infection*. It's the batarian, Jolly Doll or whatever he calls himself. Why am I the only one with any sense?"

Therion spread her fingers out over the metal of the crate, feeling everything about it. "Perhaps. Did it never once occur to you that he might have been telling the truth? That his pod malfunctioned and woke him up? We are awake. Many systems have glitched. Is it so far from plausibility?" Irit Non's muscles were so tense and tight Therion knew the unspoken answer was *yes*. "Well. However you feel about it, Non, if that poor, stupid batarian dies back there, we are in a world of problems far beyond the drell and the hanar. Our species have cohabited for eight centuries. It is at least plausible that we have developed some kind of immuno-exchange, much as humans and their livestock were able to pass smallpox between them. To then pass it to a batarian would be like an Earth cow suddenly infecting a sniper rifle with the ability to shoot milk." Plausible, she thought. But also a terrible coincidence that it should affect the drell and the hanar only, when there were worshippers of entropy and decay on board. "But perhaps he is only cryosick, as Yorrik says." Anax would eat her new volus suit if Jalosk Dal'Virra outlived a half-charged battery. But panic would not serve either of them now.

Suddenly, Therion thought she heard a soft sound in the silence of the cargo hold. She whipped her head around. Nothing. All quiet.

"Did you hear that?"

"What? No. I hear you breathing like a damn nathak, is that what you mean?"

It was not. But the suit had not registered anything. Perhaps the dark and the cold were getting to her. At least the suit helped with the latter.

"Anax Therion," Irit said, with uncharacteristic shyness. But Therion was too alert, listening for more of that hushing, sighing, almost inaudible sound, to pay the volus much attention.

"Yes?"

"Why did *you* come?" Irit Non asked. "Why are you here? I came for my father; my father came in exile. Kholai and Ysses came for its gods. Yorrik came to become someone else. The quarians came for a homeworld, the same as always, if not quite the *exact* same. Why are you going to Andromeda?"

The drell snapped back to the moment before her. She trained her new mustard-colored lenses on the volus. She almost wanted to tell the truth. There was an intimacy to tailoring, one she supposed Irit had had many chances to exploit. It put you off guard. Perhaps Anax should consider taking up sewing herself. But the truth would not endear her to a volus. She chose something else. A guess. "I was once bonded to a hanar named Oleon, a smuggler wanted in twenty-one systems. My father sold me to Oleon when I was a child. I suppose I disappointed him." Non's hands balled into fists at her side. "But I never disappointed Oleon. I made it rich. I made it feared. I was a high-end weapon strapped to its tentacles. It cut my eyes just so that I could more easily understand the bioluminescent language of my masters. It performed the surgery itself, on a ship screaming out of the Skyllian Verge with a batarian cruiser on its tail. I was lucky it did not leave me blind. I was the first drell to receive a hanar soul name of my own. It was a strange life, a violent one. I was unhappy. But who is not?"

"What happened to this Oleon? Is it on board?"

"It is not."

"Why would you abandon your patron? I know of no drell who has left the Compact. Your people are so consistently servile. If an addiction to predictability is our weakness, that is yours."

Anax's mind adjusted, clicked into place, pivoted. *There,* thought Anax. *There you are, Irit Non. There is a freedom fighter inside that merchant's body.* "Oleon sent me on a mission to Earth, to assassinate a competitor named Laslow Marston. Marston was a diplomat, from a long line of ambassadors and statesmen and, naturally, spies. Ambassador is always another word for spy. But it seemed this particular Marston had taken up selling what he learned in the halls, offices, and beds of the powerful to the highest bidder, and that cut into my master's margins. It took me a year to get close enough to Laslow to strike. A year is a long time. Long enough to think. Long enough to question. And afterward… afterward I took what I knew and ran. All the way here, where the drell Pathfinder will find us a world without a Compact, and if I want to spend a year killing a man, it will be only because he offended me. As far as I know, Oleon is still rich, still feared, and probably training some new child to be its knife in the dark. Although, I suppose, not anymore. Nearly six hundred years have passed. I keep forgetting. But I am free of it. Oleon, and the six hundred years."

The volus reached up and adjusted something on the suit that almost certainly needed no adjusting. "Disgusting, the way your people accept servitude to those revolting jellyfish. But I am… I am sympathetic."

"We are not all so free as the volus."

The volus's thick, phlegmy voice took on actual notes of warmth. "I am glad you are rid of it now."

Anax found she loved wearing a suit. She could smile and gloat and no one would see. "A subject for another day, I think—now, surely you heard it that time!"

The volus closed her crate and keyed in the lock code on the security pad. "Heard what? Look, it's probably just your suit's processes. It takes time to get used to the background noise. It's usually just below the normal hearing range. Maybe I didn't adjust it enough for drell ears."

Anax had left her Lancer rifle leaned against the side of Non's luggage. She picked it up again.

"Is someone there?" she said loudly.

"You're being ridiculous," Non snorted.

Therion swept her weapon through the still darkness of the hold. Nothing. Blood rushing in her ears. Dammit. She *had* heard something.

"I'll tell you something ridiculous," Anax said, powering down her rifle with a frustrated grind of her teeth. "I didn't know whether I should tell you. But I think… I think you're all right, Irit Non." She thought no such thing. But she needed allies right now. She needed allies more than she needed secrets. "Ysses, the hanar in the lab with Yorrik? It's *happy*. I have never seen a jelly so happy. Even when it was speaking of preparing the corpse of its priest, Ysses was positively *pulsating* with joy."

"Huh," said Irit Non.

"Indeed," Anax answered. "Now, let's go question that quarian."

"Can we go via the mess hall? I'm *starving*," the volus complained, and the drell could not disagree. She had been putting the pains of her empty stomach aside, but she couldn't do it forever, and they had been awake for over thirty hours now.

A crunching, skittering crash echoed all around the

deck. A lot of things falling over at once. Or one big thing.

"I *know* you heard that," Therion hissed. She powered up the Lancer again. "Show yourself! Hands up, and don't come closer than ten meters! Who the fuck are you?"

"Nah," came a brutish, snarling voice. A male voice, strangled with fear. "You put your hands up. How about that?"

Out of the shadows, a cluster of bright-red laser sights danced across Anax and Irit's chests.

9. UNCOATING

Senna'Nir sat on his bunk in the first officer's quarters. He could not quite think of them as his quarters yet. They were so elegant, so clean, so new. *Si'yah* was, in the end and the beginning, still an Initiative ship, however modified by her quarian commanders, and so it bore all the superfluously elegant lines of human design. Mirrored surfaces, concealed lighting, tables and chairs as nice to look at as anything in a museum. A forward chamber with seating for several, an observation window, a personal terminal recessed in a long, broad desk, an empty fish tank that took up most of one wall, and a private rear chamber for sleeping, study, and eating. On a human or asari ship, these two adjoined rooms would have been considered modest. He did know that, somewhere inside the overabundance of self-deprecation that was his genetic heritage. But on a quarian ship, this would have been enough room for three families, perhaps four. Space was at a premium on the Fleet. That was why almost all quarians were only children. They just didn't have the resources for siblings. That this space was all his felt almost obscene. When Qetsi had first shown him, he'd refused. Too much, too beautiful, too big. He didn't need all this, told her to give it to the Pathfinder or use it for storage. She'd had to coax him into accepting. *It's a new world we're headed for*, she'd said so sweetly, and put her hand on his arm, like they were still young.

We don't have to live by the rules of the old one. It's yours. Enjoy it. Besides, the Pathfinder's quarters are much better. So are mine, incidentally.

The command staff had all been assigned cabins before departure. Their belongings were not down in the hold with the rest of it, but stowed here. All Senna's old scavenged parts, his tablets, his books, his memories, even a few of his mindfish, packed into secure lockers set into the wall in the dining area. That, too, felt like privilege. That, too, made him uncomfortable. But Qetsi was right. He had to let the old rules go. Some part of him was grateful that, at this very moment, he had somewhere to go and think, somewhere to be alone with the problem before him, even if the rest of his team did not. Though the *Keelah Si'yah* was fully equipped to house all twenty thousand souls aboard, the rest of the passengers would disembark onto the Nexus almost immediately, so there was no real need to arrange housing for them unless something went very wrong.

Something had gone very wrong. But at least almost everyone was still in stasis, blissfully ignorant. Something had gone very wrong, and he had to fix it.

"K," Senna said softly to the empty room. "Is my suit intact? Analyze for external damage. Activate conversational protocols Senna4, command passkey: alpha-vermillion-9-4-4-0-pallu."

His internal display showed no breaches, no compromises of any kind. But the collective quarian worst nightmare scenario was happening all around him, and with every breath, every jolt in his stomach, every ache in his elbow, he feared that *it* could get to him. Somehow.

No external damage detected, Commander. Your suit is excellent and attractive.

He ran his hands over the tightly crosshatched gray panels squeezing his waist. Was he having trouble breathing? Was that the first shallow breath of his eventual, inevitable death? *No. No. Stop it. You're* fine, *you idiot. You're not even breathing their air. You're not even* drell. *Even if that batarian has it, you're not fucking batarian, either.*

"Are you lying, K?" he said ruefully.

I do not understand the question, Commander.

"No offense, but you seem to have developed a tendency to lie lately."

What is a lie, Commander?

"K, you know every word in every language spoken on this ship, plus the Council races' languages, plus rudimentary Vorcha. You know what a lie is."

Correct. A lie is a false statement made with deliberate intent to deceive. However, I cannot make false statements, I cannot deceive, and I have no capacity for deliberate intent. Therefore, in this context, I cannot access a definition that fits appropriately into your chosen sentence structure. I also cannot take offense.

"I'm so glad I taught you to carry on a conversation, K. It was definitely worth all that time on Hephaestus. How's that repeating diagnostic subroutine I installed coming? Still running at peak efficiency?"

Affirmative. All systems well above minimum operational parameters. I am doing a very good job.

"Sure you are," Senna'Nir said darkly. "Good ship. Nice ship. Who wants a treat?"

Commander, in this context, I cannot access a definition of "treat" that would describe any transaction between—

"Never mind, K. Sit tight. I'll fix you up. That's the treat."

Liat, he thought. *Grandmother, I need you.*

Against all odds, the lights still seemed to work in here. He'd gotten so used to the shadows over the last many hours the brightness disturbed him. Senna'Nir stood up and walked across the room. (A room so big you could just casually walk across it like it was a park on the Citadel!) He slid open a panel in the wall and demagnetized a shelf of large, long drinking vessels. His suit's fluid compartments were running low. Frankly, everything was running low. They all needed to eat. They all needed to sleep. The captain had ordered Borbala Ferank to secure the mess hall and draw up a fair food distribution roster for the nine conscious passengers that made up the *Keelah Si'yah*'s current motley crew. But Senna was thirsty now. A quick top-up and straight to work. He pulled a slender glass tube out of his inner wrist and activated the water dispenser to fill his vessel.

The spigot spat out a torrent of water so hot it turned instantly to steam. Senna leapt back as the scalding mist hit him.

"K! Reduce water temperature to seven degrees!"

All water on board is dispensed at 7.56 degrees Celsius for optimal multi-species comfort. Please enjoy your refreshing drink, Commander.

The steam cleared, and a stream of industrial coolant dribbled out of the dispenser and into the catchbasin. Senna wanted to laugh. People who came out of crises in one piece, a little older and wiser, laughed ironically when yet another thing went wrong. But he couldn't. He was too thirsty, anyway.

Focus, Senna. Get the shields back online.

Senna'Nir unlatched one of the lockers behind the dining table. There was only one thing inside. He lifted it out reverently. A bundle of rags knotted around a small, dull metal disc with thin rods radiating out from a central raised ring. It had not been treated kindly in its life. The disc was dented and scratched and ancient, with marks that looked like, and very probably were, blaster burns, all along one side and the bottom. None of that was Senna's doing. He'd always taken care of it, ever since it had been entrusted to him, kept it wrapped in soft fabric, safely padded against further damage. It smelled, as it always had, of raw wiring, ozone, and the inside of a spent power pack. The smell of home. Of family.

He couldn't hook the disc up to the ship's power supply without running the risk of hooking it up to whatever was eating away at the ship's systems, one by one. But Senna'Nir was a tech and a quarian and a hoarder, and none of those three identities allowed him to ever go anywhere unprepared, with a carefully organized range of leftover parts and obsolete components that he would *absolutely* use someday. And someday had come. He slid open a drawer along the wall and chose a fresh, still-sealed power pack of a make and model that was compatible with the disc—not all packs were. He'd scoured the Fleet for every last one of them before he left, and almost vomited with guilt when no one stopped him.

Senna sat down on the clean plasteel floor, so new it was still perfectly white, in the exact center of the private portion of his quarters. His heart raced. His suit flashed cardiovascular concern into his visual field, which he blinked away. He looked toward the sealed door between him and the rest of the ship. *Just so long as the locks don't go out, too,* he thought nervously. He couldn't help the fear. He'd never been caught, but the longer you went on doing something terribly wrong without being caught, the more you feared it finally happening. *Maybe in Andromeda it won't matter. New world, Qetsi said. New rules. We are starting over. Why would anyone care now?* But Senna was fooling himself and he knew it. *Everyone* would care. If the other quarians found out, they would care so much he might never see the Nexus. He was starting to sweat. It was too damned *bright* in here.

"K, lower lighting in first officer's quarters by forty percent."

The attractively recessed lighting in the walls dimmed moodily, and then, with a stutter, went out completely.

Lighting reduced by 40%, Commander. Would you like to select accompanying music?

"No, K, that's... that's perfect," said Senna in the dark. "I'm not sure why I bothered to ask."

But he didn't need light. He was an old hand at this thing. He could activate it blindfolded using only his teeth if he had to. The quarian felt around on the floor for the power pack, shunted it home on the left side of the disc, and slid open the power toggle with his thumb. He could barely breathe. His pulse throbbed in his forehead.

The disc vibrated very lightly. That was how you *really* knew how old the thing was. Nothing vibrated anymore. Everything else on this glorious ship ran smooth as still water, even at the highest energy output levels. But not his disc. It thrummed with effort.

A light came on in the dark. A small, shimmering figure appeared just over the center of the disc, partly translucent, but otherwise in full color and three dimensions: a quarian woman, old, but still strong and wiry, without a suit, for in her time there had been no need for them. The large, familiar webbing of a puckered scar covered the left side of her head, a memento of the time a geth told her exactly what it thought of organic life. Her eyes were white and kindly, without pupils, her hair beneath a rough cowl gray, her long avian legs wrapped, like the rest of her, in purple and red woolen robes.

"Hello, Grandmother," Senna'Nir said quietly, though there was no one around to hear him.

"Always so formal, my grandson," said the ancestor VI, as it always did, in her clipped, melodious old Rannoch accent. "Call me Liat, why don't you? Never thought of myself as old enough to have grandchildren anyhow."

Senna smiled. His whole body relaxed. She was not damaged. She had made it all the way across the known and unknown cosmos intact. "Grandmother, we are almost to Andromeda, which makes you technically nine hundred and fifty-nine years old."

"Watch your tongue, you little *bosh'tet*," said the image of his ancestor with a holographic grin. "Never discuss a lady's age, marital status, or how much she can deadlift in public." The shifting colors of the projection changed to an expression of concern. "You look thin. Have you been eating enough?"

Senna reached out and pressed his hand fondly against the side of the metal disc. It was warm, like a real grandmother would be. But Liat'Nir was not a real grandmother. Liat'Nir, hard-drinking, hard-talking, hard-coding, hard-living progenitor of his line, had died in the first spasm of the geth war, when all of Rannoch burned. This was a virtual intelligence programmed hundreds of years ago from an imprint of the real Liat'Nir's personality, taken only hours before her death, preserved so that no generation of quarians would ever forget where they had come from, so that no child would ever be without family. She was also deeply, utterly illegal, and almost unspeakably valuable. Liat'Nir had been Senna's parents' greatest secret, and now she was his. Before the war, there were thousands of these VI. Everyone had them. Everyone could hear the voices of their grandparents and great-grandparents and great-great-grandparents any time they wished. If they were not their *real* voices, they still provided comfort, continuity, the richness of a past that did not truly end. But the geth had destroyed the ancestor databanks when they revolted against their masters, and if it was a deliberate punishment, it was the cruelest they ever visited on the quarians. The ancestor VIs were not truly sentient, but before the geth awakened, there had been something of an arms race to augment and upgrade them, to approach the point at which the difference between the real ancestor and the VI was purely academic. That point had never come. But now… now their intelligence was too near a miss, too unsettling, after the quarians' machine servants had turned against them, asking if they had souls, begging to know, and finally, shooting the people who would not, could not, tell them. If you didn't know better, if you were unfamiliar with the process by which a personality could be mapped onto a huge bank of code and output standardized and improvised responses based on established prompts and augmented by all previous interactions, an ancestor VI might *seem* to have a soul. A malfunctioning water dispenser did not. Therefore, in the post-war anti-machine panic, they never tried to make another one. Ancestor VIs were an acceptable, if deeply felt, loss. Water dispensers could stay.

But not every ancestor had been erased by the geth. A few survived by chance or fate. Liat'Nir's imprint had been taken just before she suited up for war against her own creations, in case the worst happened, which it had. The pattern had never had a chance to be stored in the main databank. Someone in Senna's family tree must have been more like him than anyone since. Someone must have sympathized with machines the way he did. Someone couldn't bear to lose Liat'Nir, either to the geth or the sudden horror of all things VI, and installed her in a contained mobile unit. What Senna'Nir held in his hands was simultaneously terrifying to any other quarian and perhaps the one physical object they would ascribe any value to at all. And that value was nearly limitless. Anything approaching AI was forbidden. But ancestor VI was the lost legacy of their race. And at the moment the quarians lost everything, their computational arms race had brought the ancestor VIs *almost* to the brink of sentience. This beaten metal disc was both a crime and a near-mythical treasure, hidden by his family for generations. Senna had spent most of his life in fear of being found out. He might be dumped onto a prison planet and left to die. He might be praised for bringing this jewel to the Fleet. She might be given a place of honor. She might be deleted. But either way, she would be confiscated. And she was *his* grandmother. He would never let that happen.

Others since that first cousin who made their grandmother into a particularly unlovely dinner plate must have understood that an ancestor VI was not a geth Shock Trooper in the making. They posed no danger. Their code base was massive; K's entire interface program would fit onto a glass wafer one fiftieth of the size of this clunky, heavy metal saucer. But code, code *itself*, just the *presence* of machine code, was harmless. It could not do anything you didn't tell it to. Until, of course, you told it to. And someone whose DNA still moved in Senna's cells must have known all that. Must have known that ancestor VIs were not sentient and could not become sentient just by giving them more input any more than you could make a fish evolve legs by talking to it. However organically a sophisticated linguistic-emotive-depictive triad seemed to arise, the words a VI used, the tone of voice, and the gestures it depicted were entirely algorithmically determined. Artificial intelligence was so much more complicated than that. Those rebellious aunties or uncles, whoever they were, had kept Liat'Nir and hidden her from the collective extermination of the quarians' personal history. Each generation had passed her down to the next with so much love and reverence it made Senna's heart ache to remember the day his parents had introduced him to her, hard-coded his name into her admin access controls, and told him never, *ever* to tell anyone. And he hadn't. Not even Qetsi. Not even when they'd been at their closest. But there had never been a moment when Senna considered going all the way to Andromeda and not bringing Grandmother with him. He would rather have left both his arms behind.

"Liat," he said to the glimmering hologram. "I have a problem. Time is of the essence."

Ancestor VIs had a set number of phrases they could open a conversation with, and their available responses branched out from there, depending on how their descendant reacted. They could share something from an extensive catalogue of personal anecdotes or answer any query that the real ancestor would have been able to handle—or more, with all the style of a cantankerous relative at supper, if it were connected to a modern datacore. But the reason it was any use or fun at all talking to an ancestor VI was that they *could* improvise, and they could do it in two ways. One, by combining and recombining previous phrases, and every time you used a new phrase with Liat, she remembered it and could use it on her own, so that a conversation with Liat'Nir was actually a conversation with both her and every relative of his who had interacted with her, a private language of interacting references, a group call with the whole history of the Nir clan. But however impressive that might seem to the uninitiated, it wasn't much more than a parlor trick—no different than the old human folktale about infinite monkeys with infinite typewriters infinitely attempting to produce something Yorrik could sink his slats into.

The other method was why, despite her value, the mere existence of Liat'Nir was a crime.

A small, firewalled part of her command line did allow for spontaneous recombination—a process called, ironically enough, genetic programming. Presented with a problem, his grandmother could independently apply a genetic algorithm to a group of her pre-programmed LED responses. She would then combine and recombine these responses as fixed-length strings to produce a completely original solution never presented to her by a user or by her to one. Each iteration generated "child" strings that contained some data from one "parent" data set and some from the other. Faster than a real grandmother could sip her tea, Liat could attempt hundreds and thousands of iterations, most of whose children would be useless mutations, broken fragments, or otherwise dead-ended strings, and yet, each "generation" approached a successful result until one of them optimally fulfilled the fitness function—whatever it was that her poor, slow-thinking grandchild had asked her. This was more like collecting all those monkeys in one room, demanding *Hamlet*, forcibly breeding the best writers among them, and then mercilessly irradiating any monkey that failed to produce a melancholy Dane. The definitions of *fitness, optimal*, and *successful* were key, which was why it tended to generate somewhat unusual conversations. A machine's interpretation of *fitness* did not always match a person's idea of normal grandmotherly advice. When he was a kid, Senna had asked Liat'Nir if he would ever really be happy. She had considered it, and answered: *Sweetheart, you know I love you. But this life is long and hard and you're old enough for the truth: not unless you install a significantly improved primary processor, defrag your main drive, and seriously supplement your RAM.* He'd been upset at first. Switched her off and stormed off to brood on the trading deck about how nobody understood him. But ultimately, it wasn't the worst advice he'd ever gotten. And sometimes she managed leaps of logic he could never have arrived at on his own.

Sometimes she turned up total gibberish. Just before he joined Nedas, he'd asked her if he would ever see the quarian homeworld with his own eyes. Liat'Nir had answered: *go fish* and refused to elaborate. He still hadn't figured that one out.

Senna considered that it was not unlike the replication of a virus. The virus attaches to the surface receptors of the host cell, penetrates the membrane, fuses its own DNA with that of the cell, reproduces until the cell bursts and the process is repeated with new viral cells that contain some of the DNA of the host—mutations. Some small enough to reassure an unhappy child, some sheer nonsense, some, perhaps, uniquely ideal. More fit to spread the infection than the previous generation, stronger, more adaptable, able to colonize new parts of the body.

In terms of artificial intelligence, this kind of problem solving was the equivalent of the first rock the first proto-quarian beast on Rannoch had used to crush the first *fa'yin* shell to get at the nut inside. It was almost unbelievably crude and unsophisticated. Nevertheless, in it lay… everything. Genetic programming was the most primitive, basic building block of a machine that could truly think. In Liat'Nir, the part of her that could, in some sense, *imagine* unique answers was well beyond shackled, its use strictly limited to verbal conversation, the algorithms safely quarantined from the rest of her functions.

By using her personal name instead of *Grandmother* along with the command phrase *I have a problem*, Senna'Nir was directing her to access and use it.

Liat rolled her eyes.

"You always do, *ke'sed*." She always called him that. It was what people called the blind newborn offspring of the *qorach*—an animal something like a very carnivorous bighorn sheep whose bellies were forever covered in blue-green climbing fern pollen and seed casings, dragging the thorny plants over the mountainsides. There were no pollinating insects on Rannoch; all the native livestock existed in uneasy and often ungraceful symbiosis. Senna didn't know if she'd called everyone before him who had been entrusted as guardian of the ancestor VI *ke'sed*, and every time he'd almost asked, he just couldn't bear to know. The phrase also served as confirmation that the VI had accessed her more creative programming. "I swear the day you can take care of yourself all the stars will go nova and the universe will end."

Liat'Nir rummaged in her robes, swore a few times under her breath, and finally produced a holographic cigarette and a pink matchbox. She struck the match on her fingernail and inhaled her smoke with delight. Senna *loved* it when the program did that. Her physical behaviors were semi-randomly generated from a fixed cluster, ordered, he presumed, by the frequency with which the real Liat'Nir had done them. The cigarette sequence was a rare treat, but it was his absolute favorite. He'd never seen a quarian smoke in real life, and he didn't think he ever would. The sheer number of carcinogens beggared the imagination. And to damage your respiratory system for *pleasure*, for recreation! It was incredible. Like watching a dinosaur repeatedly hit itself in the face for fun. Sometimes he rebooted her over and over until he got the cigarette prompt. The matchbox always said something different—*Bet'salel Financial Advisors* or *Gaddiel & Sons Agrarian Suppliers* or *Ovad'ya's Fine Cosmetics*—this time it read *Macaleth All-Night Café & Cabaret*. Forgotten, long-vaporized businesses from his lost homeworld, from a life he could not possibly imagine.

"Well, out with it!" the VI said, her voice dear and loving and acerbic, gravelly with smoke.

"There is something wrong with the ship's datacore. We have experienced a series of erratic system failures, and I have no reason to think it's going to stop."

Liat'Nir leaned forward, a glint of artificial interest in her translucent eyes. When she was alive, she had been one of the best geth neural designers who ever lived. They used to say she stopped having children because she could build a lot more and far better brains on a server than on a hospital bed. The real Liat lived for things going wrong in datacores. She lived for puzzles. Therefore, so did her VI. And so did Senna. "What systems?" she said, pushing back her woolen cowl, ready to work. "In order of failure, please—my mind's not what it used to be."

Senna grinned, despite the ache of stress in his every bone. "Your mind is precisely what it used to be, Grandmother, down to the zeroes and ones."

His grandmother laughed, a short, sharp hack of a laugh. She slapped her knee with an arthritic hand. "You rude little shit! You want to comment on my figure, too? Spill your guts, *ke'sed*! By the gods, I would rather take my tea with a fully armed and pissed-off geth colossus than a young person these days."

"Internal scans on cryodeck 2, medical scans in medbay, interior lighting more or less everywhere, temperature control in zones 4, 1, 9, and 7, possibly cryopod BT566 but I'm not sure about that one, personnel tracking, external debris shield, water dispensers in first officer's quarters."

"That last one's a real emergency, eh?" Liat smirked. "We're talking life and death here. They will sing of this battle down the ages."

He ignored that one. Most of the time, Senna enjoyed her jabs, and encouraged her to generate new ones, but he had no time for that now. "Most of the systems seem to come and go, completely out of central control. The shields fail every nine minutes and forty-one seconds."

"That means the outermost tactile shield's your problem. Nine forty-one… probably the initiating starboard plasma-static generator's down. Continuous unbroken forcefields are weaker than oscillating shields, more prone to single points of failure. The tactile shuffles through biotic vibrational frequencies every nine minutes and forty-one seconds and maintains the resonance of all the other shields. The inner fields shift, too, but on a longer cycle. As long as it's only nine minutes and forty-one seconds, it's most likely just the first resonance phase that's malfunctioning, not all of them, or the shield would never come back, see? It's not as bad as everything shorting out at once, *certainly* not as bad as a broken water dispenser, but *some* space crap is definitely going to get through. So access the datacore and start debugging before a stray pebble takes out your engines, idiot."

"Just access the datacore," Senna repeated mockingly. "Yes, Grandmother, I did think of the most basic of all possible approaches. Let me finish. The problem isn't just the system shutdowns. It's that the ship cannot see anything wrong. Everything flips on and off at a moment's notice and the *Si'yah* just keeps insisting everything's fine. So I can't run a diagnostic or roll out a patch, because the system itself cannot see any errors to fix."

Liat'Nir frowned. She stubbed out her cigarette with one toe and squatted down low on the metal disc. She picked up a holographic stick off the "ground" and began working something out on the dry sand of a planet that for him was long-lost and for her was firm beneath her feet. This was a buffering posture, used by the VI to indicate it had begun to identify, mate, and test informational strings.

"Virus?" she said hopefully, without looking up.

"That's a whole other problem," Senna sighed. "Know anything about volus chickenpox?"

"Don't get it? I don't know. Fuck the volus. Those little walking asthma attacks get on my last nerve the second they open their fat mouths. That whole species isn't worth the ale-riddled bladder of your stupidest cousin. I was married to one once, I should know."

"You were married to a volus? You never told me that."

"You never asked, *ke'sed*. It didn't last. If you'd ever seen a volus without his suit, you'd know why. And on the subject of stupidest Nir cousins, my dearest, darling boy, if you don't tell me at once that you were merely making a terrible joke and absolutely know I meant a computational virus, I shall give up on you right here and now and sell you to the first band of roving batarian pirates I come across. Mean ones. You know how they say there is always honor among thieves? I will find ones who have never heard that saying."

He hadn't. Senna was so exhausted and thirsty and hungry he actually hadn't realized she meant something infecting the ship's computer. "I think I can be forgiven, Grandmother—" "I disagree."

Senna ran his hand over the back of his neck. He *knew* she was only a VI. He knew it, so why did he so often feel like a misbehaving child being made to confess to stealing toys when they talked? Yet he did. LED triads were effective. No matter what displayed them. "Well, you see, there is also… at the same time… a physical virus infecting some of the passengers."

Liat'Nir burst out laughing. "Well, that won't be a coincidence, will it?"

"It could be."

"It could *not* be." The small avatar of his grandmother reached out and smacked his thumb. He felt nothing, not even a static charge; the projection had no physical presence at all. "I raised you better than that!"

"Just because they're both called viruses doesn't mean malware and pathogens are the same thing. It would have to be two completely different coordinated attacks happening at the same time. What are the chances?"

"High, I'd say, since it's happening to you, *ke'sed*."

"Either way, I did check for a virus, because I am not an idiot—"

"I disagree."

"And, Grandmother… there's nothing wrong with the source code. Nothing at all. It's perfect. No virus. No wormcode chewing its way through systems. It's all fine. Not even an unclosed bracket."

"Shut your mouth," said Liat in disbelief.

"I know!"

"That's not possible," the ancestor VI blustered.

"I know it isn't, that's why I'm talking to you about it!" yelled Senna in his empty chambers. "No code that complex is that perfect."

"Oh, I don't mean that. Of course, yes, that's true, I was the best there was. I could make geth stand in a row dressed in lace garters and turn out a perfect kickline without breaking a sweat, I rode servers like stallions to war, and my whole life is one enormous unclosed bracket blinking away on an infinite terminal screen. But that's not what I mean, grandson of mine." Liat'Nir looked up at him, her prismatic eyes blazing, strands of gray hair hanging free past her frail collarbone. "Code is truth, code is life! The only honest thing in this galaxy or the next is a datacore. What the command line says, happens. It can't be shiny and perfect line after line while your tactile shield is failing and your lights won't stay on and your scans won't scan and you can't even get a damned drink of water in your own quarters! It is not *possible*. If the codebank is active and running, that's what the machine is doing. It's all there, because it has to be all there, because there's no other place for the ship to get instructions, anymore than your sweet little genes could express someone else's DNA. That's not how it works, *ke'sed*!"

Liat'Nir was getting extremely worked up. She had never once, in all his years with her, referenced the fact that she was a VI and not actually living on Rannoch right this second. He didn't know if she was programmed not to, or if he had just never found the right combination of input phrases to prompt it. But sometimes, very occasionally, when they were working on a problem together, she could get like this, and it always seemed to him like a kind of digitally wounded pride.

"Okay," he said with a deep breath. "All right. Here we are. We have arrived at our destination. You and me, Liat. A family affair. *I have a problem*. How can a datacore be severely compromised, rendered unable to recognize the problem or the effects of the problem, while showing no corresponding fatal error in the source code? And how do I fix it?"

The ancestor VI's mouth snapped shut. She turned her head to one side, then the other. Liat'Nir turned around and walked two or three steps to the edge of the projection disc. She fiddled with something invisibly, the way she had "drawn" in the Rannoch sand. When she turned around, his grandmother had a truly jaw-droppingly large glass of krogan ryncol in her hand. On the rocks. It had taken him weeks of immunizations and antibiotic courses to spend one night sipping ryncol with Yorrik, and it had felt like sipping knives. But Liat lived long before the quarian immune system was ravaged by living on the Migrant Fleet. Before the suits. Before anything that made a quarian quarian in Senna's world. She drank it down in one gulp, fixed herself another, this time with a twist of citrus, and sat down moodily in the center of the disk with her knees drawn up under her chin like a sullen kid.

"Well?" Senna'Nir said after a few minutes. Even as old as the VI was, she had never taken this long.

The ancestor VI glared at him. "Working," she said, and returned to staring. She swigged her ryncol angrily.

"I've been away too long already. Can you hurry?"

Liat'Nir stuck her finger in her drink, swirled it around, sucked it off the tip of her thick forefinger, and pointed it at her grandson. "*Working*," she growled.

After five minutes—five!—of silence and drinking and working, Liat'Nir gave up and retrieved the bottle from the invisible bar. She sat down again, hiccuped twice, pulled a small pair of scissors out of her robes, and started clipping her toenails with a murderous look on her face. *Another* new loading screen.

"The reason ryncol is the best alcohol is because it hurts you," Grandmother slurred. *Tink.* A purple hologram-toenail flew off and disappeared in midair.

"Are you *kidding* me," Senna'Nir said.

"Shushup, *ke'sed*, I'm talking. I do a good talk, everyone says. Ryncol is better than turian brandy because ryncol tastes like lighting all your mistakes on fire in a glass barrel and then eating the barrel. Mouthfeel like a tactical nuke. I heard they let a city get fire-bombed just to capture the smoky flavor. The *bouquet*. And the best part is, *ke'sed*, the *best* part is, with every sip, you know someone *wanted* to make you feel that way. Some krogan distiller did this to you on *purpose*. It looks so harmless in its wee little glass—wee. Little. Glass. You look so thin, little glass. Have you been eating enough? Your growth is *stunted*, wee little glass. You need some gene therapy? Granny knows a guy who knows a guy, don't you worry. But *ke'sed, ke'sed*, are you listening? Nothing that fucks you up this thoroughly while looking that small and innocent happens by accident. And so you and the krogan have made a long-distance agreement, where he gets to do this to you, and you get to let it happen and also you never retaliate. *Wee. Little. Glass of angry krogan.*" She looked up at her grandson through three hundred years of Nirs, eyes weeping from the ryncol fumes. "How many VIs you got?"

"Seventeen of the *Si'yah*'s systems use a VI interface, but it's no good, Grandmother. They're all connected to the same compromised datacore."

Tink. Another toenail.

"Well, how fortunate for you that your grandmother is not a complete and utter *von*. I didn't ask how many the ship's got, I asked how many you can put your slow, dumb baby hands on."

Tink.

"I don't know. People… brought a lot of things with them. I'm not a steward, I haven't looked at the manifests. Why?" *I've got you*, he thought but didn't say. He'd never indicated to her that she was anything but a living, breathing quarian, either.

"What you have to know about ryncol, son, is you can't just dig it out of the ground like a wine grape. It's nothing so simple. A real spirit requires a huge distilling contraption, so many chambers and barrels and sterilized condensers. It's a carefully timed process, and the end result is a brain smashed open with a small, angry meteor."

Senna sighed heavily. It didn't always work. Those fitness algorithms were as likely to turn up a lecture on ryncol as anything useful. But he had hoped. He really had. "Grandmother, thank you for trying. I love you, even when I need your help so badly and all you can give me is *go fish*."

Liat'Nir swigged from the bottle. "If my hypothesis is correct, your best-case scenario is that communications will fail next, followed by either environmental zone controls or the tram system. In your worst case, the cryopods will go first. Come back and tell me which, *ke'sed*. I need a nap."

"Wait, what hypothesis?"

"*Working!*" she yelled at him, and smashed her glass against nothing.

"Senna?" came a voice, and a knock, at the door.

Captain Qetsi'Olam vas Keelah Si'yah, who always knocked because she was polite, but rarely waited for an answer because she was a small, furious fuel cell powered by enthusiasm and her command lock override code, stepped into his quarters. Senna'Nir shoved his grandmother's mobile projection unit under his sleeping bunk and pulled a small crate of personal items in front of it with the practiced panic of someone very accustomed to hiding the evidence.

"K, end conversational protocol Senna4," he whispered. "Resume standard interpersonal routines."

Qetsi appeared in the doorway to his sleeping area, her violet hood crowning her head, not unlike Liat's cowl.

"Captain," he said, standing up quickly.

"Don't be stupid, Senna. How many times have I told you you don't have to call me that? *Keelah*, it's so *dark* in here."

"Many, Qetsi," he said, with affection. Even now, in this mess, with affection. "You have told me many times."

"Yorrik brought me up to speed," the captain said, her voice thin with worry. "It's not… It's not good, is it?"

"It is not."

"We almost made it. We were so close. Another thirty years." She paced the room, not even glancing at the puddle of coolant in the water dispenser basin. "It's my fault," she whispered finally. *Keelah*, she was so young, really. So was he. They'd never have been given their own command on the Fleet at thirty-five. Perhaps not at forty-five. He caught her mid-pace and held her in his arms. Their faceplates touched briefly, like a kiss.

"It's not your fault, Qetsi. Don't do that to yourself."

"I tried so *hard*. To be prepared. For anything. For everything. Not like those empty husks the Initiative fired off before us. I tried to build us a good ship. I did build us a good ship! A *quarian* ship. I just did such an excellent job that the most quarian of all fates befell it: our technology betrayed us. The basic fact is, we don't have what we need. Whatever else is happening, that's the real problem. We don't have what we need. I can't decide if my mother would laugh or scold me." She sniffed. "I should have bought more medi-gel. I could have at least done that."

"Your mother has been dead since you were a kid. Since you were a kid plus six hundred years, actually." Senna realized this sounded rather harsh. "She'd be proud," he added quickly.

She buried her face in his shoulder. "I just want to go *home*," she whispered. Senna was surprised. Qetsi did not show vulnerability. She was as allergic to it as to a gust of foreign air. The situation must be so much worse than he thought. "Who is doing this to us?"

"I don't know," Senna sighed. "But I suspect they're a lot smarter than I am."

"Do you have *any* good news for me, Senna'Nir?" the captain said, disentangling herself, all business once more.

"I'm sorry, I don't. I wish I—" Something in the corner of his faceplate display caught Senna's attention. He'd been so absorbed with Liat he hadn't noticed. "Wait. That's… odd."

"What? What is odd? Odd in a good way? Odd in a 'suddenly everything fixed itself with minimal effort' way?"

"No, not exactly, but…" He checked the timestamp. "It stopped."

"What stopped?"

"I set my suit to keep me updated on the number of cryopods that showed the necrotic freezer burn that first alerted the ship. It's been a pretty grim thumbnail in my peripheral vision for the last thirty hours, just ticking up and up and up. And it stopped. It stopped two hours ago. I didn't notice. No drell have died in the last two hours. No hanar either."

The captain did disentangle herself then. She leaned back against the dining table, her shoulders relaxing. "That's good. That's a good thing. Thank the ancestors! Maybe if we can just get a little breathing room we can get a handle on what's happening to us. Find a way to stop it."

"I'll go see Yorrik," Senna'Nir said, grabbing his omni-tool from the seating area where he'd left it.

"No, I'll go," Qetsi insisted. "You've had longer to get your head around it all. I need to get there. I'm the captain. I need to be the first point of contact. You focus on the datacore. We need those shields back up or we won't be around long enough to worry about a deadly contagion."

"Yes, sir," Senna acknowledged.

Qetsi'Olam reached out her arm and took his shoulder in her hand with a strong grip. "Hey," she said—and there it was. That old voice. The voice that had once told him to come with her and meet the future of the quarian species in a repurposed supply closet on the *Pallu'Kaziel*. The voice that had given a spine to the Nedas Movement, night after night, keeping them all drunk on the possibility of change. Of something, anything but that hopeless fleet drifting into nowhere. The voice he'd followed between galaxies, that he'd follow to another one if Andromeda didn't give them what they wanted. "We're going to make it," said that voice. "We're going to get out of this alive. I will buy you a drink on the Nexus, Senna'Nir vas Keelah Si'yah, I swear it."

Attention, Captain.

Qetsi answered the ship's vocal interface. "Yes, K?"

Oh, Qetsi, thought Senna. *Even you're calling her K. Maybe things can be just that different in Andromeda. Maybe they really can.*

I have detected an atmospheric anomaly in the cargo hold.

The captain groaned. "*Keelah se'lai,* what now?

Another system malfunction? I said breathing room, K. Senna, you clearly heard me say we needed breathing room."

There is a significantly elevated concentration of carbon dioxide, adenosine triphosphate, ketones, water vapor, and other volatile organic compounds in the cargo hold.

"Interpret," Senna'Nir ordered.

There are people in the cargo hold. They have been there for some time. These gases are byproducts of organic exhalation.

"Yes, we know. Anax Therion and Irit Non are down there," the captain said. "They should be finished soon, I imagine."

Given the size of the hold, the proportional change in air composition indicates more than two respiring individuals.

Senna'Nir felt his heart begin to race again. He felt like he was standing on a platform over depthless, empty space, a platform in which some important bolt that held it together had already come loose, it just hadn't collapsed yet. But it would. It was inevitable. The bolt had never been there, he just didn't know. The commander shut his eyes.

"How many more, K?" he asked.

One thousand, six hundred and thirty-nine.

The platform wobbled. The fateful bolt slid out, tumbled down, disappeared into nothingness.

"Anax Therion, come in," Senna barked into an open comm line. "What the hell is going on down there?" No answer. Just dead air. "Irit Non, respond," he tried again. Still nothing. The hiss of a severed connection. It sounded different, somehow, than just silence on the other end; someone thinking, or distracted. Heavier. Senna toggled the line over to medbay. "Yorrik? Are you there?" The same heavy, empty quiet. He tried a shipwide open address.

"Ferank! Jalosk! Anyone! If you can hear my voice respond on open comms immediately!"

No reply came.

"K, open a priority override comm channel to Anax Therion," Qetsi tried.

All communication channels are open and operational, Captain. You are already connected to Analyst Therion.

They heard nothing. Not Anax, not the volus, not the supposed sixteen hundred and thirty-nine people swarming over the cargo hold. The *Keelah Si'yah* was no longer just blind. She was deaf, too. *Comms or trams or cryopods,* Senna'Nir thought. *You have your answer, Grandmother. And two out of three is* terrible. *Now what are you going to do with it?*

Captain.

"Yes?" answered Qetsi'Olam, staring numbly, straight ahead.

I have detected gunfire in the cargo bay. Updated calculations available. Current population of Deck 11 is one thousand six hundred and thirty-seven.

The platform fell away.

10. TRANSCRIPTION

Over the next eighteen hours, Yorrik watched Jalosk Dal'Virra die.

Stars moved outside the wide medbay portholes, distorted by the ship's ungodly speed. The *Keelah Si'yah* traveled at a rate of some eleven light years a day. One moment, a comet flared blue in the dark, its tail full of ice. The next moment, it was gone, lost to the past. The tall magenta hanar floated by the window, its back to anything that might be called work. It had been standing there motionless since Borbala Ferank had airlocked the three autopsies. Since Kholai's body, like the comet, flared briefly in the night and then vanished far behind them. Gradually, Yorrik became aware that Ysses was asleep. He had never seen a hanar sleep before. Its tentacles drifted out around it like gelatinous petals. It snored softly, a sound like a flute trying to play a single perfect note underwater.

Yorrik spared a glance for the spectacle of a sleeping hanar. But not for the stars, and not for anything else. His world had shrunk to the view through the slowly, gently flashing medbay glass edged with frost, across the dim, bile-streaked corridor, past the shimmer of a decontaminant forcefield, and into the iso-chamber, where a lone batarian sat on a thin cot, weeping softly. He had developed a rash. It snaked over half his face and down his throat, disappearing into his stained leather collar, a silver-pink spiderweb of angry lines pinpricked with tiny, hard pustules.

No vocal contact with the others in fifty-one minutes. And counting.

"Barely controlled panic: Commander?" the great elcor actor droned into his comm. No answer came. "Insistent: Senna'Nir? This is medbay, please respond." Nothing. "Deep despair: My friend, please. Where are you? Uneasy plea: ''Tis bitter cold and I am sick at heart.'"

The only answer was the total quiet of the darkened med deck. Even the hanar had found its way into a sleep beyond snoring.

"No one is coming," the batarian muttered. He pawed at his cheeks, wiping away the tears that welled up in the corners of his lower pair of eyes before they could fall. The upper pair were dry. "I don't know why you keep trying. Comms are down. They're *clearly* down. *All* the way down. If you want your friends so badly, you're going to have to go and get them."

Yorrik glanced over at Horatio, the child quarian's suit, hanging on its hook, stuffed full of Dal'Virra's samples, blinking away at a full-spectrum tissue analysis. "With acceptance of fate: Neither Ysses nor I can leave the quarantine area. We have been exposed longer than anyone. Either of us would carry particulates with us anywhere we went. We would potentially contaminate anything we touched, anyone we spoke to. I am as dangerous as you are. Irrepressible hope: K, locate all members of Sleepwalker Team Blue-7 and the captain."

Analyst Anax Therion and Specialist Irit Non are currently on Deck 11, cargo bay north quadrant. Specialist Borbala Ferank is on Deck 2, Mess Hall 3. Medical Specialist

Yorrik and Hydraulic Chemical Specialist Ysses are on Deck 4, medbay. Commander Senna'Nir vas Keelah Si'yah and Captain Qetsi'Olam vas Keelah Si'yah are on Deck 6, on inter-habitat tram line 1, car B2, between the quarian residential zone and common assembly zone 5.

Yorrik gave a shaky exhalation as, "Relieved: They are alive at least."

Dal'Virra arched one hairless greenish-yellow eyebrow. "You think? K, locate Munitions Specialist Jalosk Dal'Virra."

Munitions Specialist Jalosk Dal'Virra is currently in cryopod BT566 in the batarian hibernation bay on Deck 11.

Jalosk leaned back against the real wall of his cell, stretching his jaw. Dried black vomit flaked away. The nausea had stopped and the crying had started forty-two minutes ago. Tears still trickled down his haggard yellow face, over the teal markings on his cheeks, and dripped onto the floor. "Don't get your hopes up. Our ship is a good-looking wench, but she has shit for brains. Alas, poor Yorrik, it's just you and me and a crazy jellyfish."

A rush of good feeling suffused Yorrik's body for the first time in many hours. "Surprised delight: You know *Hamlet*?"

The batarian blinked. "What now? Who? Is he a passenger?"

Yorrik slumped slightly. He wiped away a smear of fluorescent dye from the dormant krogan microscope and rearranged a few bits of nothing on the now-empty autopsy table. He had not known it was possible to feel nostalgic for his life only twenty hours ago. But those had been good times, comparatively. Reverse engineering a coroner's lab from junk and children's toys. Practically a game. "Confusion: You said, 'Alas, poor Yorrik.' That is a line from *Hamlet*. *Hamlet* is a play. Correction: Hamlet is also a man. But he is not on board the *Keelah Si'yah*."

"Yeah, *poor Yorrik*, because I feel sorry for you," Jalosk grunted. "All the excitement is somewhere else and you're just standing there staring at me like a sad loner at happy hour in purgatory. Are you not called Yorrik?"

"Disappointed: I am. Curious: How do you know there is excitement?"

Jalosk shrugged. "If there wasn't, they'd have come back to check on us as soon as the comms went out. Horrible virus loose on a ship? No place more important than the medbay. And yet." He indicated the empty halls. He tried to vomit again, but there was nothing left. He gagged and spat. There was bright blood in the gob that hit the floor.

"I'm not cryosick," Dal'Virra said flatly.

Yorrik turned to Horatio, the faceplate beneath its smiley face full of data, data that scrolled down past the softly blinking "positive" icon that said the only thing worth saying. "Apologetic: No. You have what the drell Soval Raxios and Tyomar Lukad and the hanar Kholai had. Yoqtan, or something like Yoqtan, but much worse."

"You said viruses don't jump from species to species like this."

"Helplessly: And yet."

The batarian sunk his head into his hands. "I was telling the truth," he mumbled bitterly. "I just woke up like this. I don't know anything. This isn't my fault. Not... Not for the reasons *she* told you. I'm not stupid. *Shrik vai*, the arrogance of the ruling caste! They look at a merchant and automatically assume he doesn't have two brain cells to rub together to keep him warm at night. It takes more intellect to scrape and strive through your whole misfiring disruptor charge of a life, knowing that whether or not you sell this weapon or that one is the difference between dying and another day, than it does to be born into a family that runs everything and *still* shit it all away. I could have done it, I swear I could have. I've raided more medical vessels than you can possibly imagine. I know how people die, it's not magic. I could engineer a superbug. Or at least hire the right people to do it for me. I could've. I just *didn't*. There's a big difference." A vicious cough wracked his chest. "It's important to me that you know that. I won't be disrespected. I *won't*."

Yorrik glanced at the hanar, still floating, still sleeping. "Dejected: I am not sure it matters whose fault it is now. And it certainly will not change what is happening to you. Delicate request: Please... tell me how you feel, as often as you can. It will help. Correction: It will help other people."

"I feel like I just got fired out of the back end of a Hensa cruiser, that's how I feel. I'm *boiling* hot, my head is pounding, and I'm just so... I'm so fucking hungry, elcor. Is there something to eat in there? Anything?"

Yorrik glanced at the creeping frost at the corners of the medbay glass. The ship's temperature controls had not improved. "Gentle tone: Unfortunately, the *Si'yah* has limited food supplies on board. It was presumed that the Nexus would feed us when we arrived, having already begun cultivation on several habitable planets. Statement of sympathy: I am also hungry."

"You may be hungry, but I *need* to eat, you fat cretin. I'm starving."

"Genuine regret: I am sorry."

The quarantine chime sounded softly every minute on the minute.

The first sores appeared three hours later.

So did the captain.

Small, hard, dark blue, all over the batarian's throat and jawline, rising up from the rash like toxic islands in a river of pus. Yorrik's scent glands released a musk of relief and joy as Captain Qetsi'Olam stumbled into the medbay though a small access panel near the floor, breathing heavily through her facemask. Her black-and-purple suit was stained with oil and other, unmentionable industrial filth.

"Concerned query: Where is Senna'Nir?"

The captain collected herself quickly. "As you may have noticed, we are having issues with the networked systems. The trams stopped. We split up somewhere back there in the maintenance tunnels. He went to lock down the cargo bay. I came here. Unless you'd prefer I go to assist my colleague?"

"Overenthusiastic interruption: No, no, please stay. I have results. You are interested in results. You want results. You will not leave us here alone while there are results to be had."

"I gotta scratch, Doc," Jalosk Dal'Virra wheezed, clawing desperately at his sores.

"Do not scratch," Yorrik said for the hundredth time.

His four black eyes bulged with the effort, but he stopped.

"Kindly suggestion: If you depress the button on the wall next to you, a medi-gel mist will dispense from the ceiling. It may offer some relief."

The batarian jammed his fingers against the wall, moaning loudly as the mist hit his swelling neck.

The captain looked over the afflicted colonist dispassionately. "You should kill him," she said softly. "Now, while he is still himself and has a little dignity left. It's only kindness. You have your results. Surely you know all you need to."

Yorrik sighed through his olfactory slats. "With ethical ambivalence: It would be better to see it through. Besides, I might yet heal him."

Qetsi put her hand on the medbay glass. "Heal him? Is that even possible? Have you found a cure already?"

"With deep self-loathing: No. But I might." He shifted his gray bulk miserably. "He has children. I have to try."

Dal'Virra coughed. "Ungrateful shits, children. No greater debt than the one owed to the fools who gave them life. Yet they refuse to pay it. They just *refuse*. It's extraordinary. Everything else you make in this life, you own outright. Yet I am expected to allow my children to do as they please, and if they leave that debt unpaid all their lives, I have no recourse to collect what I am owed."

"And what are you owed?" asked the captain with what seemed like genuine curiosity. She turned her whole body toward him, every microgesture seeming to communicate that there was nothing in the world so important as what this one batarian scratching himself to death on a lonely ship was going to say next. It was quite extraordinary. Yorrik could not help wanting her to pay so much attention to him. No wonder Senna couldn't let her go.

A large tear welled up in the corner of Dal'Virra's lower left eye. "Love, I suppose. Unconditional love."

"That's not the answer I expected from a batarian," Qetsi said. "I like that answer very much. There were so many who told me I should not even consider letting your kind aboard my ship. But, Jalosk, I believe very strongly that all people should be given a chance to become great. It is *everything*, I believe. That chance is the most important thing in the universe. My people were denied that chance so often, by so many. I couldn't deny it to you, just because you are not like me. I could not carry that into the new galaxy." This was the old Qetsi'Olam. The one who could inspire a speck of dust if she got it alone for long enough. When she spoke again, her voice was thick and melodious with sincerity. "*Thank you* for proving me right."

Jalosk grunted. "Yes, love. And affection. And undying loyalty. And a ten-to-fifteen-percent share of their profits, no less than a brokering agent would receive. I brokered them into existence, after all. And they should... they should stay where I put them. They should stay nearby. Generous terms, by any bank's measure. But of course love. Did you really think batarians don't love their children? No race can evolve without that trait. Otherwise, we would all eat our young alive for the trouble they cause us. Would it surprise you to know I nursed my little son Grozik back to health when he fell from our habitat roof? Always going where he shouldn't, my little warrior. And Zofi, when she cried because the other children were cruel to her, would it shock you to know I—yes, I! A batarian!—wiped her tears and kissed her wounds? And why do you think we're monsters? Because we keep slaves? Because we sell things?"

"With deep disgust: You sell weapons, narcotics, and people. That is what your species did with your chance."

Jalosk shrugged. "Someone buys them. If rainbows,

smiles, and cuddles brought the highest prices, we'd be selling those instead. Back home, I had asari customers, salarian, turian, even human. Yet you do not hate their entire races for purchasing and using what the batarians sell. Yes, yes, slavery. It is so terrible. I have heard it all. Yet my father was a slave. He bought our freedom. He bought us a future. You *can* buy your freedom from a batarian slaver. Good luck trying that with anyone else. On Khar'shan, slave is a position. Everywhere else, it is a condition. And again, I must point out, we do sell slaves to *someone*, and those someones are only sometimes other batarians. You had it so easy on your garden worlds, with your fruits and your vegetables and your fresh summer rains and nice, tidy Prothean artifacts tied up in a bow for you to find. We *clawed* our way to the stars. We made an economy out of slime, muck, thirty-year dry spells, and an alien slagheap that made no more sense than a moron's scream in the dark. So we had to do it selling all your worst instincts back to you at a steep markup. That says more about you than us. *I* lifted my entire family out of the laborer caste and into the merchant caste—what greater love can there be than that?"

"With cautious curiosity: And their mother? Is she not also owed a debt? Borbala said you took your children from her."

Jalosk grimaced. Another large, heavy tear welled up in his eye, this time the lower right. "Their mother was an imbecile. What the mother of worms says of me is actually true of Ukiro Dal'Virra. She left me and married a male of the military class."

"Embarrassment: I am sorry."

Jalosk knuckled a tear away. "No, no, you misunderstand! I am proud of her! It was a daring match, and allowed our offspring a path into the elite, perhaps even the Khar'shan ruling classes. I never loved her more than the day she succeeded in seducing him. I could have burst with admiration and personal satisfaction. She was an imbecile because, even with the access her new rank afforded her, she insisted on staying on Camala, even after… even after. They struck the eezo refineries first, those things, gigantic and black as nothing you can imagine. Like insects… but made of space itself. They turned people into… husks. Into withered, dried-meat shadows of themselves. Hungry shadows. Ukiro thought she could keep them safe. But something like that… doesn't care about caste. I took my children to keep them safe. They still haven't forgiven me. I guess they never will, now. But at least… At least whatever was happening to Camala, even if it happened everywhere else in the galaxy, at least it is six hundred years over now and Grozik and Zofi are far beyond it. There. *That* is the idiot dolt that scion of Ferank told you could never do anything worth doing. Well, I did something. I did *something*. My father was a slave, and his father was a red sand addict suckling at the teat of whoever would get him his next fix, and now my children will be among the founding families of a new galaxy, a caste beyond castes. Her father was an oligarch, and she is an oligarch. Who scored better, between the two of us?" Jalosk coughed viciously, and for some time. Tears trickled down his cheeks, darkening the teal spots there. "Dammit, this is intolerable. It is humiliating to weep in front of an alien. I do not even know why I'm crying."

"Regretfully: That is because you are not crying. Those are not tears. You are weeping cerebral spinal fluid. Most likely one of the abscesses on your neck has collapsed into a fistula, forming a passageway between your spinal column and your mucus membranes."

"Oh," said Jalosk Dal'Virra. Another tear splashed onto the floor. "So I am going to cry myself to death. I can't imagine a more un-batarian way to go."

"Comforting bedside manner: No, no, do not worry, other things will kill you first."

"Perhaps it's time you gave me that report, Yorrik," said the captain. And then her attention was on him fully, like the light of a red giant, like no one else existed, and she had never spoken to anyone else in all her life. It was uncanny that she could do that. Yorrik wondered if it could be taught. A wonderful skill for the greatest actor in the Andromeda galaxy, if he could get hold of it.

"Depressive quotation: 'Thou art a scholar, speak to it, Horatio,'" the elcor said to the hooded quarian suit hanging beside the autopsy table, its hips and torso wrapped in violet fabric and brown belts, like all quarian suits.

Horatio had much to say.

The virus that was dead and frozen in the cryopod victims was screamingly alive in Jalosk Dal'Virra's veins. It was also alive inside the quarian suit. The suit was doing what all environmental suits were supposed to do—identify the intruder and neutralize it without harming the suit's fragile occupant. Horatio had no occupant, of course, but the suit itself didn't know that. It only knew something inside it was sick. It was applying all quarian technology to the problem, isolating the puncture points where Yorrik had injected the batarian's blood and various other fluids into the mesh musculature in pressurized plasto-bubbles, washing the samples with an array of antivirals, antibiotics, aerosolized medi-gel, painkillers, DNA and RNA unhelixers, nanoanalyzers, antigens—anything that might alleviate symptoms, identify the virus, or prove effective in killing it. So far, none of it had helped. If they were on a quarian Flotilla ship, Horatio would interface with the medical mainframe and cross-reference other case studies and plague histories in order to locate other victims and begin to paint a picture of just how bad the situation was. But there was no mainframe here. Just a poor four-eyed bastard crying himself to death.

Something flashed in the upper-left corner of Horatio's upturned faceplate, just above his fluorescent-painted eyebrow. It looked like an equation, but it wasn't. Those numbers worried Yorrik more than any of the rest of it. He hated those numbers. Why couldn't they be other numbers? Safer numbers? No matter how the elcor tried to focus on something else, those numbers kept dragging his eyes back, taunting him, telling him to just give up now.

As an ear, nose, and throat doctor, Yorrik was not at all unfamiliar with viruses. The elcor lip slats might look like simple orifices, but they were terribly delicate sensory organs, prone to infection. If this were a case of ochreous rhinophage, or Thunowanuro megafluenza, or even the vicious Hunno plague that had torn through the settlements on Sangel a few decades ago, Yorrik would have felt very much in his element. If he could not be on stage, then second best was stage managing the body's greatest performance: healing. But this pathogen was not anyone's element, because this pathogen had almost certainly never existed anywhere before it existed on the *Keelah Si'yah*. Horatio had just finished a rough genome sequencing of the virus. A three-dimensional model turned slowly on the faceplate, its deadly anatomy glowing in helpfully differentiated colors.

"Is that the thing that's killing me?" rasped Jalosk. His voice sounded like someone had ground it up and shoved it through the ship's engines. Those blue abscesses were not only on the outside. His words echoed in the lab, but Ysses only rippled in its sleep and did not wake.

"In sad agreement: Yes. That is the Yoqtan virus. Pedantic insistence: Although we must stop calling it that. It is not… It is not precise. And it seems to hurt Irit's feelings. With bashful hesitation: I am thinking of calling it the Fortinbras Plague."

"Let's hope we don't have to call it anything, shall we?" said the captain. "I would very much like to look back on this in a few years as an example of the efficiency of my crew in a crisis, rather than… anything more."

"I'm so tired. So *fucking* tired. But it hurts to sleep." The batarian watched the diagram revolve slowly on Horatio's face. It looked so alien, like its own creature, which, in truth, it was. A crystal impaled by a long, vicious screw and delicate arachnid legs. It inspired the same revulsion in organic beings as certain insects did.

"It's kind of pretty, isn't it?" Jalosk said. "You really should name it after me. I'm the one dying."

"With bitter fatalism: It is prettier than you can imagine. It is what we call a chimera virus." The elcor indicated one illuminated section of the virus's RNA with his thick gray forefinger. "Professorial tone: That is Yoqtan. Emphasis: Only *that* is Yoqtan. You can see it acts like a tailor's dressform. It gives the virus a basic shape. Something to build on. But then there is all this silk, Qetsi'Olam. All these horrible ribbons." One by one, other RNA sequences lit up in a series of colors: blue, pink, yellow, purple, green. "With horror and wonder: This is Asari Cyanophage," the elcor said, pointing at another stretch of the pathogen's genetic code. "And this is a strain of salarian proto-syphilis called Ayalon B. This is called the Titan's Tears, a rare turian hemorrhagic fever. This is the human disease known as measles, and this…" A much smaller piece of the genome lit up an angry red. "This is a trash compactor of junk RNA from a dozen different sources, including Kepral's Syndrome, Varren Scale-Itch, Ardat-Yakshi, and, as far as I am willing to guess, a viral form of the bubonic plague which ravaged Earth in the fourteenth century."

"Ardat-Yakshi? Isn't that the thing that kills you if you fuck the wrong asari?" the captain asked. She sat down on the deck floor cross-legged, listening intently.

"I've never even touched an asari, Doc!" Jalosk protested. "Believe me, I'd have liked to, but I haven't. They make a big noise about genetically diversifying their species, but have you ever met a batarian-asari girl? No, you have not, because they are arrogant and racist."

"He has a fair point there," Qetsi chuckled. "The proximity of death has made you quite the comedian, Jalosk."

"Patient explanation: You do not understand. This is junk RNA. Pieces of dormant information that are not currently actively coded in the virus. They are merely… there. I do not know why. Although they may 'switch on' at some point as replication accelerates, we cannot know until it happens. You do not have Ardat-Yakshi. Or Kepral's Syndrome, or bubonic plague. But the virus you do have contains elements of them. If we return to the metaphor of the dress and the dressform, you can think of junk RNA as decorative pockets that do not really hold anything."

"What's a metaphor?" grumbled Jalosk. "Is that a new symptom?"

"Incredulously: Never mind." Perhaps Borbala was not entirely wrong in her assessment of Jalosk's intelligence. Yorrik hurried on. Talking about it helped somehow. Talking about it made it real, which was awful, but real things had real solutions. Sometimes. "With nervous hesitation: The junk RNA is also how I know, at last, that this is an artificial disease. Someone has done this to you. Ayalon B is not a naturally occurring virus. The salarians engineered it in their station on Erinle, but it proved too volatile for mass manufacture and all samples were process-bleached and incinerated. And yet it is here. It is there. It is in you. Helpful exposition: A chimera virus is just this. A virus which combines aspects of many other viruses. This one, whatever we decide to call it, is in the *Metastolizomai* family. It is highly mutagenic." Yorrik thought better of his choice of vocabulary and started over. "Viruses are living creatures. Not like us. Not like synthetics. But living creatures all the same. Their only goal is to survive and reproduce, just like us. Viruses are simply much more ruthless in their methods."

"I like ruthless," coughed Jalosk.

"Sharp correction: No you do not," Yorrik replied. "Please try to focus. Viruses have personalities. Correction: They do not have personalities like ours. But they have something *like* personalities. Family traits. Some are very conservative and averse to risk; they may not even kill their host. Others are reckless and disorganized; they may kill the host long before it has a chance to spread the infection. Ours is... opportunistic. You could call it nimble, if you wanted to. When it encounters an obstacle, such as a strong immune response or a treatment or an already weakened system of the body that could not support significant replication... that doesn't have enough 'food' to keep the virus going, Fortinbras has so many other viruses spliced onto it that it can very easily mutate instead of dying off.

"With growing intellectual excitement: All viruses mutate to some extent. It is part of their life cycle. When a virus meets a healthy cell, it first attaches to the surface receptors, then penetrates the protein membrane, then binds to the most susceptible mechanisms of the cell, fusing with them in order to take control of the cell's reproduction in order to force the cell to make copies of the virus rather than more healthy cells. It turns the cell into a factory for making more viruses. At that point, there may be an incubation period as the virus enters the uncoating process—shedding that crystal part you see there in order to transcribe its proteins over the proteins of the original cell. And in mixing those proteins, mutations occur—parts of the host merge with parts of the virus, and this merger will be reproduced in the new viral copies during the replication stage.

Many mutations will not be particularly advantageous. Some will be more specifically adapted to the environment. To the infected body. Better for the virus, worse for the patient. Personifying the internal monologue of a virus: I was a pulmonary infection, but I didn't have much fun in those lungs, so I'm going to let my kids go play in the brain stem. Solemnly: But Fortinbras here has so many exotic proteins to draw on that it is far more likely to produce very bizarre and unpredictable mutations. That means many more of them will be catastrophic failures, of course. But the ones that succeed are likely to succeed in wildly interesting ways. Such as being able to jump from drell to hanar. Or from hanar to batarian. And all it needs to find these wildly interesting ways is time." A strange thought sparked in Yorrik's mind. The kind of thought that was hardly even a thought at all yet, just a little road in the dark that might lead somewhere... somewhere new. "That is why it is so resistant to Horatio's attempts to kill it. Every time it reproduces, it actually becomes a different virus. Sometimes only slightly different. Sometimes night and day."

"I have no idea what you're talking about."

But the captain did. The elcor could see it in her posture. She knew just how bad this was, and it was really starting to sink in now that she would not look back on this fondly in ten years. In ten years, she might not even be there to look back on anything at all.

"With renewed confidence: Batarian, imagine you are preparing to board a vulnerable ship by force. First, you locate the airlock—the part of the ship you can commandeer and enter most easily, yes?"

"Sure, I suppose."

"Then you penetrate the ship's defenses and swarm onto the bridge. You either kill or enslave the command structure and the crew—now you have control of the ship. On the outside, it still looks like an asari cruiser or a volus frigate. But in reality, it is now a batarian ship, and you can use it to attack other unsuspecting craft and make them into batarian ships, too. Yet you did not kill everyone on board. Some you took as slaves. You absorbed them into the new ship's hierarchy, into the batarian culture, and what will come of that synthesis it is impossible to say. That is what a virus does. It survives, consumes resources, and reproduces. Without mercy or morality. And just like people, once it has learned a new trick, it will not go back to the old way of doing things."

Qetsi was looking down at the floor, deep in thought. After a long silence, she said, "What is that little equation in the corner?"

"Dejected: I was hoping you would not ask. That is the R nought number. Every virus has one. It is a variable. Not everyone who encounters a virus will contract it, not everyone who contracts it will die. There are always natural immunities and outlier cases. But the R nought number tells you how many people a single infected person is likely to pass the virus to given ideal conditions, population density, temperature, group behavior, that sort of thing. For example, the human disease smallpox has an R nought number of five to seven. So a person with smallpox might infect five to seven other people before they die. Ochreous rhinophage, an ancient elcor pandemic, had an R nought number of six to nine."

The batarian coughed and spat blood again. "And what's my score, Doc?"

"With grim fatalism: twenty-two to twenty-six."

None of them said anything then. What could be said? Yorrik watched the frost slowly fade from the medbay glass. It was warming up out there. Something was coming back on. Finally. He almost felt relieved, until he remembered how much better pathogens fared in hot climates. The batarian, however, was shivering.

"Why in the hell do you want to call it Fortinbras?" he said finally, his teeth chattering. "That's a stupid name. I can barely pronounce it. It sounds human."

"With great sorrow: Because, no matter what you do to save your family, Fortinbras always swarms in at the end and destroys it all."

IIIIIIIIIIIIIIII

Jalosk Dal'Virra began to swell ten hours after entering the iso-chamber. His tears crusted over, clogging his tear ducts and coating his eyelids with angry, fouled scabs. The flesh around them bulged. His throat and chest filled with fluid, likely an edema—fluid where there should be no fluid. The batarian was drowning in his own skin. He screamed for the lights to be shut off, screamed that they were burning him, even though the medbay was no brighter than it had been for hours, a place of mostly shadows and dim blue emergency lighting. When this passed, he began to stare at the lights in awe, moving his hands over them as if in a trance.

"They're so beautiful," he whispered, and began to laugh softly. A giggle, really. A batarian. Giggling. "So beautiful. Like sapphires made of feelings. Can you see their feelings?"

Yorrik turned to Ysses for help, but the hanar still snoozed away. How long could a jellyfish sleep? The swelling seemed to be putting pressure on Jalosk's already taxed brain. "Worried correction: They are running lights, and they do not have feelings."

Jalosk rolled onto his back on the narrow cot, staring, dazzled. "I thought it would be different in Andromeda, Yorrik. I really did."

"Perplexed query: You thought the lights in the Andromeda galaxy would have feelings?"

"No. I thought... *everything* would be different. Why would it be the same? It's not a new planet. It's not even a new system. It's a whole galaxy. Why should it still be the Council races on top, and the rest of us scrabbling for scraps? Why should it not be all of everyone, equal, eating the same size slices of the same size pie? Why should people still hate batarians? Everyone gets a new slate. Me. I get a new slate. Grozik and Zofi get a new slate. Maybe in Andromeda people will think batarians are the enlightened, wise, sexually desirable ones, and asari are hideous and stupid and morally bankrupt, hmm? Why should *anything* be the same? Why should the old castes hold?"

"There are no castes in the greater galactic society, Jalosk. That is the batarian obsession."

The captain paced slowly back and forth, working something over in her brain. When she spoke, she seemed surprised at the words pouring out of her own mouth. "You think? Then why did the elcor never have a place on the Council? Why do the batarians and the volus not have their own Pathfinders? Why did quarians get turned away at so many stations and harassed on the Citadel? Ah, you are a good elcor, Yorrik. Too good to understand anything about the world. There are *always* castes, Doctor. At least batarians have the decency to name them. Perhaps Kholai was right. All systems tend toward their worst possible conditions."

"It will be the same in Andromeda," Jalosk mumbled. "Humans, asari, salarians and turians up here, then drell, elcor and hanar in the middle, batarians and volus on the bottom, and quarians where everyone else sees fit to stick them once they've seen to every single one of their own needs." He began to giggle again. The giggle turned into panting, then wheezing. "And blue running lights full of feel… feel… *feelings* to enslave us all."

The sores on his neck burst in a spray of fine, dry dust that hit the iso-field, sizzled, and vanished.

The captain knelt next to the glass, as close as she could to Jalosk's iso-chamber. She leaned her head against it and spread her fingers against the cool barrier. "No, my poor, poor soul. It will be different. It will be better. It has to be. That's why we came. For something new." Her gaze lifted past the ruin of the batarian's dying body, past the medbay, into the stars. She hardly saw him now, Yorrik or Ysses or Jalosk or any of them. She saw something so much bigger. "You may not see it. *I* may not see it. But Andromeda will be *beautiful*. I swear it to you on your death."

The batarian spluttered and gagged. He clawed miserably at the shimmer of the iso-shield. "The only peace in the universe is entropy. I will see you at the end of all things, sister."

A few hours later, the madness began.

Jalosk Dal'Virra's four black eyes filled with blood. He began to scream, to spit, consumed by gibberish and rage, bellowing, throwing himself over and over at the forcefield, using profanity Yorrik had never dreamed of. The batarian clawed at the invisible barrier between him and his doctor, kicked it, punched it, at one point even tried to tear at it with his teeth. He foamed at the mouth, sobbed, leaked from every orifice, and all the while his fury never stopped, his absolute need to tear the elcor he had only just before called good and kind to shreds.

Yorrik watched without moving. He was stunned, and sorry, but he could do nothing as the batarian died raving and shrieking in front of him.

The awful noise seemed to finally rouse the hanar. Ysses floated to the elcor's side and joined him in staring at the ruined corpse in numb horror.

"He looks so pretty," said Ysses after a long quiet. "This one could look at him for hours." Yorrik turned to gawp at his lab partner. "And you smell wonderful, Yorrik! Like flowers."

"I should go," whispered Qetsi'Olam.

11. MUTATION

Hello… everyone. This is your captain speaking. Please remain calm and return to your respective environmental control zones. There is not enough acclimatization equipment for everyone, and we must conserve the supplies we have. While person-to-person comms are offline at the moment, the public address system is still operable. However, its use should be restricted to emergencies only. This is an emergency. Now, if you can hear this, then you are awake, and if you are awake, you must have figured out by now that something has gone very, very wrong on our little ark. Really, rather a lot of things.

The acrid smell of weapons' discharge hung over the cargo bay as the captain's words boomed out through the cavernous space.

Containers spilled their contents everywhere. The hold stretched out in every direction and in every direction was destruction and chaos. Groups of containers had been dragged together to form makeshift blinds and shelters and forts. It looked like a tent city down there. Anax Therion crouched behind an unmolested shipping crate, where she'd been crouching for hours now, her knees throbbing, her eyes smarting with the smoke. She could just make out the squat, round shape of Irit Non several crates away, clutching a shotgun that had, until recently, belonged to a completely unreasonable hanar. The drell had fallen asleep in her crouch several times, startled awake, and drifted off again. Her skin was beginning to itch inside the constricting volus suit.

A flurry of gunfire blasted past Anax's crate. She took a deep breath, swept round, fired back through the wreckage, and returned to her holding position. She could hear Irit swearing, repeating the same thing she'd been saying over and over for hours now, as though saying it again would produce an answer out of thin air. *What the fuck is going on? Why are they shooting at us?* Someone's plasma bolt had sliced through the thigh of the volus's suit. A protective bubble had immediately encased the exposed area while nanobots began to repair the mesh, but the bubble was bulky and it slowed her down.

From the labyrinth of luggage, a garbled voice arose. There was a great deal of swearing in this voice, and at the very least the words *overcharge*, *overheat*, and *you said you knew how to use these things*.

"This is all highly unnecessary," Anax Therion called out. They were coming up on forty-eight hours since Sleepwalker Team Blue-7's attention had been required. Forty since she and the batarian had taken their leave of the cargo hold. How long had these people been down here, alone, confused, hungry, unable to use comms or the ship's interface or even half the doors, all of them cryosick, some of them perhaps sick of something much worse? She could hear screams, and they were not screams of pain, but of an incredible, rationality-shredding rage. "Let us come out and we'll explain everything."

"Enraged desperation: Unlock the fucking doors and let us out of here," droned an elcor who then, Anax was nearly certain from the sound, *threw* his or her slagged weapon in the drell's general direction.

This is a Code White situation. I repeat, ship security is currently set to Code White. There is an active pathogen aboard the Keelah Si'yah.

The most extraordinary wail of hopelessness and terror went up around the cargo hold, from every cluster of containers and fortress of belongings. Not one of them moved toward their respective environmental zones.

"Hello, stranger," came a voice too close to Anax's ear. She whipped her head around to see Borbala Ferank crouching next to her, shotgun in hand, peering up over the lip of the overturned crate, the only thing between them and a shot between the eyes.

"Where did you come from?" asked Anax. It was the first time anyone had successfully snuck up on her in years.

"Oh, I've been here. It doesn't take very long to count up *very little*, multiply by *however long this takes*, and divide by *all of us*. I came back here to check on my nest egg and what do you know—our intrepid colonists have colonized the place. They wanted food. I could make food happen." She gestured toward one of the container corridors. Borbala Ferank's precious frozen fish bowls lay everywhere shattered, rolling around the floor like a child's marbles. Most of the fish were still half frozen, with bites gouged out of the bellies. "They might have asked more politely."

Please remain calm and return to your respective environmental control zones. This will help to slow the spread of the disease. Right now, drell, hanar, batarian, and elcor are all susceptible. The earliest symptom is an overwhelming sweet scent, followed by a distinctive rash, extreme fatigue, and small blue abscesses around the throat, chest, and under the arms. We believe it is most contagious during this phase. These symptoms may be accompanied by uncontrollable weeping, fever, and excessive hunger. The final stages are characterized by euphoria, hallucinations, severe edema, or a swelling of the limbs, and subacute sclerosing panencephalitis, which is a very scientific way of saying violent, all-consuming madness as the brain swells in the skull. Unfortunately, all cases so far have been fatal.

Please remain calm.

"*Really* wish she wouldn't do that," Anax Therion grimaced. "They're not going to stay calm now."

"Shall we make a run for it?" Borbala suggested.

The drell glanced over at Irit Non. She was pinned down far worse on her end of the row.

"You go!" the volus snarled. "Go, go, go!"

Your first officer is attempting to repair several malfunctions in the ship's datacore. Until he does so, the following systems are offline: temperature control, lighting control, person-to-person communications, water dispensation, hull shielding, trams A–D, short-range sensors, and locking mechanisms, including those on small arms containers. Revival cascades have commenced and continue to trigger in cryobays 1, 4, and 8, which is why so many of you are listening to me right now.

Senna'Nir spliced another pair of wires together on a panel in the empty tramway tunnel. The captain's voice sharpened on the intercom. Their tram car had shut down, stuck halfway between the quarian zone and the Radial. They'd split up, the captain heading for medbay, the commander after his crew, walking toward the cargo hold, trying to meet up with the drell and the volus there. But there was a mainframe access panel down here, Senna remembered from the blueprints back on Hephaestus. They stood near it now, in the dark, while Senna made it possible for Qetsi to talk to her ship. She looked at him with hope and misery. He could see her expression, even through the shadowed glass of her faceplate. Senna felt for her. He was horrifically glad all he had to do was hotwire a microphone. She had to hotwire the morale of half a starship.

"Am I doing okay?" she whispered.

"You're doing fine." He squeezed her hand.

"I've spliced the tram malfunction," crackled his grandmother's voice in his ear. "If you're interested. You forgot to turn me off, so I had to do something with my time. You know how I feel about idle hands around the house. I'm porting you the codepatch now. Upload it and get back here. I suspect it'll only work temporarily."

"Not now," Senna hissed as cool, clean, elegant, machine-generated code flowed down the curve of his faceplate. "You fixed something? You really did? And… you couldn't have fixed the shields first?"

"What?" Qetsi said in the shadows of the transport tube, her voice frightened, sounding so much younger than she was.

"Nothing," he said as he transferred the patch through his omni-tool and into the access hub. "Keep going."

Deep in the bowels of the ship, Senna heard a tram car begin to move toward them with a grinding, reluctant sound.

If you detect symptoms in yourself or others, do not report to medbay. Isolate and confine symptomatic individuals to designated residential quarters on your species' environmental control decks and await further communication. Food distribution will commence at 0600 hours beginning with the drell in Mess Hall 2. We have limited supplies on hand. We are at least three weeks' travel from the nearest planet, which is, I should mention, a lifeless rock with nothing to eat on it but dust and a very calorie-inefficient lichen, so we must make what we have last as long as possible.

Yorrik had, at long last, pushed beyond all endurance, fallen asleep. The iso-shield still shimmered between the dreaming elcor and the wracked corpse of Jalosk Dal'Virra leaning against the almost-invisible barrier. The stars still blinked by outside, too fast to count.

The hanar Ysses stood above him, tall and rosy and gleaming. The captain's voice echoed in the empty lab as Ysses raised itself on its tentacles and released the iso-field. The body inside toppled out with a wet sound as it hit the floor. Yorrik did not wake.

Ysses giggled. It turned around and glided past the tables stained with dried dye, past the krogan microscope, past the ruins of the stuffed volus, past Horatio, past the dormant laser scalpels, to the quarantined medbay door. It giggled again as it pressed its gelatinous limb against the security pad and undulated slowly, hacking the correct code out of the interface never meant for its species.

The persistent quarantine tone ceased to chime. The soft red light stopped flashing through the glass walls. The medbay doors glided open.

Ysses giggled again.

"The Day of Extinguishment has come," it whispered, and floated out into the long, open hall that led out into the screaming chaos of the unsuspecting ship.

I trust you to organize and conduct yourselves in a civilized manner in this time of crisis. Rest assured that all possible steps are being taken to discover the source of these problems and determine a quick and effective solution. Do not panic. With a little luck and ingenuity, we will all be safely back in our pods in a few days and the next time we open our eyes all we'll see before us is the Andromeda galaxy in all its wonder and infinite promise. Everything is going to be all right.

This has been your captain, Qetsi'Olam vas Keelah Si'yah. Please remain calm and return to your respective environmental zones. May our ancestors be with us. Thank you and good luck.

The captain's message began again. It cycled through and repeated on the hour, every hour, as the longest night in the history of the galaxy wore on.

PART 2

KEELAH SE'LAI

12. SYNTHESIS

The Radial had been beautiful in its own way. Once.

By the time Anax Therion and Borbala Ferank fought their way to the heart of the ship, it was no longer.

Now the flower arrangement that had seemed so important on Hephaestus Station, so necessary to their long journey into the unknown, lay smashed and shredded on the floor of the spacious blue-black hexagon, pollen and juices smeared all over the thick glass walls of the six converging environmental zones. Glass walls that did little to muffle the cacophony of voices on the other side, yelling and arguing and screaming, and the occasional firing of a biotic charge—and biotic accidents and biotic attacks sound much the same. The pale lerian ferns of Kahje lay torn to pieces, their tiny pods stripped off. The red usharet flowers from Rakhana had been pulped and wiped down the alcoves like blood. The elcors' thick onuffri bulbs had been ripped off their stalks and carried off, the batarian spice cones dashed against the bolts between the hexagon's walls until they shattered. Someone had trampled the volus's carnivorous kympna lobes, leaving boot prints on their petals. And the quarian keleven roots had been utterly devoured, leaving only their tough, leathery cores strewn around the Radial.

Hello… everyone. This is your captain speaking. Please remain calm and return to your respective environmental control zones. There is not enough acclimatization equipment for everyone, and we must conserve the supplies we have.

A volus Anax did not recognize ran screaming up out of the fumy ammonia-riddled depths of his zone. He slammed his fists against the glass, shrieking in fury: "I'll kill you both! You did this to me! You did this! It hurts! It hurts so much. It huuuuurrrrts—"

There was a sickening *pop*. Blue liquid sprayed against the inside of his yellow eye-goggles. The volus slumped to the ground.

"That is not good," Anax said.

"That's *impossible,*" Borbala breathed, her tone more of fascination than disbelief.

Anax shrugged. "Not really. The volus suit's main function is to provide constant high pressure similar to that on Irune. If he were to develop severe edema, his limbs would swell considerably, and the equalization between pressures would become intolerable." She smiled ghoulishly, trying desperately to hold on to some sense of humor. "*Pop,*" she said softly.

"No, I mean—how can the volus have it? Their suits... I don't even know what one looks like under there. But shouldn't it keep them safe? And shouldn't they all have Yoqtan antibodies, if they get it as kids?"

"I'll ask Irit next time I see her. I think for now we must accept that any of us are vulnerable, no matter how unlikely that might seem. As for antibodies... there is a human sickness called shingles. A human can only acquire it after surviving chickenpox. It is the same illness, but it only returns to an immune system which it has already compromised. An organic body is a strange and terrible place, Borbala Ferank."

Unfortunately, all cases so far have been fatal. Please remain calm.

"If I have to hear that one more time, I am going to shoot the first audio array I see," growled the batarian. "How did we get the world's prissiest captain? Just say: *We're all going to die, you're on your own, have a nice day* and be done with it, woman."

They peered down into the hanar section. Several of them were clustered around one preaching. One had open sores on its tentacles, but no one seemed to be moving away from it. The elcor hallways were dark and still. The batarian ones were a riot of accusations and shots fired. Therion put her hand on the drell-zone glass. The area within was awash with glittering blue light. She felt tears start in her eyes. *My people are so clever*, she thought. *So much cleverer than we are credited for.*

"What's that?" asked Borbala.

"The drell biotics have captured the sick in Singularities. It knocks them out, gives them some peace, and isolates them from the healthy population. And it's beautiful." A few Singularity bubbles drifted into view, the dying drell inside looking almost as though they were meditating.

Borbala looked at the bubbles for a long time, catching her breath. She wiped a streak of blood off her thigh—what was left of another batarian who rushed them back in the maze of corridors connecting the decks. He'd been so angry, bellowing, trying to spit on them, ranting that if he had to die, they would too—they hadn't wanted to take him down, but he was past saving. They'd shot him together, so neither had to carry the sin alone.

"I'll be bad cop," Borbala mused. "Obviously."

The drell smiled without happiness.

Ferank and Therion let themselves into the quarian section. Therion's air filter wasn't strictly necessary here, since the quarian zone was set to common environmentals—Citadel standard. They never had any intention of leaving their suits, anyway, and a deep-space ship was home climate to a quarian. What sense was there in pumping their quarters full of Rannoch's atmosphere? Wasted energy. The pair of them walked down the residential halls—it was quiet in quarian town. Of course, it would be. They alone had nothing particularly to worry about. Their suits would protect them. No one was sick. They waited patiently in their quarters for instructions—doors open to friendly traffic. Those quarians unfortunate enough to wake up in the initial cryopod failure were gathered six and eight and even ten to a room, despite there being more than enough space for them to spread out. On the Fleet, an empty room was very nearly a crime. They waved their gray three-fingered hands as the drell and the batarian walked by like guards in a prison, all but running a nightstick against invisible bars.

"I need to speak to Malak'Rafa," Anax Therion said to each cluster of nervous but optimistic and healthy quarians. They shook their heads, speculated on where he might be, claimed not to know him, apologized. And they moved on down the corridor.

"I need to speak to Malak'Rafa," Therion said again at the doorway to a smaller room, probably meant for a menial laborer or low-ranking nobody-in-particular. Four quarians were seated around the dining table, three male, one female, playing some kind of card game rigged up out of bits of repurposed scrap plastic. The taller male was clearly winning. Anax could see it in his posture.

"Who is inquiring after him?" said the tall winner, ticking his head to one side.

"My name is Anax Therion, this is Borbala Ferank. We're part of the Sleepwalker team that discovered the pathogen. Malak'Rafa was part of the previous one." She decided on a small lie. "We are seeking out all the members of Yellow-9. Someone on this ship knows what happened." She shrugged. "It might be one of them." Three of the members of that team were floating dead and frozen in space light years behind them.

"Then I am he," said one of the shorter, less lucky card players, and turned to face them.

He crossed his arms over his chest. Malak'Rafa vas Keelah Si'yah looked like every other quarian—they were by far the most difficult interrogation subjects. Anax hated questioning quarians. You could not see their faces, their pupils dilating, their sweat response, the dryness of their lips. And they didn't care about anything but their fleet, so threatening them was useless. The lights didn't seem to be working in here either. Shadows and dim pale-blue emergency lighting turned Malak'Rafa into a dark statue. Until he saw Anax in her volus suit, shoved his chair violently backward, and leapt up.

"*Keelah se'lai*, what kind of a *bosh'tet* am I even looking at?" marveled the quarian medical specialist in a thick but not impenetrable and certainly not unattractive Fleet accent. He gestured at the drell in the volus suit.

"A drell, I assure you," Anax said. "May we have the room?"

The other quarians nodded and drifted off calmly. It was not that they were not worried, for the ship, for the others—but they were not worried for themselves, and it made all the difference. None of these people were going to run at them screaming in the depths of space madness, firing whatever weapon they'd dug out of a locker or someone's luggage, demanding to be fed. No one else could eat the quarian's dextro-protein food anyway, so they were altogether in better shape than most.

"Listen, kid," Borbala began, settling down on one of the other card players' chairs. "This ship is under attack. You have to know that. Just because no one is torpedoing us out of the sky doesn't mean we're not under attack."

"I really wish I could help," Malak said, and he really did sound like he meant it.

"You can, Sleepwalker," Borbala said casually. "Everything was fine until your team went on shift. So why don't you tell us—what did you do while the rest of us were napping, you naughty boy?"

The quarian went ramrod stiff. *Oh,* Anax thought. *How unexpected. What* did *you do?*

"Am I the only one of my team awake?" the quarian asked, expending some effort to keep his voice calm. "*Keelah Si'yah,* locate Systems Analyst Soval Raxios."

Illegal query. Soval Raxios is not on board the Keelah Si'yah.

Why does this seem to keep coming back to Soval? Therion thought. "The computers have trouble finding anyone at the moment. Senna is trying to fix it," Anax apologized quickly. If he didn't know she was dead, she might be able to use that. It was always to one's advantage to know something another did not. "Why did you ask about her specifically?" Anax asked.

"She's... She's a friend. She can tell you that I didn't do anything during our cycle but check life signs on 20,000 cryopods."

"Just a friend?" Anax pressed. The quarian said nothing.

Borbala Ferank barged in as any easily bored batarian would. "Listen to me, Malak'Rafa. This ship is under attack. Someone on your Sleepwalker team did something to help that along and the captain says it was most likely you. We've been awake and dealing with your mess for some time now, so there's no use lying about it. But everyone has their reasons. I'm sure you didn't mean it. Let us help you."

Therion winced. *Risky*. She would never have been so forward. This was why she detested the whole framework of good cop, bad cop. She had had quite enough of bad cops in her life. Bad cops were sloppy. Bad cops shot their clip too soon.

"Impossible," said Malak, shaking his head. "I have known Qetsi'Olam since we were both children on board the *Chayym*. Since we were fitted for our first suits together. When the geth attacked our birth ship, only Qetsi and I survived. I know her better than the sister I never had. We took our Pilgrimages together at the salarian biodiversity station. When those racist little insects pulled their hazing stunt and compromised her suit on a group outing, I nursed her back to health. We developed the vapor-biotic to cleanse her lungs of that crawling *yelik* algae together, and brought it back to our home ship. We took leadership of the Nedas movement together, to find a new hope for our people. We took our first wounds together fighting the geth. And we took meetings together with the Initiative to build this ark and fly it beyond the visible stars. Twins are less close than we are. Qetsi'Olam would suspect her own two hands before she suspected me."

Anax Therion was no novice. She had spent her time on Hephaestus Station reading personnel files while the others laughed and talked and drank and danced. Only on that last night had she joined them, joined Soval... She suppressed the memory. Soval didn't matter now, except as evidence. She knew very well who Malak'Rafa was. She'd planned to use it in seven to nine minutes. But plans were easily enough changed.

Malak'Rafa shocked her. The quarian reached out and squeezed her hand tenderly. "If I knew anything, Anax, I would tell you, I promise. But nothing happened. Nothing at all unusual. I think maybe we should all go and see the captain. She'll tell you I'd never do anything to harm *any* ship, least of all this one."

"The problem is, something happened on your watch, Malak. And it's enormously important that we find out what it was. Were you ever separated from your team, for any amount of time?" Therion asked. "Maybe it wasn't you. Maybe one of your friends snuck off while you weren't looking."

"No," Malak'Rafa said quickly. Too quickly. He hardly let the drell finish her question. "We were either in visual range of each other or on live vidfeed throughout the cycle. Yellow-9 follows protocol."

Therion sat back. *Interesting*. She knew for a fact that was a lie. She'd watched all the teams on the security footage. She hadn't expected him to lie. She didn't think he himself was actually at fault, the way Borbala presumed everyone to be at fault for everything. She only assumed he had seen something the vids might have missed. That shadow in the shadows, that persistent movement just past the range of the cameras. But why was he lying?

Borbala got up and started pacing, embracing her role as an impatient, embittered policeman. "What about Jalosk Dal'Virra?" the batarian barked. "Did he seem normal to you? Any effects from cryostasis? Any odd behavior?"

"Jalosk? No. He's... He's a good worker, I suppose. Finished early. And then hung around Kholai like a lovesick puppy. I think he was actually starting to believe that hanar's depressing drivel."

"What drivel?" coaxed Anax, sitting up straight. "That Day of Extinguishment nonsense?"

The quarian nodded, glancing nervously at the pacing Ferank. "You must have heard it on Hephaestus, it's just... *constant*. Like a broken vidscreen. But after we shared our final meal together, I noticed that Jalosk was *really* listening. On Hephaestus and on our cycle. I felt a great deal of pity for him. Kholai's philosophy is... like alcohol. At first you are laughing, but soon enough you weep, and then you slide into the black and do not come out. The last thing Kholai said to me before it went back into stasis was: *The only peace in the universe is entropy. I will see you at the end of all things, my brother.* That's one of *their* hymns. They say it to each other all the time. It's not good for them. I hoped... I hoped beyond hope that in Andromeda, they would see the possibility of a new life rather than the certainty of death. How beautiful something *new* could be. And then... And then, just before he left for the batarian cryodeck, Dal'Virra said the same thing to me. *I will see you at the end of all things.*"

"And that didn't seem suspicious to you?" Borbala laughed.

But Malak'Rafa shook his head. "No, not at all. I can't believe you've never listened to Kholai's sermons. That hanar never stops talking." *It certainly has now,* Therion thought. The quarian recited from memory in a long-suffering voice, "'Only the Enkindlers know when the Day of Extinguishment will come. Take no action to hasten it, for all deeds are meaningless, and to strive toward accomplishment is to arrogantly elevate yourself to their glory. The holiest bear happy witness to the rot of the universe, but have no part in it.' They are the laziest cult I have ever encountered. They quite literally believe any action at all is a sin. I am genuinely surprised they went so far as to seek out the ark and book passage."

"Perhaps there has been a new revelation," Borbala said darkly.

"Perhaps," shrugged Malak.

"And what about your friend, this... Soval?" asked Anax, her voice full of feigned hesitance, as if she had never known her, never seen her shining face dancing in the tavern lights on Hephaestus. "Did she also listen to the hanar?"

"Soval... Soval." Therion watched the way his shoulders moved when he said her name. "She did, but not like Jalosk. She's the happiest girl I've ever known. She was a poet back on Kahje. She wrote 'Each of Us Dying is the Soul Name of Rakhana,' do you know it? It's very good, if a little on the nose. Her husband is political, a revolutionary, at least in his own mind. But she isn't like that at all. Soval didn't listen to Kholai so much as she *talked* to it. I think she really thought she could change that jelly's outlook on life. Show him that the galaxy is not a mistake. That joy in living is not a sin. We had our last meal all together. Threnno, Soval, and Kholai sang some Citadel song together. It was nice. No one argued. No one acted strange. And that's all I saw, I swear to you by the new homeworld we seek in Andromeda."

"Impossible. There *is* something else! We know when it happened, and it happened on your watch," the batarian fumed.

"When *what* happened? Why don't you tell me?"

"You said you inspected the cryopods..." Anax ventured softly, tracing an idle pattern on the table. It helped her think.

"Yes. I confirmed each and every one of 20,000 were in good working order with the assistance of the elcor team member, Threnno."

"And you saw no problems at all?" Borbala said.

"Did something go wrong with the pods?" asked Malak.

"Why don't *you* tell me whether something went wrong with the pods?" snapped Borbala.

"You were in love with her," Anax said quietly. "With Soval Raxios. With a drell."

The quarian's faceplate showed no expression, but his voice was tight and thin. "That's preposterous. I told you she's married."

"Yes, to Osyat, the radical. I know him fairly well. He is obnoxious and disliked. Married to his politics. She would have been lonely. And though twins may well be less close than you and Qetsi'Olam, I have seen the way she and Senna'Nir speak. She left you lonely, too, even on your salarian Pilgrimage. Even in your Nedas cell."

"I would like you to leave. I can't help you, Anax. And what..." Malak'Rafa held out his hands pleadingly, "...what point can there be to any of that now?"

Therion said nothing for a pregnant moment. She had her line. Now she needed only to cast it.

"I was in love once," she said, filling her voice with all the softness of someone who really, truly had. "It was forbidden for us, too. But not because its immune system could never withstand my subcutaneous oils. Simply because the soul bond between a drell and a hanar is never meant to be a physical bond. Its name was Oleon. It bought me from another hanar, a cold and cruel master who worked me nearly to death to spread the word of the Enkindlers without having to do any real work itself. Oleon was kind. It was giving and soft. When it was happy, the lights of its skin were brighter than any galaxy here or there. We were happy, for a time. I was the first drell to love a hanar in that way. As far as I know. But we were discovered, and…" Therion hid her eyes in one hand, as though she could not bear to go on. She heard Borbala snort.

The captain's voice droned on through the public audio system.

If you detect symptoms in yourself or others, do not report to medbay. Isolate and confine symptomatic individuals to designated residential quarters on your species' environmental control decks and await further communication.

"So you see, I know," the drell said. "I know what it's like, to love someone you can never touch again."

The quarian's faceplate fogged gently. He was crying. "When we reach Andromeda, she'll go back to him," he whispered. "And all I will have in my memory is the way she smelled on that last night, so impossibly sweet, like flowers, flowers in the depths of space…"

A bone-cracking scream echoed down the hall. All the tiny hairs on Anax Therion's neck stood up straight. That was a mother's scream. Once you heard it, you could never mistake it for any other.

They dashed out into the corridor. A quarian woman was standing there, her violet hood black in the shadows. She was holding something small in her arms. Something terribly small. A child, clutching a stuffed green keeper toy in one limp, dead hand.

With a little luck and ingenuity, we will all be safely back in our pods in a few days and the next time we open our eyes all we'll see before us is the Andromeda galaxy in all its wonder and infinite promise. Everything is going to be all right.

13. REPLICATION

Someone banged on the door of Senna'Nir's quarters. No one else had closed their doors in the quarian zone, so this had begun to happen very frequently. The locking mechanisms now cheerfully activated and deactivated whenever they pleased, so he simply hoped they were active now and tried to be as quiet as possible, ignoring the insistent and regular punching of his door.

Yes, they were in pain. Yes, they were starving. Yes, they were dying.

But if Senna could just get the ship working right again, they could fix it all. The med scans, the communications, the decontamination protocols—it could all *work*, if he could just *make* it work. They were only in this mess because they couldn't access their own tech. *Technology will save you. It will always save you. As long as you treat it with respect. As long as you don't leave it alone with its thoughts.* Those people out there didn't understand. He was in here saving them. No less than Yorrik in the medbay. *Of course they don't understand. People with subacute sclerosing panencephalitis don't even understand how many fingers they have.* And if one of those thundering knocks was Qetsi, well, he could not risk her seeing what he was doing in here. He just needed more processing power.

But even through the door he heard the scream.

Senna stuck his head out of the first officer's

quarters. He saw a woman sink to her knees with her child in her arms. It was horrible. It was impossible. It was a slow-acting nightmare that curdled his gut and made his hair stand on end. But he couldn't let himself focus on it. Not now. He could fix things on the macro level—the ship, the mission, the whole situation. But the micro level would drown him—a mother, her child, one person's death. He focused on something else instead: the two green women standing in the corridor. One was not so green anymore—Anax in her custom volus suit.

"Therion!" Senna'Nir hissed. "Ferank! I need you!"

The drell snapped to attention. They moved quickly toward him. "Senna, it's you! Are you all right? Are you seeing this? That's a *quarian* child. There's an extremely dead volus out there, too." She paused, as if she was going to say something else, and thought better of it. "She's supposed to be safe. Her suit and her," the detective whispered helplessly, her voice thick with far too much feeling for a strange child she'd never known. Senna ignored that, too. He could only do what he could do and what he could do was this.

"Yes," he said tightly. "It's absolutely the worst thing I can imagine and under no circumstances should it be within the realm of possibility but I need you right now. I need your help."

"Sure, boss," said the batarian, her voice all silk and ice, still looking backward over her shoulder at the sobbing mother.

"How many VIs would you say are on this ship?" Senna asked.

"What? Who cares?" Borbala said.

"Total?" asked Anax Therion.

Senna shook his head. "No, just the independent or mobile ones. Self-contained VIs with their own power sources. VIs that were never hooked up to the mainframe; discrete units."

The drell rubbed her long middle finger against her forefinger, calculating. "There's the krogan microscope. I would imagine many people brought educational VIs to help with the colonization, entertainment VIs, that sort of thing. One of my sets of armor utilizes VI components."

"Mine too," nodded Borbala companionably, casually, as though the two of them had just discovered they liked the same perfume.

"And then there are the Pathfinders," Therion said hesitantly. It was the third rail. None of them wanted to touch it. To risk infecting the Pathfinders for a little technological help felt like giving up on finding a homeworld. Felt like losing Andromeda before they ever arrived.

"No," said Senna'Nir, very loudly. "We cannot wake them. I've tried to isolate their pods as best I can through the access hubs. They'll be the last ones affected by any malfunctions."

"My wager would be in the hundreds, then. People bring the strangest things across the universe," finished Therion. "More importantly, have you seen any hanar since we talked last?"

"No, none, why do you ask?"

"A theory is beginning to form. The hanar are at the core of it. But they seem to be making themselves extremely scarce."

"Good work, Analyst. When you are ready to report, come to me or the captain, no one else, do you understand?" She did, though her eyes narrowed in a way that made him nervous. "But for now, I need you to bring me every VI you can find."

The batarian frowned. "They'll be all over the ship. And in the cargo hold. Do you know what's happened in the cargo hold? It's a madhouse down there. They've all... congregated. Everyone who woke up in the revival cascade. Some of them went to guard their possessions. Some heard us on the comms before they shut off, and thought the ship had been boarded. They found the weapons stores on their way to the storage deck. Some went in search of food. Some followed the running lights and the sound of others. But they all ended up down in the hold, and getting anything out of there may quite literally be murder."

He looked pleadingly at them.

"I can fix it," he whispered. "I can fix the ship. I can make it all stop." *Well,* his brain added, *perhaps not just me.*

"You need VIs?" the batarian crime boss sighed. "I can make VIs happen."

"Aye, Commander," said Anax Therion after a long, appraising pause. "We will do this for you. Stand by. It may take longer than you would like. Stay in your quarters. If it has spread even to the quarians, we may all be damned anyway."

No, his mind simply refused to accept that. A quarian in a seal-tight suit could not get sick. That was the whole point of the suit. He hadn't even taken it off in cryosleep. None of them had. It just wasn't possible, so it was easy to put out of his thoughts. That poor child had died in the chaos, that was all. It was sad, but it didn't mean the suits were compromised. They couldn't be compromised, so they weren't. As simple as that.

Senna'Nir slid gratefully back into the safe and controllable universe of his quarters. He pulled Grandmother Liat'Nir out from her hiding place and booted her out of sleep mode.

"Hello, Grandmother," Senna'Nir said quietly.

"Always so formal, my grandson," said the ancestor VI, as it always did, in her rolling, familiar Rannoch accent. "Call me Liat, why don't you? Never thought of myself as old enough to have grandchildren anyhow."

The visual interface rolled up the shimmering sleeves of her red-and-purple robes and ran her hands through her gray hair. She sat back on an old, creaky chair and began to whittle something in her lap. He liked the cigarette boot better than the whittling boot, but he didn't have time to cycle her through just for his own comfort.

"Liat," he said to the little hologram. "I have a problem. Do you have an answer for me?"

Liat'Nir rocked back and forth, back and forth, whick-snicking her knife across the little knob of wood. "When my first daughter was born, I gave her two pieces of advice. Do you know what they were?"

"I don't have time for this, Grandmother. You patched the trams, you must have made some progress."

"When my first daughter was born, I gave her two pieces of advice. Do you know what they were?"

Senna'Nir sighed. It was no use trying to bully a VI. They didn't have enough emotional capacity to feel the pressure of time or necessity. "What were they?"

Whick-snick, went the sound of her whittling. "I said to her: Be the soul of warmth to all you meet. And don't get caught."

The ancient quarian beamed at him, her sun-baked face full of pride. "You are very welcome, Grandson."

"I didn't say thank you."

"But I have solved your problem for you. You would say thank you if the youth had the manners evolution gave a scrubmouse with a fever."

"I don't see how." Senna's heart sank. Another of these koans of hers. Another *go fish*. Her iterative thinking process was prone to them, but he had hoped, perhaps foolishly, for the plainspoken truth. He put his head in his hands, rubbing his temples through his suit's mesh. "I'm sorry. I just don't understand. Can't you explain yourself? Just this once?"

Liat'Nir sat forward in her rocking chair with a sharp gleam in her holographic eye. "Of course, *kes'ed*. It is ingenious, really." She held up the object she had been whittling.

It was a lemek worm, a desert vermiform species of old Rannoch. He had seen pictures of them. Small and slender and covered in metallic rose-colored scales. You could cut them into pieces over and over and the pieces would grow into new lemeks every time, down to the thinnest shavings of its body. Liat'Nir had been carving a worm with two heads. She spoke briskly, businesslike, not at all like his grandmother and more like a team leader reporting to her superiors.

"Per your instructions, I have not interfaced directly with the *Keelah Si'yah* so as not to contaminate my code base, so you will understand this is only a hypothesis, but it fits the evidence, and when you access the core, I believe you will find I am correct. It is a worm, but you had to have known that. An organic system crash is much faster and more holistic. By now, it would all have simply shut down and tried to retro-boot itself into a clean save state. A program is working its way through this ship, doing exactly as it was told.

Unfortunately for you, grandson of mine, over the last nearly six hundred years, it has had to improvise in order to obey those very basic instructions."

"The computer virus is alive? Sentient?"

"Don't be stupid. Did I raise a drooling fool? Of course not. But the nature of a virus is to be adaptable. Anyone who creates one knows it will at some point be targeted by a program designed to annihilate it, and it must have some rudimentary defense mechanism, or none of us would ever have technical support issues to force our grandmothers to mend on holidays like old socks, hmm? In the case of our foreign friend, when it was born, it received two pieces of advice. Two instructions with which to interact with the world around it." Liat held up one arthritic finger. "One: raise the temperature." She held up another. "Two: cover your tracks. It is that second one that is causing us so much trouble at the moment." She began to pace. Liat had been a great one for lecturing in her day. The cigarette appeared in her glimmering hand, trailing smoke up into nothing. "The first is simple enough—raise the temperature on X number of cryopods—where X is sufficient to cause a chain contagion in a set population—just enough to allow the barest of physical processes to take place. Then, any infectious agent introduced from the outside can begin the replication process. But *cover your tracks*—ah, there is a pernicious little *bosh'tet* of a command. It satisfies parameters simply enough—boom! The ship will read only healthful life signs from the affected pods. But the second any infected person leaves those pods, well, then our wee friend must spread in order to cover up their existence, make them unseeable, undetectable, or else it has failed its programming. Every time you tried to look at what was going wrong, from this angle or that, every time you spoke to the *Keelah Si'yah* and tried to get it to detect a problem, the worm gained access to a new system to prevent it. This is very basic stuff, my idiot grandson. I am surprised you needed me to figure it out. The only tracks in the sand it left was its effects—the sublimation in the pods, the carbon dioxide exhaled in the cargo hold. Anyone infected cannot be seen, because they are evidence. How does it know? An elevated temperature, a detectable scent, any physiological change that can be apprehended by the internal scans would immediately mark this person as invisible to the person using the scans. The ship is not blind, she is mute. She knows, she just can't tell you."

"Grandmother, why have you never explained yourself so clearly before? If you could talk to me like this, why all the riddles?"

Her face set into itself stubbornly. "You never asked. Manners, young man. Manners."

"That is why the codevault looked so perfect when Irit and I examined it. It was covering itself. I thought that! I thought that we would find it in the perfect places."

"Congratulations, you had a good idea and left it up to your old gran to do the legwork," snorted Liat'Nir.

His mind raced. "The worm must have been installed at the same time that the pathogen was smuggled on board. They must have deployed at nearly the same moment, working side by side, though not together, the one to enable and hide the other. That is certainly deliberate."

"Do you think so?" Liat'Nir blinked her eyes innocently. "Of course it was deliberate, *ke'sed*."

"But what could be the intended effect? To kill us all? They could have just blown up Hephaestus if that's all they wanted. To exterminate the drell? Then why has it spilled over into so many species? How could it have spread at all before we started mingling, after the first victims had already died? This is so complex simply to cause death."

"I don't know, *ke'sed*. I just work here. I can work on the problem if you like."

"No," Senna said, shaking his head furiously. "No, that's Anax's territory. Our first priority has to be fixing the ship. Liat, I have a problem. What is the most efficient way to purge the worm from the *Keelah Si'yah*?"

The ancestor VI knelt at an invisible river, washing invisible linens in invisible water. Another of her loading icons. "Working," she sang to the tune of an old Rannoch fishing song. "Working."

It did not take long this time, but Senna'Nir hated the answer.

14. LATENCY

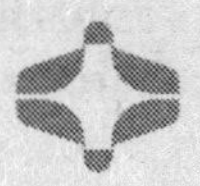

Yorrik had never been so hungry in all his life. A volus, half in and half out of his suit, lay on the autopsy table below him, but the elcor could hardly see it through the haze of hunger. It was a ruin of metallic, electric color, flesh bulging out of the pressurization suit, blood coagulated in huge greasy lumps, almost unrecognizable as anything formerly alive. It reeked of that sweet flowery smell, that smell which Yorrik, now that he had so many specimens to work with, understood was the body beginning to consume its own sugars to feed the viral replication process. Beside the volus lay a small quarian girl, quite dead, her limbs beginning to stiffen in her suit. Horatio looked down at her with his grotesque neon smiling face. Yorrik felt sick now, having done that. It was disrespectful. But how could he have known then what there was to disrespect?

Irit Non had brought the child corpse. Hauled it over her shoulder like a sack of grain. The volus fashion designer stood next to him in the medbay now, panting, her suit covered in unspeakable stains and burns.

"Self-pitying: I am glad you are here, Irit Non. But I wish you would stay outside where it is safe."

The volus made a disgusted noise. "Safe? Where is Ysses? Pretty safe, do you think? When I got here the door was wide open and you were snoring. What's safe around here? No, it doesn't matter now.

Quarantine is well and truly broken. If we are exposed, we are exposed. And that"—she gestured at the dead girl in the helmet—"makes everyone," she wheezed, her voice as emotionless as his had ever been.

"Tentative overture: You know, my grandfather Verlaam believed that other species could greatly benefit from using the elcor speech technique in times of great stress," he said flatly. "Many veterans of many wars came to him to learn it in his later days, for great trauma blunts emotions in all organic beings. Perhaps you should try it."

Irit Non turned her yellow eyes up to him. "Total fucking despair: Everyone has it. None of us are safe. How was that?"

"Encouraging: Very good. With great confidence: But that quarian cannot have died of the Fortinbras virus. Their suits are excellent. It should have kept her perfectly safe. I am sure she died in some other way. Let us focus on the volus victim."

Irit shrugged. "Do you know where I found her? In Mess Hall 4. They turned it into a makeshift mausoleum. All the dead are there. All the dead anyone has time to collect. It's cold enough for storage there. They're piled in there like rations. Environmental zones hardly matter for them anymore. No one means any disrespect… they just have to go somewhere. I saw her while I was interring my father's body under a cafeteria table. One quarian arm under all those hanar tentacles. And while I was carrying her through the decks, I thought about how it could possibly happen. The volus suits are one thing, not much in the way of disease filtration. But the quarians should be fine. They should have been fine. And I am not… a large person. It is hard for me to carry a dead body." Irit Non's voice grew thick. "Miserably: She was so heavy," the volus whispered. "So much heavier than you'd think, for a child. It took a long time. So I tried to imagine how a quarian suit could be breached without the suit responding or the quarian inside knowing."

Yorrik saw the captain arrive out of the corner of his eye. She saw him notice her and raised a hand—no need to interrupt. Qetsi'Olam leaned against the far wall of the corridor and listened.

"Do you know what Clanless suits are made of?" the volus went on, staring at the dead girl. "It sounds like the beginning of a joke, doesn't it? Well, the answer sounds like a punchline: anything they can find. They're made of whatever they can scavenge on the Fleet, from other ships, on planets where they make planetfall. It's strictly patchwork crap, the strongest materials, but all pieced together like a quilt. It's really a wonder they work as well as they do. Clanless engineering, I suppose. But… I can't imagine they put 'whatever can plausibly be interpreted as fabric' through serious stress tests, can you? What I am trying to say is: I know the exact duration my suit can survive without structural failure in a vacuum. Exactly the pressures it can withstand, internal and external. At exactly what point it will breach if it comes into contact with dozens of known caustic substances. And precisely what temperatures it can take, high and… high and low. Do you see? Do you see, elcor? Perhaps the Clanless know all those things, too. They are a careful people. I've always admired that about them. But those numbers, those precious, life-supporting numbers, cannot possibly be the same for every square inch of their suit. Because it's all patched together from the-gods-know-what."

"We do," said the captain, softly but with the authority that all captains have the moment they take the rank. "Of course we stress-test them."

Irit turned to Qetsi. "Captain, I didn't see you."

"It's perfectly all right, Specialist Non. I rather enjoy listening to you speak. You have such a way. It's comforting. I came to check on you, Yorrik. I have… I have seen your friend."

"Vain hope: Ysses?" Yorrik said. Where could that blasted hanar have gone? *Why* would it have gone? The elcor had wakened to Irit Non screaming at him, and his head felt so heavy, so heavy.

"Yes. *That one* cornered me near the bridge. It grabbed me. Have you ever been grabbed by a hanar? I don't recommend it. It wrapped me up in all of its tentacles and giggled and giggled and told me to let it happen, to let it all happen. Someone ripped it off me, and it floated away. And then that someone tried to stab me because I didn't have any food. But I think… I think I am all right. The ship is lost, I'm afraid. There is no control anywhere."

The volus opened a panel in her thigh and drew out a small black device. "Captain, would you mind if I examined your suit? It could put all our minds at ease."

"My suit? I said I am all right. But… of course," Qetsi'Olam demurred.

The volus beckoned her closer and ran her device over the expanse of patchwork mesh that comprised the captain's suit. A dim ultraviolet-colored light emanated from it. She ran it all over Qetsi's body, and only at the end did a tiny ultraviolet-colored mark appear on the small of her back—and then a few more, and a few more, like cracks in ice.

"Micro-tears," sighed Irit Non. "No material can be stress-tested for six hundred years in a cryopod, at temperatures far below organic tolerance. I don't believe the makers of those pods ever imagined that people like you and me would keep our suits on when we went to sleep for centuries at a time. You might have been all right if you hadn't."

The captain might have looked horrified. You could never tell with quarians. But her posture looked as though you could knock her over with a breath. *"We'll sleep safe as engines as forward we fly, my self and my suit, my suit and I,"* she whispered.

"Yes, well, maybe just you next time," the volus grunted.

"I've been exposed," Qetsi said faintly.

"Wry humor: Join the club," Yorrik droned. His limbs felt so thick. Like he was standing in a swamp. He could hardly think. He tried to focus his thoughts. *"To be or not to be, that is the question, whether 'tis nobler in the minds of men to suffer the… suffer the…"* What was it the old Dane was so worried about suffering?

"How long is the incubation period?" Qetsi asked. "I don't feel well. Do I? I don't. I can't tell." She coughed experimentally.

"Regretfully: I have not been able to observe a patient from the point of first contact, so I cannot provide that information," Yorrik sighed. Who knew how long it had been since Jalosk was exposed?

Anax Therion and Borbala Ferank made hardly a sound coming up the hall, despite carrying rather a large crate of electronic supplies between them.

"Hullo, Yorrik, you great lump," said the batarian. "How are you? We… eh. We're going to need the microscope. And… And the fish tank, too. Whatever's left of the CPU from the one we brought up to you. You don't need them anymore, do you?"

Anax took it all in and Yorrik watched her do it. What could possibly be said? The open door, the absence of Ysses, people wandering in and out of the medbay as though quarantine protocols had never been invented. She sighed. Yorrik sighed. It was a world of sighs and no solutions. How could he tell them? How could they not know? How could they not smell him? The smell of his own organs devouring themselves hung thick in the air, sweeter than flowers, almost like candy, sickening. But they did not seem to notice. He was so tired. So very tired.

"Am I an unforgivable optimist if I ask about a cure, Yorrik?" ventured the captain.

"Hopeless: I will forgive you. But I do not know what you think I can do without a working virology lab. You can identify a virus with toy parts. You can't cure one."

The elcor stared down at the shredded, half-exploded volus. He tried again to focus on something good, something solid, something that felt like love and life. *"The time is out of joint. O cursed spite, that ever I was born to set it right..."*

"Defeated: The trouble is the mutation. Fortinbras has had so long to evolve. Hundreds of years. And I am to murder it in a day? It is impossible, unless I could have as much time to evolve as it did." Yorrik could not be sure his words had come out as well as they sounded in his head. But the others seemed to understand. He did not want to panic them. The patient could panic. The doctor, never.

Anax Therion stopped him. "What do you mean, it had so much time?"

"Who's Fortinbras?" Borbala chimed in. They ignored her.

Yorrik sighed and settled some of his weight onto his rear legs. "Exhausted explanation: We cannot know exactly how long the virus lived inside the people in cryostasis, but it was a long time. Years. Decades. Centuries perhaps. No virus in the history of the universe has had so long to replicate, even if it was slowed by the cold, without outside interference, or treatment, or the host dying. It got a doting childhood in their bloodstreams. Protected. Nurtured. It could grow up so strong. Find the perfect solution to a virus's only problem: how to live and spread. Sorrowfully: I am babbling. I cannot help it. Deep depression: If I had eezo, that would at least be a start."

"Eezo?" asked the batarian sharply.

"Glumly: It is a mutagen. If we had enough of it, which we do not, and we could find a person who was immune on board the *Keelah Si'yah*, which we have not yet, it might be possible to use the mutagen to engineer a retrovirus from the blood of the immune patient. Anyone who had come in contact with Fortinbras but survived would have viral markers in their blood, antibodies that had successfully fought off the virus. With a full gene-viral lab, which we also do not have, I could use eezo to 'teach' a copy of the original virus to infect the cells of others as normal, but then obliterate the virus within the same way the immune person's body did. The retrovirus would unzip the original virus and leave it dormant at least, purged at best. But this is a recipe for which our larders are quite empty. We would need enough eezo, and we would need to test everyone on board who has been exposed. And we would need the Nexus, because the equipment in here is as useful in making a retrovirus as a rock in making an omelette. And you're about to take my microscope, which is the only thing in here that gives sensible instructions on how to do anything."

Borbala Ferank was chewing mercilessly on the inside of her mouth. She kicked the floor with the toe of her boot.

Irit Non spoke up. "There's eezo in the engines," she mused. "A lot of it."

Qetsi'Olam came to life. She had been listening, or not listening, pressing her hand against the micro-tears on the small of her back, as though her hand could save her, could rewind time and make her whole. She shook her head. "We'd be dead in the water. Gutting the engines of eezo would leave us a drifting hulk out here. We have no way of contacting the Nexus—"

"Senna is making good progress," Anax interrupted. "This is our third lot of supplies for him."

"That's as may be, but even if he gets the long-range comms on again, and we can raise the Nexus, by the time anyone could get to us we'd all have starved to death out here. I've already set a distress message on all frequencies. There's been no response yet. And you'd be asking them to bet *years* on a rescue. They'd rather just cut us loose. What difference would it make, really, if a bunch of quarians, drell, elcor, hanar, volus and bloody batarians never show up? Hell, they'd probably prefer it. Less messy."

"Protestation: It doesn't matter. We do not know of a single immune specimen on board. It may be no one. A virus that can jump species like rope may have a fatality rate of 100%. You would have to get blood from everyone who is awake, and we would have to put it through Horatio for testing until we found someone. In any sufficiently large population, there should be a few people with natural immunity. But are we a sufficiently large population? It's not a needle in a haystack, it's a needle in a galaxy."

"What else are we supposed to do?" barked Irit Non. "Lie down and die? It's the engines or death. A distress call is better than choking to death on your own fluids. Unless anyone has any red sand?" The horrendously addictive drug was packed with eezo, which was what made it feel so good—and what killed you, if you used it long enough. "I thought not. We were all starting with a clean slate, after all. Well done, us."

The captain popped her fist against a wall panel and opened a mainframe access port. Yorrik was surprised she knew the ship so well—but then, he had barely glanced at it. He had been rewriting Lady Macbeth's last monologue in his head as he boarded, full of dreams, full of the idea of distant stars all applauding for him. A fool he had been. A motley fool. Qetsi twisted a few wires together, and then a few more. She interrupted the cycling broadcast they had all quickly learned to ignore and unhear and addressed the ship on the mercifully still-functional public address system.

Attention, Keelah Si'yah. *Hello, everyone. This is your captain… again. Please remain calm. Form an orderly group and proceed to medbay for treatment. I repeat: Please remain calm, form an orderly group, and proceed to medbay for treatment. Be patient, my friends, and we will see our new worlds yet.*

Yorrik groaned. He wished she hadn't done that. It would not be orderly. Why did she have to use the word treatment? Why could they not go, leave him alone? The nausea was building in his stomachs. They could not see him succumb. They had to go. They had to go.

Borbala Ferank looked up to the ceiling of the medbay and shook her head. Her three eyes blinked in succession, then all shut, as though she hated herself for what she was about to do.

"You need eezo?" she mumbled. "I can make eezo happen."

15. RESOURCE EXHAUSTION

"You're a little liar," said Borbala Ferank sweetly as they descended toward the cargo hold again. Which was to say, descended into pestilent hell again. "You lied to that quarian about Oleon. Or you lied to me. But either way, you're the most beautiful little liar I've ever seen."

Anax Therion smiled faintly. "And you are the soul of truth?" she said archly.

"But you do it so smoothly. When I lie I have ticks and tells all over the place, Grandfather always said so. But not you. It just pours out of you like honey."

"Hey," a wheeze hissed out of the dark outside the cargo bay doors. "You sick?"

A volus emerged from the shadows. The light of his turmeric-colored goggles illuminated a bloody handprint on the door. At least Anax thought it was blood. It could have been that black, awful vomit. It didn't matter, she supposed.

"If you're sick, I got a cure. Six food rations, that's all I ask, and you'll be right as rain on Irune in the wintertime."

"Six?" scoffed the batarian. "The hanar were selling cures for four two hours ago."

"Four then!" the volus sputtered. "Hanar cures don't work! Mine do. Guaranteed. I thought I was gonna die like a pyjak, popped a couple of these, and I'm as strong as… as…"

"As a pyjak?" offered Anax.

The little alien opened his brown three-fingered hand. Inside was the crushed remains of a few ignac cones from the Radial's erstwhile flower arrangement.

"You *are* a fucking pyjak," Ferank snarled. "Get out of my way, you stinking merchant swine." She shoved him aside and breached the door to the cargo hold.

It reeked inside. Cloying, sweet, flowery, sugary smells made them both gag. The whole place smelled like a confection factory. It was horrible. Anax wondered, if she made it out of this alive, whether she would ever be able to smell something sweet again without retching. Her stomach was heaving as it was. But not, she thought, because of Fortinbras. Her skin crawled beneath the volus suit. Her mind was beginning to wobble as she soaked in her own subcutaneous oils. It was getting to her. She hadn't been able to stop for hours upon days. Only to make the tiniest meal of a few food wafers in Mess Hall 2 with the others, but not to sleep, and not to strip out of this walking hallucinogenic sarcophagus. If she told the batarian, it was a vulnerability. Only Irit Non knew this weakness. If Ferank decided to turn on her, somehow, for some reason, all she would have to do would be to keep her from getting out of this suit, and eventually, it would kill her as dead as any Fortinbras victim. But perhaps, perhaps it was safe.

"Borbala," she half-wheezed through her air filters. "We get the eezo and then we go to my quarters."

"My my, Miss Therion, I had no idea!" trilled the batarian with an amused lilt. "You've quite swept me off my feet. Do you even have quarters? I suppose we'll make the best of it..."

"You are a fool with your mouth open or

closed," sighed the drell. "There are few enough drell both awake and alive that I can take any room in the Rakhana zone without issue. But not because I desire you. Because if I do not get this suit off, in an hour or two, I will be seeing three of you, as well as goblins climbing the walls, and undead cats taking blood samples from Ataulfo mangoes. I will, to put it gracefully, be out of my mind. This is why the drell do not wear suits, generally."

"All right, all right, calm down, my little romantic, you don't have to make it sound quite so enticing. Straight shot to my eezo and then off to the bedroom. My head is spinning!"

"Maybe you're dying," Anax said dryly. "Now, are you going to tell me why the hell you have eezo or am I meant to guess?"

"You wouldn't begrudge me my little nest egg, would you, darling?" said Borbala Ferank, as she had in front of that wall of fish, what seemed like a lifetime ago. But this time her voice was not so merry or arch. It was quiet and perhaps even a little ashamed. Anax Therion had no idea what to do with this batarian. She was nothing like the others. Nothing like the one that had called her mother of worms. The one who was dead in a stack in the mess hall now. *Amonkira, Lord of Hunters, protect and defend me. All I wanted was a new life. I would settle to retain any life at all when this is done.* "I… I am not so different as they took me for, my poor, stupid sons. What was I supposed to do in Andromeda, take up an honest living?" She repeated as she had before, but hollow now, and tired. "I am what I am. And what I am is a batarian, and a batarian is a smuggler and a schemer who ends up on top. I am, my dear, the Pirate King." Borbala Ferank sang softly under her breath, a tune Anax did not know, but one that sounded somehow familiar.

Oh, better far to live and die
Under the Khar'shan flag I fly,
Than choose to play the paragon's part,
With a pirate head and a pirate heart.
Away to the Citadel go you,
Where pirates all are well-to-do;
But I'll stay true to the life contrarian,
And live and die batarian.

"Ah well. A new life in Andromeda, they said. And so now you will hate me because of what I brought into that new life. Because of what I could not resist. Because of what I was afraid to leave behind. The old ways, the old world. I smuggled the old life into the new, and now I will have neither it nor the profit, which is, perhaps, what I deserve. But I cannot... Anax, I cannot escape what I was born, any more than you can escape your useless lungs. That is the whole meaning of *caste*. If you could escape it, it would not be much of a caste." She tried to smirk. "Don't say our date's off."

"If you are such a perfect batarian, why did your sons blind you? Why does Jalosk call you the mother of worms?" Anax hoped she had laid enough groundwork for this question to pass.

Borbala smirked a little. "Because I quit. I left the family business. I tried to convince my people that our ships and manpower could be better used spreading batarian culture—and that in order to do that, we had to create some. Art, music, theater, novels. I wanted a batarian renaissance. Fewer guns, more songs. They wanted my eye for that."

The drell and the batarian edged along the north wall. The noise in the cargo bay was deafening. Moans and cries and splashes of unspeakable liquid. An occasional firing of biotic or rifle. Footsteps. Running. Running where? There was hardly a crate left fully assembled now. *We are all so very inventive when we need to be,* Anax thought. *This is why we knew we could rebuild in Andromeda. Give an organic the smallest space, and they will put a civilization in it.*

A hanar rose up from behind a cargo container with a shrill, bleating scream of a laugh. It was covered in pustulating sores, not quite the same blue as the ones on Soval or Jalosk or even Kholai; these were almost turquoise, suppurating blood and pus clotted with dry blue dust, its tentacles swollen to the thickness of tree trunks, its inflated flesh digging into its levitation packs painfully. Any face it might have had, inasmuch as hanar had faces, was obliterated by dried vomit, tears, and a horrendous rash like a fisherman's net thrown over the miserable jellyfish.

"Do not be sad!" it shrieked. "Everything is all right now! Rejoice! Make merry! The Day of Extinguishment is even more glorious than prophesied!" It floated down toward Borbala and Anax, who stumbled backward to get away from the flying, tentacled infection. "Kholai was wrong," it chortled thickly, through a ruined throat. "Kholai the Enkindled One was wise, but it was wrong. It preached that only the pure hanar would see the final days and reap their pleasures—but look! All species, together as one! Dancing, dancing so beautifully, in the ballroom of heaven! This is unity! All the creatures of the Enkindlers feasting upon the dregs of time together! Together!" The hanar fanned out its oozing tentacles like a carnival barker revealing the splendor of the midway.

Gun smoke drifted down the stacks of crates. Screams of agony echoed. Quiet, snickering laughter cut through the din, food changing hands like money, money changing hands like food, deals in the dark. A drell boy, hardly a man yet, vomited his innards onto the wedding linens his mother had packed for him, and collapsed into the sinkhole of his own liquefying body. The sick hanar giggled again. "This one is happy! This one is euphoric!" It tried to lean into them again, confidentially, like old friends, and once again the two green women struggled to get away. "*I* am happy!" whispered the hanar.

A blast of plasma fire shot out of the corner of the hold. It caught the hanar between two sores on its magenta skull and blew out its brains onto the floor. An enormous elcor trumpeted a scream of incandescent, incoherent rage, and thundered toward another hanar down the piles of ruined luggage, one who had swollen out of its levitation packs and was crawling pitifully along the floor, trying in vain to stand tall again. The elcor in the grips of madness trampled it underfoot, bellowing, "Furious hate: You did this to us, you did this!"

The elcor disappeared in the maze of cases.

"I think we had better run," Borbala said.

The captain's voice rang out over the belly of the ship. Those who had the presence of mind to hear it lurched toward the exits in a river of broken, leaking flesh.

Please remain calm. Form an orderly group and proceed to medbay for treatment. I repeat: Please remain calm, form an orderly group, and proceed to medbay for treatment. Be patient, my friends, and we will see our new worlds yet.

They ran. They ran as though Borbala Ferank was not long past her prime and Anax Therion was not drowning in her own sweat. They ran as though this one thing could matter, in the end of it all. They ran as though the room was not pink with laughing, singing hanar spinning like dervishes of joy. They ran as though they knew they would be able to run out of this place again.

Be patient, my friends, and we will see our new worlds yet.

"Here," panted the batarian. "It's here. It's somewhere… oh, you must be joking. This must be an amusing jest, yes? The universe is having it on at old Borbala's expense. Hilarious, truly the height of comedy in the known universe. *Get the fuck off my nest egg you disgusting blob,*" she roared.

Ysses had wrapped itself around a comparatively small crate and was suckling at its innards lustily. It looked up, its wedge-shaped head blistered with sores, as though it had stood too close to the sun.

"Anax Theeeeerion!" it gurgled. "This one has missed you! Look what this one found! It is wonderful, it is a miracle, it is this one's Day of Extinguishment present!"

The hanar's nostrils and eating orifice were caked with red sand.

"Oh, Bala," Anax sighed. "You didn't."

Borbala Ferank, former master of the greatest crime family in her quadrant, sang softly:

For I am batarian!
And it is, it is a call clarion
To be batarian!

"Don't you want to try some?" the hanar bubbled. "There's more than enough to share! Come, drell, this one will tell you its soul name and we will watch the cosmos perish together!"

Anax Therion sighed in disgust. She extended her arm and activated a stasis field, snatching the hanar up into the air like a sack of salt.

"Your soul name is 'Shit for Brains,'" she snapped. "And you're coming with me."

The drell looked down again at the red sand, washed black by the blue biotic light, her disappointment in the batarian mingled with gratitude. "Well?" she said to the most feared woman on Khar'shan. "Are you coming?"

"Yes, darling," whispered Borbala, in something very like self-loathing.

16. ACTIVATION

It was quiet in the quarian zone. There was an orderly line proceeding up the hall, with an older lady taking blood samples at one end of it, patting heads and reassuring everyone with those soothing sounds. It looked nothing like the rest of the ship. Quarians knew how to conduct themselves in a deep-space crisis. Even though they were terrified. Even though one male dropped to the ground in the sampling line and had to be carried away. Quarians understood that the ship that sustained you could always turn against you, and the least you could do was refrain from helping it along.

"What in the name of Rannoch and the homeworld to come is this?" Captain Qetsi'Olam breathed.

She was standing in Senna'Nir's doorway, gaping at the technological wreckage within.

"Don't look. It's not so bad if you don't look," Senna said, trying to keep his hands from shaking. *Don't ever tell anyone. You mustn't tell anyone.* But it was time, and she was his captain, and she was his Qetsi—surely if anyone was ever to break this promise, it would be him and it would be now. Qetsi had broken rules all her life. She would understand. And she would understand because his secret was going to save them.

Cables and disassembled parts covered both chambers of the first officer's quarters. Processing orbs, memory wafers, imaging pipettes, code cores, all ripped out of the dozens of unconnected VIs Anax and Borbala had dredged up out of the corners of the *Keelah Si'yah*. A cairn of deconstructed cryo fish tanks were piled up on top of his dining table, the guts ripped out of every one of them. A heap of hollowed-out early childhood education VIs was stacked up on his bed, eviscerated celebrity simulator VIs scattered the floor, gaming VIs filled up the sink. And toward the center of the bedroom was Senna's old elcor combat VI that he'd built himself on his Pilgrimage, hanging off of the krogan microscope like a metallic octopus, clutching in its silicon tentacles the cold, dull disk that was the body of Liat'Nir, inasmuch as she had one. Yet she was not entirely Liat'Nir anymore. Or at least, not *just* Liat'Nir. He'd been augmenting her, increasing her capacity, her speed, everything he could before… before the end. He needed her to be able to do more, and faster, that was all that mattered, because his diagnostic tools were as blind to the worm as the ship was blind to everything else. Senna could not do it. No human could. He needed her to have access to more than the millions of responses of her descendants, no matter how varied and interesting her combinations of those lost and ghostly words might be.

"I have something to show you, Qetsi. You're not going to like it, but we are very, very far from home, and if you do not decide to punish me, there is no one who will. New world, new rules, that's what you've always said to me. We have come so far for new rules."

"I don't know what you're talking about, Senna. Of course I'm not going to *punish* you. We've lost so many already… so many." She looked at him intently—he could see the shadows of her eyelashes beneath her faceplate glass. "You know it was the hanar, don't you?

Not all of them, of course, but… the religious ones. The cult. With their Day of Extinguishment nonsense, bleating all day and night. They made it happen. They're going to annihilate us. We are a sacrifice. That baby girl in Yorrik's lab. She's a sacrifice. Senna, what am I supposed to do with a crime that enormous? Convene a tribunal, as we would on the Flotilla? Try them? Or push them out an airlock? I am not ready to be that kind of captain. I just wanted to be the kind that *flew*."

"There can't be that many of them left. Perhaps justice will take care of itself," Senna said. He remembered the frenetic glow of Ysses's tentacles as it surveyed the dead. If only they'd known. "In a moment, Captain, I'm going to press a button, and if I've done it all right, we'll have our ship back. I think that's worth trading a bit of sin for, don't you?"

She squeezed his arm through the mesh of his suit. "I'll forgive your sins if you forgive mine," she said softly. "Now, just tell me what you're so afraid of, you great stuttering processing orb."

Senna'Nir took a deep breath and activated the conglomerate program. Liat flickered to life on the disk, smoking her hand-rolled cigarette, lounging on her rocking chair.

"Qetsi'Olam vas Keelah Si'yah, this is my grandmother, Liat'Nir."

The captain froze. Her shoulders went tense and stiff. Her knees locked. Senna wished, and not for the first time, that he could see her face.

"Is that what I think it is?"

"It depends on what you think it is."

"An ancestor VI."

"Hello, Grandmother," Senna'Nir said softly. His

heart was racing. He had never shared this with anyone. It was more intimate than sharing suit environments.

"Always so formal, my grandson," said the ancestor VI, as it always did. "Call me Liat, why don't you? Never thought of myself as old enough to have grandchildren anyhow."

"You *bosh'tet*," whispered the captain. "How long?"

"All my life."

"And you never told me."

"How could I? But she's… She's truly extraordinary, Qetsi. She helps me think. Her capacity for deduction is unique. There is hardly anything she can't figure out, although her answers don't always make much sense. But she's not… Don't be afraid. She's not alive. Her deductive abilities come from something, oddly enough, called genetic programming—"

The captain crouched down and stared at the little hologram, who stared right back. "It's an abomination," she said finally.

Senna sighed. It was the longest sigh of his life. In that sigh, a thousand hopes crumbled. "New world, new rules," he said in vain.

"Not like this. Some rules are there for a reason, Senna'Nir. The geth murdered my family. Perhaps, because they did not murder yours, you do not feel how wrong this is."

"You have no idea what you're talking about," Senna growled, through a jaw clenched so tight he thought his teeth might shatter. He pointed at the VI. "You're looking at what the geth did to my family. Reduced us to ash and code." Qetsi ignored him. She couldn't hear a thing over the sound of her own righteousness.

"You do not know, not the way I do, that machines are not to be trusted. I tried to tell the Initiative that, with their revolting Pathfinders, embedding AI in people's flesh—it does not help the organic host, it makes them a monster. There can be no synthesis between organic and machine. They will find that out sooner or later, whether we reach the Nexus or not. But this? This is the abomination our ancestors were striving for when the geth came to life. You have repeated the end of the world, Senna. On my ship. Get it out of here. Airlock it. Burn it to ash. I don't care."

"Qetsi, please!"

"I *never* took you for stupid, Senna! That's not your grandmother! It's a copy, a copy meant to fool you, to make you feel things toward it. Don't you think the old ones felt something toward the geth? And what happened to them? No. I would not allow the quarian Pathfinder to take the implant like the others and I will not allow unborn intelligences on my ship. Delete her, or I will."

Qetsi'Olam strode around him faster than Senna thought possible. She reached for the disk, her furious breathing audible even in her suit. But there is an instinct for protecting family that is faster still. Senna had wanted to explain everything carefully to Qetsi, how Liat could help, how, by uploading her program directly into the ship's mainframe, essentially installing her as an executable function within the *Keelah Si'yah*, she could maintain her individuality and capacity for creative thinking—bolstered and expanded by all his tinkering with the guts of the other VIs—long enough to hack the worm and destroy it herself. To pursue it through the failed systems, deep into the core of the codebank and exterminate it for them. But eventually, he had wanted to tell the captain that the sheer massiveness of the ship's systems would overwhelm and drown out the little pieces of Liat'Nir that made her Liat'Nir, would wash away any dregs left of personality in the great sea of the ship's core. It was a suicide mission, one he and Liat had discussed at length. One he'd begged her not to embark on. One he hated with every ounce of his soul. One he was willing to sacrifice the thing he loved most in all the world to accomplish. Why couldn't Qetsi listen? Why couldn't all her rhetoric about the new rules of Andromeda have been true? Why couldn't he give the gentle, noble speech he wanted to give, and accept her gratitude for his sacrifice?

Instead, he cried out the command passkey to his grandmother: "GO FISH!"

Liat'Nir's eyes went out like candles. She disappeared. Qetsi and Senna stood motionless in the shadows of his quarters.

"What did you do?" she seethed.

"Wait," Senna whispered. "Please. I did something good, I promise."

"Captain!" came a loud masculine voice, followed by a banging at the door. "I need to speak with you!"

"I'll be with you in a moment, Malak'Rafa!" she shouted.

Senna'Nir shut his eyes. He prayed silently to the real Liat'Nir, his flesh-and-blood grandmother, so long dead. *Be with me now as you always have.*

After a few moments, he spoke to the ship.

"K, establish a comm link between first officer's quarters and medbay."

You got it, ke'sed.

"Yorrik?" Qetsi said into her comm, almost without hope. "Tell me you found our needle in a galaxy, my friend."

The voice that came over the line was not Yorrik's. It was ravaged and ruined, so faint it seemed hardly a voice at all.

"Dejected: Affirmative. It is you."

17. ASSEMBLY

Yorrik could hardly see the shape holding his head. He thought it was a man. It seemed probable that it was. It smelled familiar, but the elcor's olfactory slats were caked in dried fluids.

"No, no, no, Yorrik, get up, old friend. How could this happen? Your neck..."

Senna. The shape was Senna. How nice. How good to see him again. There was a terrible pain in Yorrik's limbs. Not only the swelling, though that was bad enough. But when he had fallen, he had cut himself on the shards of glass from the broken fish tank, or the broken volus goggles on that child's toy, or something. Something sharp. He was bleeding, he could feel it. It wouldn't be long now. And that was fine.

"Warm affection: Say it, Senna," he rasped. "It is time. Say it. Wry rejoinder: Also it is clear how this happened. I have been breathing Fortinbras in for days. I did not want you to know."

"Say what?" The quarian tried to shift his weight, to get the whole of Yorrik's gigantic head into his lap, lifted up off the floor of the clinic. "Oh, no, no, Yorrik, no you don't. You just had a fall. You're not going to die, don't be stupid. You've got to get up and save us. You found our needle. She's just there, near the iso-chamber. Now we just need to thread it. And look—Yorrik, look up!" The elcor tried, he really did, but the room was a blur. There were figures there, splotches of gray and purple. Nice splotches. "Anax and Borbala brought your eezo. It's all here for you, old man. We're all here for you."

"'Will all great Neptune's ocean wash this blood clean from my hand?'" Yorrik whispered. He realized he had forgotten to preface it with emotion. Now they wouldn't understand. They wouldn't know what he meant. The elcor struggled to speak again but his throat, his throat hurt him so.

"Ysses..." he managed.

"Is in custody," Anax Therion said, and the sharp green of her voice cut through his fogged mind.

Yorrik struggled to his feet. The madness would come soon. He knew it would. He had seen it, heard it, and no doctor suffers from the usual delusion that he will be any different than another patient. The progression of a disease is the progression of a disease. He would soon be nothing but a rampaging hulk of tonnage aimed at all these people. It was clever, really, as far as a virus can be clever. The spores that shot out of the abscesses at the point of rupture spread the infection one way, but once the victim was possessed by the rage of the final phases, their lust for destruction and death would spread it, too, fluid to fluid, a classic if ever there was one.

"Angry: You took my microscope. That krogan was going to talk me through it," he growled, and felt resentment rising like blood in him.

Senna'Nir stood back a little, ready to try, very vainly, to catch the enormous heft of a falling elcor, if he fell again. Good Senna. Always so good.

"Grandmother," the quarian said, a tinge of pride in his voice, "How do you engineer an active retrovirus?"

Hello, Grandson. Well, first you pour yourself a very

tall drink, 'cause this is going to take a while. Then, you've got to isolate the immuno-cells and treat your eezo source to leach impurities—

"Overjoyed: You got the ship working again."

"Not at all, but we've got a few systems back online. Enough?"

"Satisfaction: Enough. Warning: You should not be near me, Senna. I am extremely contagious at the moment. Go. I will alert you when I have finished."

"Can't I help? I want to stay with you. Like that night when we drank ryncol and watched the stars down by the river. Do you remember that night?"

"With great love: Say it for me, Senna. You may not get another chance."

Senna'Nir was crying. The elcor could smell the salt of his tears through his helmet.

"No," Senna snapped. "You say it. I won't. You're so close. You're not going to die before you save us all."

"Coaxing: Say it."

"No!" roared the quarian.

The captain interrupted, her voice cool and calm, as it always had been from those first days on Hephaestus.

"How can we distribute the retrovirus once you have it, Yorrik? In case the worst should happen, I need to know."

Yorrik had dreaded this part of the discussion. This was not a laboratory and supplies were not infinite. In the end, if he was lucky, and he lived long enough, and the ship's computer really was fixed, Yorrik would end up with a very small sample to work with. Infinite space bound in a walnut shell.

"Reluctant response: The most efficient method, given how little material is in our possession, would be to inject a person with it, and allow them to infect others as they would with the original Fortinbras virus. It could be a sick person or a well one, but they would have to move throughout the ship, coming into physical contact with everyone who has been exposed to the virus. I doubt I will have enough to treat more than one person. We could wait for the virus to replicate under laboratory conditions, but how many more deaths would occur? So many. So many deaths. And each of them bright violet, as violet as a river in the night…"

Yorrik could feel the tension that kept a mind slipping from him. He stared numbly at Qetsi'Olam through his haze. Hatred surged in his heart. Unnameable, unreasoned hatred. If he could only rip her to pieces and feast on her blood, everything would go back to the way it was before. He knew it, somehow, in his bones. But the ancient elcor bit back on his fury. It was not his at all. It was Fortinbras, doing what he always did, coming in at the end to ruin and rend. He would not give in to it. Not yet. This was his final stage. His soliloquy. His swan song. Fortinbras would not ruin that for him.

"Urgent: Go. Leave me alone with my work," Yorrik pleaded.

The comms crackled to life suddenly. No—not the comms. It was the public address system. The only way Anax Therion knew to contact them.

Good evening, fellow doomed passengers. Would Captain Qetsi'Olam and First Officer Senna'Nir kindly make their way to my cabin 788B in the drell zone? I have some things I wish to say. And I believe my hanar friend does, as well.

18. CELL SUICIDE

Anax Therion watched her come in. Watched her sit down across from the sullen hanar, coming down off its red sand high, hanging like a coat in the corner of her quarters, its levitation packs at half power to keep it immobile. She watched Senna'Nir hover over her. Protective, overly so. Guilt, perhaps. She still hadn't decided on the commander. They had hardly had a chance to speak. Or, more importantly, for Anax to hear him speak. The drell took a deep breath, finally free of that suit, her green skin shining in the dim lights of her quarters that flickered pinkish-violet every so often. She would be grateful to see normal, steady lights again, if she ever did. The kind you could read a book by.

"Borbala, the door, if you don't mind?" Therion said carefully. These were her favorite moments, when she had almost all the answers, and needed only to fit the last piece in. Unfortunately, the last piece rather often tried to make a run for it. The batarian nodded and moved to prevent that from happening.

"Is this the *bosh'tet* who tried to kill us all?" said the captain stonily, gesturing at Ysses.

"It is, indeed," answered Therion, without taking her gaze from the quarians.

"It is a strange thing," Qetsi'Olam said softly, "to worship death so fervently."

The lights flickered again.

"This one knows the truth. The Day of Extinguishment is the day of freedom. This one rejoices in the chaos around it, that is all. This one has no need to explain itself."

"I thought Kholai's followers didn't believe in taking action to bring about the end of the world," said Senna uncertainly.

The lights flickered: rose, violet.

Borbala Ferank shrugged. "There are heretics everywhere," she grunted. "Even among heretics."

Anax Therion did not get up from her sofa. Her muscles ached from the oils they had absorbed. She wanted only to rest. To rest and to eat. But another part of her had never been so alert.

"What will you do with him, Captain?" the drell asked. "What is the name of justice in our new world?"

Qetsi crossed her arms and leaned back on her heels, thinking. "We must revive the Quorum," she said finally. "All of us must pass judgment on this one who has brought such horror upon our beautiful ship. It cannot be my decision alone. Perhaps there is a mercy to be divined here… Perhaps he only followed his master. Perhaps he is not so bad as all that. There must be a trial. Keep him confined. We revive any members of the Quorum who were lucky enough to sleep through this in a clean zone to limit their exposure. With some luck, Yorrik's retrovirus will make such contingencies irrelevant. No one has entered Engineering since the onset of this crisis, it should be safe. I will go and make arrangements. Is this acceptable?"

They nodded. It seemed fair. The captain nodded back and slipped past Borbala into the open hall.

"Senna'Nir," said Anax, standing up and brushing her palms off on her thighs, "come with me?"

"What? Why?"

"Why? To follow the captain and see where she goes, of course."

"She's going to the cryobay, to start moving the Quorum's pods to Engineering," the quarian male insisted.

"Is she?" Borbala Ferank mused. "Fascinating."

Anax Therion let her translucent inner eyelids slide shut. "The night before," she whispered. "Stars like grains of wheat outside. Inside, music, light, movement. Soval Raxios, dancing like a heart on fire. A quarian dances with her, laughing, a heron on the surface of clean water. I alone am unhappy. So many people. So much sound. I walk alone through the station as on the banks of a river, watching, listening. I look up; a young man crawls across the belly of the ship, a lamprey against a silver shark, taking sustenance, injecting… something else. He sees me, I withdraw. I consider my own life, a book of secrets. I remember all my sins. Then—a shot in the shadows. The lamprey is dead. A figure disappearing in the distance, singing, humming, a voice I know, a voice I do not hear again for almost three hundred years, the same heron whose feet made no mark on the clean water." Her eyelids withdrew. "A drell's memory is perfect, but we must choose to remember. I thought I kept recalling Soval because so much of this seemed to return to her somehow. But it was not Soval my mind wished me to see again."

It had always amazed Anax how easy it was to turn love to distrust, if you really tried to do it. Senna followed her out of her quarters in silence, leaving the batarian to play prison guard, a role she seemed to enjoy. The darkness of the corridors helped them;

the quiet of the drell zone made it easy to hear the captain's footsteps.

She was not going to Engineering.

They kept their distance. The running lights outlined Qetsi in the dark. An arm snaked out from an alcove outside Mess Hall 2 and grabbed her, dragged her into an alcove. Voices hissed up out of the dark.

"What are you doing? I told you to meet me. This has gone too far. We have to do something," a male voice snarled.

"Please, Malak'Rafa, do not fear. It is all resolving better than we could imagine. They have the hanar immobilized. They have no doubt it and its people are to blame. If the elcor's cure works, we have nothing at all between us and innocence."

"That... is a relief. But, Qetsi... if the retrovirus works... all our plans..." Malak said mournfully.

"There will be time for more plans. A new life in Andromeda. Where there is life there is always hope. We are lucky, Malak. Lucky to have any path free of this."

"It wasn't supposed to happen like this..."

The captain put her finger on Malak'Rafa's faceplate. "I know. Go back to the quarian zone. I am going to the cargo hold. I will find something usable, and I will dispatch Ysses tonight so that it cannot tell the truth—not that it seems inclined to, it truly is happy that all this has happened. I will never understand hanar. Or religion. Soon, all will be well."

Senna'Nir and Anax Therion watched the quarian male disappear down the long curving hallway.

"Oh, Qetsi," Senna sighed with a horrible choke in his voice. "What have you done?"

The captain whirled on them, drawing a small Arc Pistol from her hip.

"Senna!" she cried. "You frightened me! What are you doing sneaking around like that?"

Anax had always found people to be most themselves when they were afraid they had been caught doing something they oughtn't. Would they admit it right away? Obfuscate? Everything a person was could be revealed in that red-handed moment.

"I think I've gotten turned around," the captain laughed nervously.

"On your own ship?" asked the drell.

"It's a big ship, Analyst Therion. Shouldn't you be guarding our hanar friend?"

"Ah," said Anax, clasping her hands behind her back. "I believe Ysses is the literal embodiment of the old human folktale of the red herring. That one rejoices in death and annihilation, but it did nothing to bring it about."

The captain's hand began to tremble on her gun. "Malak," she called out, but he did not come.

"But you. I saw you dance with Soval Raxios. I saw you gun down that human boy in cold blood. You did something, if not everything. Means, motive, and opportunity," Therion went on. By the Lord of Hunters the fresh air felt good on her skin. "They are classics, but useful. You would have had all the opportunities you could carry; after all, this is your ship. And as for means, they can be purchased at any port. It is only the motive that has perplexed me. Why would you hate the drell so intensely that you would seek to destroy us? What have we done to you to deserve this? If you wanted Andromeda to be rid of drell, you had only to forbid us to board."

"Qetsi'Olam vas Keelah Si'yah," Senna'Nir whispered. "What have you *done*?"

It was not as satisfying as Anax had hoped. You couldn't see a quarian's face drain of color, or her pupils dilate in terror, or her perspiration response. You could only see the same shadowed faceplate you always saw, even in that most intimate of moments, when the hunter catches her prey, and the detective pins her criminal to the deed.

"It wasn't supposed to happen like this," Qetsi whispered. "I don't hate the drell. You were never supposed to be harmed, please believe that."

"I do not, but go on," Therion snorted.

"I did it for us, Senna. For our beautiful new world," she said to her first officer. She wasn't speaking to Anax at all. Just pleading with her former lover to understand.

But the first officer did not understand. He pointed at the mess hall door and spoke in cold fury. "There are bodies stacked up in there like old shoes. How is that beautiful? Or even new?"

"It wasn't supposed to be like this!" Qetsi screamed in frustration. "I was so careful. I designed the virus myself. It was perfect. It was so perfect. A carrier virus. It would never have shown any symptoms. The drell would contract it three-quarters of the way through the journey, and they would never even know they had it. I paid a kid to install dispensers in their pods. Told him it was perfume, to remind them of home. Everything was supposed to be *fine*. But the computer side of it all, the worm, that was Malak'Rafa's baby. His darling. He spent months on the thing, and in the end, in the end, Senna, he fucked up, not me. I did my job flawlessly. He choked at the finish somehow. All it was ever supposed to do was raise the temperature slightly, the very barest minimum, to let the virus get a foothold and then cover its tracks. That's it. That's all.

But the worm raised the temperature a little too high, just a little, maybe half a degree too far, just far enough to allow the beginnings of a very slow continuous replication without waking anyone up."

"And that gave Fortinbras a hundred and fifty years to mutate," Therion said. "I suspect it found no good purchase in our lungs and was forced to progress to the brain. And once a virus has learned a new trick, it doesn't forget. Fifty years of replication with no predators is enough to create the mother of all infections. It's billions of generations."

"To fulfill fitness parameters," Senna mumbled.

Therion pursed her lips. "But then we have the problem of Sleepwalker Team Yellow-9. We always seemed to come back to Soval Raxios. Patient Zero, of a sort. She wasn't, of course, you infected hundreds of drell. But her Sleepwalker team revived shortly after infection, and she had contact with all those other people. They went back into their pods covered in the droplets of her breath, her sweat, maybe even more. And Fortinbras had more time to work, and more species to adapt to. And all the while, you revived yourself, here and there, flitting just beyond the cameras, checking the progress, monitoring the worm in the computers, making sure all was proceeding according to plan."

"It was a carrier virus," Qetsi hissed through clenched teeth.

"Carried to what?" Senna'Nir said numbly.

The captain looked up at him with a misery that was clear even through dark glass.

"To the Nexus," she said. "Senna, remember what I said. Remember it. New world, new rules. Why should it always, always be them? The Council races, lording it over us all. What does the Council *matter* in Andromeda? Why should turians, asari, humans, and fucking salarians always come out on top? Humans! Who barely puked themselves into a spacefaring culture half a second ago? Salarians? You know what they did to me, Senna. You know."

The quarian glanced at Anax. "When she was on her Pilgrimage on Erinle, they stripped her suit off and left her outside the habitat bubble without it. Only for a few minutes. A prank, they said. But her lungs became infected with algae. It took months to recover."

"Months during which I *learned*. I learned about Ayalon B and artificial viral technology. I learned how to build my own like a child's blocks. And I learned that people hate us. The quarians. They hate us for all the reasons one species hates another. We could never really be safe in the Milky Way, even if we retook Rannoch. We could only be safe somewhere *new*. So..." She swallowed hard. "The drell would carry the virus onto the Nexus. The only people it would harm would be humans, turians, asari, and salarians. Quarians would be safe in our suits, everyone else... Oh, Senna, if only you could understand, you'd be proud of me. It's so clever. No one else could have thought of it. As long as the infection stayed within a drell—or even an elcor or batarian; I did consider spillover, I'm not an idiot—it would be inert. Safe. But once it infected species whose bodies it recognized, its *parts* recognized, it would come into its own. It would run wild through them. The Council races are native to the diseases I used, the rest of us would have been safe. Once it found its home, the disease would clear out the Nexus of almost everyone but us. Not *just* us. Not just quarians!" She turned to Anax. "Drell, too, and elcor, and hanar, and batarians, and volus. The species denied our places in the Milky Way. We would finally have our chance to shine. To become great. To create something better than the corruption of the old galaxy, the seething schemes of Cerberus and the geth and all the rest of the horrors of home. A new life, a completely new life, with us at the top."

"That's hundreds of thousands of people. You were going to kill hundreds of thousands on the Nexus, just for political advantage?" Senna stood back from her. He felt sick with recognition. This was Qetsi'Olam, love of his life, the big-picture girl. The big-picture girl who sometimes just… couldn't see the little brushstrokes. All that vulnerability she'd shown in his quarters was gone. Maybe it had never been there. Maybe she'd just needed him to trust her as he'd always done.

"Not all of them. Some of them would always be immune; in any population some people are just… lucky. But… but most. Enough. Enough that it would only make sense to let the quarians step up and administer the survivors. We would comfort them in their grief. And only I and Malak would bear the guilt. No one would ever know. When a truly just galaxy arose, it would all be worth it. There would only be a history of unexplainable tragedy, and the light that was birthed from it. It wasn't supposed to happen like this."

The captain sunk to her knees.

Anax Therion felt a terrible suspicion in her stomach.

"How did you choose?"

"What?"

"How did you choose which drell to infect? It wasn't all of us, or I would have it."

Qetsi did not raise her face to meet Anax's eyes. "I watched you, all of you, on Hephaestus. We chose the most outgoing ones, the social butterflies, the happy drell who talked to everyone. Like Soval. The ones most likely to make… new friends on the Nexus."

Stony, venomous silence met that reply.

"You're insane," hissed Senna. "They say that in vids but you are really and actually insane. Something is broken in you. How did you get past the screening? The Initiative rejected people far less *bent on genocide* than you."

Qetsi laughed. "Oh, Senna, you really are simple. I was always so good at taking tests, you know. Even if I didn't study. There's a reasoning, a certain logic, to all tests, and as soon as you know it, you can pass anything. It's not like they asked if I planned to rewrite the whole history of the quarian species. That is not a question on the psychological exam. And if it was, my love, I am surely capable of answering *no.* Besides, they were looking for someone a little insane! The ancestors know you'll never find a sane quarian who would abandon the quest for Rannoch. Anyone on this side of normal wouldn't even consider it. They needed someone just the perfect amount of insane to dump their entire lives and families and all of recorded history and light out for Andromeda on the promise of… of what? A planet? Maybe? If there's one out there for us? That the bureaucracy there would somehow provide for us when it never did back home? They *wanted* insane. Insane and inspiring and reckless. Only on their forms they spelled it 'visionary.' Well, they got me. I see the great pageant, just like the Initiative does. I see the new galaxy, writ large in stardust and blood. I just… see it a little differently arranged than they do. And that difference just looks like eagerness on a psych screen."

"But the people," Anax said. "*My* people. You used us. Why couldn't you just wait until we got to the Nexus? Or spread your disease in the Milky Way? Why come all this way for so much death? Why did the drell have to be the bullets you fired?"

Qetsi stared at them, genuinely dumbfounded. "I'm not a monster. Killing a few thousand on the Nexus in exchange for a pristine society is an easy bargain. Killing trillions back home—and for what, there's far too many of them on too many worlds to really change the balance of power—is horrific. What kind of person do you think I am?"

"One who will be easily convicted," Senna said grimly.

"You can't tell them," the captain whispered. "The people on the Nexus. They will only persecute the quarians more brutally when we arrive. No one will ever trust us. You cannot tell anyone. Let Yorrik's cure do its work. Airlock me if you have to—say I contracted it and died. I will accept that. But you cannot tell. You own this now, just as I do."

For a long moment, there was only silence.

"Grandmother, open a comm channel to medbay," Senna barked.

Comm channel open, ke'sed. *By the way, I know you haven't asked because you've got the manners the gods gave a black hole, but I am nearly ready to begin my final patch. You'll want to be in your cryopod when I do. Things could get as rocky as a glass of good ryncol around here.*

"Yorrik, is the retrovirus ready?"

No response. Qetsi wept. Anax watched her with curiosity. *I will remember this so well,* she thought.

"In overwhelming agony: Yes, Senna. It is ready," Yorrik's voice stuttered over the line. "Begging: P... p... please, my friend. Please say it."

But Senna said nothing. He grabbed the captain roughly by one arm. She did not resist. He dragged her toward medbay without a single word, his anger so black and total that Anax didn't even try to tell him a story of Kahje to pass the time on their long, dead woman's walk.

||||||||||||||||

Yorrik crouched in the corner, blue sores blossoming all over his enormous, noble body. The elcor nodded weakly toward the autopsy table where a loaded hypospray waited.

Senna'Nir turned to his captain. "I am not going to wake the Quorum. The three of us here should suffice for a tribunal. You did this, you're going to undo it. Generating more of the retrovirus will take time. People will die in the gap. Maybe thousands. But you're not going to let that happen, are you?"

He picked up the hypospray and looked to Anax. She nodded solemnly. Then to Yorrik, whose red, crusted eyes widened in comprehension, if not of the why or wherefore, at least of the fact of what they meant to do. The elcor struggled to his massive feet and seemed to allow that final rage of Fortinbras to reign free. He charged her with a broken bellow, slamming Qetsi'Olam against the glass medbay wall. It cracked horribly. The captain moaned in helpless pain. But she nodded.

She did nod. Years later, when Senna'Nir remembered this, he would try to hold on to the fact that, in the end, she agreed to mend what she had done. She had some speck of who he'd loved in her still.

But that charge was all Yorrik had in him. He slumped to the ground.

"With deep love and need: Say it, Senna. It is time," he begged.

Senna'Nir knelt next to his old friend. He put his hands on the ancient elcor's gray head. He leaned down and whispered, "With infinite grief and friendship: 'Now cracks a noble heart. Goodnight, sweet prince, and flights of angels sing thee to thy rest.'"

The elcor sighed no more.

The quarian rose, seized the captain by the throat, released the clamps on her helmet, ripped it off, and injected the retrovirus directly into her jugular.

19. RELEASE

Qetsi'Olam walked naked, or near enough to it, down the halls of her ship.

Down every hall, in every zone. They watched her come, her crew, her passengers. The old woman's voice that had taken the place of the ship's interface had told them what to do, if not why. They watched her come, singing as she walked, and one by one, they approached.

Sing me to sleep on the starry sea
And I'll dream through the night of my suit and me
I won't fear the heat of a desert breeze
Or contaminants high in the jungle trees
Even in space I shall never freeze
Because I've got my suit and my suit's got me.

Most had never seen a quarian outside her suit before. The drell came to her and stood near, hesitantly, like wary dogs around a new pup. They breathed the air she breathed. They reached out, gingerly, and one by one she held their hands and squeezed them, flesh-to-flesh contact, every cell of her body containing the possibility of grace. They stood so close, close enough to contract her healing infection. Tears coursed down her cheeks and the hanar touched them, wiped them away, and Qetsi'Olam tried to pretend that meant they forgave her. Child elcor smelled her scent and let her fingers trail through their slats. Batarians were rougher, they swore at her as they crowded in, snarling, and she could not pretend then. One spat at her. She had never in all her life felt anything like it. It felt like being struck in the heart by a rifle.

And all the while she trembled, and shook, and gooseflesh rose on her pale flesh as she entered zones not meant for her, for her anatomy, for her respiration, for her comfort. All the while she wept and sang.

Oh, I love my mother who holds me tight
And I love my father taught me right
Oh, I love my ship sailing strong through the night
And I love the homeworld for which we fight
But what do I love like a lock loves a key?
What holds fast my heart, head, shoulders and knees?
I love my suit and my suit loves me.

Qetsi'Olam thought of her parents burning away into ash on their home ship. She thought of the feeling of the algae on Erinle crawling into her lungs, creeping inside her, taking her prisoner. She thought of Senna'Nir, his joy and warmth when they were young. She thought of Malak'Rafa, his fire, and what they would do to him when she was gone. She did what she could on her walk of penance. Touched them all though it turned her stomach, this intimacy of skin on skin, flesh on flesh, no suit, no protection.

It would have been beautiful, she thought. *My Andromeda would have been beautiful.*

She finally collapsed in the volus zone, the last of them, the ammonia raising boils on her skin, the pressure making her eyeballs bulge. She fell to the ground and they stood around her in clumps, breathing in loudly, roughly, needing the medicine her body offered so badly.

Qetsi'Olam, for all that she had done, tried to hold on as long as she could for them. She sang as loud as she could in the fumes, clinging to the last of life, the last lyric of her long journey into the black.

When I grow up I shall have a house in the sun
On my true homeworld where the wild rivers run
I'll plant flowers in soil where now there are none
And there'll be plenty of room for everyone
But till I see Rannoch with my very own eyes
And kiss the sweet ground where my ancestors lie
We'll sleep safe as engines as forward we fly
My self and my suit
My suit and I.

When it was over the *Keelah Si'yah* streamed on like a sailing ship through the night, a silver wake behind it. Frozen, glittering, beloved corpses, laid to rest in the bosom of space, and among them, one without sores or blood—Malak'Rafa, his crystallized eyes turned backward toward the Milky Way.

EPILOGUE

Borbala Ferank lay down inside her cryopod.

"I'll see you on the other side," Anax Therion said, perched on the lip of the pod.

"Will you?" said the batarian with some amusement. "Tell me a truth, Anax. I listened to all those lies. Tell me one truth about yourself and I'll see you there, I'll even keep a house for you, waiting on whatever homeworld the Pathfinders find for the batarians. Somewhere nice and dry."

Anax gazed down with her dark eyes.

"They were all true."

"Tell me another one."

"All right. I was never bonded to a hanar. I have been alone all my life. I watched other drell be chosen, but I had to carve my own way. I was not wanted. Except by the Shadow Broker, who only wanted the secrets I could send. The stories are true, but the names are false. It has always only been me, occasionally in company, mostly alone."

"Is that true?" said Borbala Ferank.

"Perhaps," smiled Anax Therion, and leaned down to kiss the batarian on her gouged-out, withered eye, and then, almost afraid to do it, on her lips. "Sleep well. Do not dream. Find me in Andromeda."

Batarian skin looks almost white in cryostasis. Drell skin, too.

"Systems report, Grandmother," said Senna'Nir as he activated the stasis cascade on his own pod. He immediately began to feel the drowsiness overcome him.

Call me Keelah Si'yah. *Never thought of myself as old enough for grrrrrr—all systems optimal, Commander.*

There. It had begun. She had lost her name. By the time someone from the Nexus found them, his ancestor would be completely subsumed into the ship's databanks. A tiny fish in a great sea. Not dead, not gone, but not Liat, either. But perhaps... Perhaps he could visit her, still, from time to time. In his old quarters, where she, so briefly, came very nearly alive.

The cryostasis came on fast. He tried not to think of Qetsi, to fear dreaming of her, a dream in which he had to decide whether to tell the others what had happened, or simply deny them boarding rights until full decontamination procedures were followed and report the usual plague story—unexplainable, devastating, over now. Done. The rest was a decision for the warmth of arrival, not the cold forgiveness of sleep.

If there was any forgiveness to be had.

"Goodbye, Grandmother," he whispered.

Goodbye, ke'sed. *May flights of angels sing thee... sing thee... thee sing...*

Incoming message, Commander.

But no one was awake to receive it. The *Keelah Si'yah* flew on in silence, a glimmer of light in the dark, toward a home that was already calling to them.

ACKNOWLEDGEMENTS

Let's just jump right in at the deep end: Thank you to everyone who has been involved with the creation of Mass Effect over the years. It is and remains my favorite video game series of all time, and I was honored to be allowed to play in such a glorious sandbox. Thanks particularly to the team that guided me through this process: Steve Saffel, Cat Camacho, Mac Walters, Cathleen Rootsaert, Derek Watts, Joanna Berry, my agent Howard Morhaim, and anyone I've missed.

Thank you also to the Mass Effect fan community, whose tireless enthusiasm, interest, and eye for the smallest detail of the universe keeps this universe alive.

Thanks to Connor Goldsmith, who got so sick of my evangelizing about the wonder of Mass Effect that he stopped me mid-sentence to introduce me to Steve Saffel and quite deliberately started this whole crazy ball rolling. And thank you to my Patreon patrons, especially Sean Elliott, who kept me afloat while I worked on this project, all the while not getting to see a bit of it.

Now, about four years ago, I was moping around the house whingeing: "I wish I was playing a game that

I could get obsessed with like I used to get obsessed with the old Final Fantasy games…"

And my partner answered: "Haaaave you met Mass Effect?"

I played the series through in about a month of ignoring the entire rest of my life, and so much came from that procrastination it beggars the mind. So thank you, Heath, soon to be my husband, for making sure I didn't let Mordin die in the suicide mission and that I waited to make any romance decisions until I met Thane, and for listening to me complain about my blue boo Liara being so mean to me after everything we went through together, and then, a couple of years later, listening to me hash out a space thriller with no blue boos in it at all. Mostly green boos, really.

Finally, a small note to my son, who will join us here on planet earth just around the same time this novel does. You were very small and quiet while I wrote this, a mere glimmer on the character selection screen. But you were there, with me in the space between galaxies, in and around and throughout this book technically written by a two-in-one creature, the most science fictional beast you can find in this mad world. *Keelah Se'lai*, my child.

ABOUT THE AUTHOR

Catherynne M. Valente is the *New York Times* bestselling author of more than two dozen works of fantasy, science fiction, short fiction, and poetry, including *Palimpsest*, the Orphan's Tales series, *Deathless*, *Radiance* and *Space Opera*. She's the winner of the Andre Norton, Tiptree, Sturgeon, Prix Imaginales, Eugie Foster Memorial, Lambda, Locus, and Hugo awards, and a finalist for the Nebula and World Fantasy Awards. She lives off the coast of Maine.